Aunt Bessie Considers

An Isle of Man Cozy Mystery

Diana Xarissa

Text Copyright © 2014 Diana Xarissa

Cover Photo Copyright © 2014 Kevin Moughtin

All rights reserved.

ISBN: 1500884286
ISBN-13: 978-1500884284

Author's Note

Welcome to the third book in the Aunt Bessie Cozy Mystery series. For those of you who are new to Aunt Bessie's world, Bessie first appeared in my Isle of Man Romance, ***Island Inheritance,*** as a distant relative of the heroine and the source of the inheritance that brings her to the island. That meant, of course, that Bessie had passed away not long before that book began. Her life story was told primarily through letters and diaries.

Unwilling to let go of such a wonderful character, I brought Bessie back to life to appear in my cozy mystery series. In order to accomplish this, I've set the cozy mysteries about fifteen years before the romance. The series begins, therefore, around 1998. I've tried to be careful with setting the stories in the recent past, especially with technology.

Some characters do make appearances in both the Aunt Bessie series and in my romance novels. In the mystery series they are younger versions of themselves and that gives readers a bit more background about them, should they be interested. The romances are all intended to stand on their own, however, as is the Aunt Bessie series.

I've used British spellings and British and/or Manx words and terminology throughout the book (although one or two American words or spellings might have slipped past me). A couple of pages of translations and explanations, mostly for readers outside of the United Kingdom, appear at the end of the book.

The Aunt Bessie stories are set in the Isle of Man, a small island located between England and Ireland in the Irish Sea. While it is a Crown Dependency, it is a country in its own right, with its own currency, stamps, language and government.

This is a work of fiction. All of the characters are a product of the author's imagination. Any resemblance to actual persons, living or dead, is entirely coincidental. Similarly, the names of the restaurants and shops and other businesses on the island are fictional.

The Manx Museum is real (and appears on the cover)

however, all of the events that take place within it in this story are fictional. Manx National Heritage (MNH) is real and their staff work incredibly hard to preserve and celebrate the island's unique history and culture. All of the Manx National Heritage staff in this story, however, are fictional creations. Please see the notes at the end of the book for more information about the Manx Musuem.

The Isle of Man Constabulary is also real; however, their members in this story are very much fictional and I'm sure I have them behave in ways that their real-life counterparts never would.

Manx Archeology and History Conference Schedule of Events

Friday, 15th May

6:00 p.m. **Welcome Reception**
Come and enjoy a glass of wine with hors d'oeuvres.
Education Level Foyer

7:00 p.m. **Dr. Harold Smythe will open the conference.**
"An Update on the Isle of Man's Roman Past."
A.W. Moore Lecture Theatre

9:00 p.m. **American-style "Dessert Bar"**
Enjoy tea and coffee with a selection of brownies, biscuits and other "American-style" sweets.
Education Level Foyer and Kinvig Room

Saturday, 16th May

8:00 a.m. **Registration and Breakfast**
Education Level Foyer

10:00 a.m. **Session One**:
Dr. Joseph Steele.
"What Paleogeography Taught Me About Archaeology."
A.W. Moore Lecture Theatre

OR

Dr. Michael Brown
"Seventeenth Century Pottery Finds and

Unique Origins."
Kinvig Room

12:00 Noon **Lunch**
Manx Museum Café (ground floor)

2:00 p.m. **Session Two**:
Marjorie Stevens
"The Hidden Treasures in the Manx Museum Archives."
A.W. Moore Lecture Theatre

OR

Bus Excursion
Visit Rushen Abbey and Castle Rushen for short tours led by experts in their history and archaeology.
Buses will load in front of the museum and leave promptly at 2:00 p.m. They will return to the Museum in time for dinner.

4:00 p.m. **Round Table Discussion**
Join many of our guest speakers as they discuss alternative approaches to archaeology and history and how best to work together to deliver the best possible research.
A.W. Moore Lecture Theatre

6:00 p.m. **Italian Buffet Dinner**
Manx Museum Café (ground floor)

7:30 p.m. **Session Three:**
Paul Roberts
"Putting Manx Archaeology into a Wider Context."
A.W. Moore Lecture Theatre

OR

	Dr. Claire Jamison "Island Doesn't Mean Isolation. Considering the Similarities and Differences in Prehistoric Cultures on Anglesey and the Isle of Man." Kinvig Room
9:00 p.m.	**Tea and Coffee** Education Level Foyer

Sunday, 17th May

8:00 a.m.	**Registration and Breakfast** Education Level Foyer
10:00 a.m.	**Session Four:** Mary Morgan, Gary Rose, Steve Duncan and Doug James Join four researchers as they each give a twenty-minute "short talk." There will be a ten-minute question-and-answer session after each talk. A.W. Moore Lecture Theatre
OR	
	Dr. William Corlett "On Establishing a Centre for History and Archaeology on the Isle of Man." Kinvig Room
12:00 noon	**Lunch** Manx Museum Café (ground floor)
2:00 p.m.	**Session Five:** Elizabeth Cubbon "Surprising Secrets from 19th-Century Wills." A.W. Moore Lecture Theatre
OR	

Dr. Karen Cross
"Harvesting Prehistoric Pollen; a Look at Environmental Archaeology on the Isle of Man."
Kiving Room

4:00 p.m. **Closing Remarks**
Join Dr. Harold Smythe and Ms. Marjorie Stevens as they discuss what they've learned over the weekend.
A.W. Moore Lecture Theatre

AUNT BESSIE CONSIDERS

CHAPTER ONE

Bessie's taxi was late. She looked at her watch again and sighed deeply. She had plenty of time to get where she was going, but she'd ordered the taxi for half five, and it was now twenty-five to six and the car was nowhere in sight.

Elizabeth Cubbon, "Bessie" to nearly everyone in the village of Laxey, hated being late. She was due at the Manx Museum at six o'clock and if the taxi didn't hurry, she might not make it on time. She sighed again and then pulled her mobile phone from her handbag.

"Doona, it's Bessie," she said when her call was answered. "I just need to talk to someone while I wait for my taxi or I might just work myself into a real state." Doona's laugh made Bessie smile in spite of her anxiousness.

"I told you I could take you to the museum," Doona reminded her.

"But you don't have any interest in coming to the conference," Bessie replied to her close friend. "There isn't any point in your driving me all the way into Douglas for a conference you don't want to attend."

"I'm just not that interested in history and archaeology," Doona said in an apologetic voice. "I'm coming to hear your talk on Sunday, though."

Bessie shuddered. "I'm trying hard not to think about that right now," she told Doona. The blast of a car horn interrupted the conversation. "Oh, that's my car," Bessie said. "I've got to run."

Doona said a quick goodbye before Bessie disconnected and dropped the phone back into her bag. As she locked her front door behind herself, Bessie frowned. The dark hair and unnecessary sunglasses she could see through the vehicle's windscreen told her that Mark Stone, her least favourite driver, was behind the wheel of the car that was waiting for her.

"Hurry up, love," he called to Bessie now. "I've got a pickup at the Sea Terminal after I drop you off."

"You wouldn't have to rush so much if you'd been on time," Bessie couldn't stop herself from saying as she climbed into the cab.

"Oh, I stopped for a quick extra fare on my way to your place," he replied with a wave of his hand. "I knew you wouldn't mind waiting a bit. It isn't like you're going anywhere important, is it?"

Bessie bit back a dozen angry replies. "Actually, I'm going to the opening evening of the Manx Archaeology and History Conference at the Manx Museum," she told Mark in carefully measured tones. "I'm giving a paper on Sunday and tonight is the opening address."

"Gonna talk about your childhood?" Mark laughed. "I'm sure you've lived through a whole lot of history."

Bessie bristled at the rude reference to her age. It wasn't like the driver was a young man; he had to be in his late fifties or early sixties. Bessie sighed to herself. She'd stopped counting her birthdays once she'd turned sixty, but that had been a good many years ago now. One of these days she would have to admit to herself just how old she really was. But not today.

"I've been doing research into wills from the nineteenth century," she told Mark. "And I'm working on learning how to read handwriting from even earlier times so that I can help with research into those periods as well."

"So this conference thing is all weekend, is it?" Mark demanded.

"Yes, it starts tonight with an opening address and then there are a number of papers being given tomorrow and Sunday. Everything wraps up late Sunday afternoon."

"At the museum in downtown Douglas?" Mark checked.

"Yes, are you interested in attending?" Bessie worked to keep the scepticism from her voice.

Mark just laughed. "Hel, er, um, heck no," he told her. "I did enough history at school, thank you very much. But if there's lots of folks from across here for the conference, they'll be lots of folks needing taxis, won't there? Maybe I'll ask the boss to rotate me into Douglas for the weekend."

"As I understand it, all of the attendees from off-island are staying at one of the big hotels on the Promenade. They'll be able to walk to the museum from there. The museum is having the whole thing catered, so no one will have to go anywhere for meals, either. I think I'm probably the only person who is going to need a taxi to get back and forth."

Mark shrugged. "From what I've seen of the schedule, it looks like Dave is going to be doing most of your picking up and dropping off."

Bessie smiled. "That's good to know," she replied. "Now I'll know who to look for in the crowds." Dave was her favourite driver by far, but she didn't want to say as much to Mark.

"Why aren't you just staying in Douglas?" Mark asked.

Bessie wondered if he was genuinely curious or just making conversation. "It only takes a few minutes to get back and forth," she pointed out. "Anyway, I prefer to sleep in my own bed every night, and I love my little cottage."

"Aye, and I can see why, with your spot on the beach and all," Mark agreed. "Anyway, there's no place like home, right?"

Moments later he pulled up along the road behind the Manx Musuem. "Wanna hop out here and walk?" he asked in a hopeful voice. "The car park is such a nightmare."

Bessie thought about arguing, but she could see the queue of traffic trying to turn into the tiny museum car park. It would take far longer for Mark to get into the car park to let her out near the door than it would for her to walk the short distance.

"This is fine," she told him. "Have them put the trip on my account."

Mark nodded and was gone before Bessie had taken more then a few steps. She made her way towards the museum,

3

watching with interest as more cars arrived and parked. She spotted several familiar faces and waved to a few old friends as she reached the museum's front door.

The museum's foyer felt quiet and cool. The day had been warm, especially for the middle of May, but the museum was comfortable. The foyer was unexpectedly empty and Bessie figured she must have just missed one crowd of people and beaten the next. She waved a quick hello at the two men sitting at the information desk. They knew her on sight and one of them quickly handed her a registration packet.

"The conference schedule is inside," Doug told Bessie. "If you have any questions, Henry and I are going to be here all weekend."

Bessie thanked him, wishing she had time to chat with them further. They were both old friends, but she didn't want to arrive at the welcome reception any later than necessary. No doubt she would have plenty of opportunities to talk with Henry Costain and Doug Kelly throughout the weekend.

The lift whisked her up to the building's top floor quickly and quietly, but the noise that greeted Bessie when the doors opened was considerable. She left the lift and walked into the spacious foyer of the museum's "education" level with a small sigh. Already there were way too many people around for her to feel completely comfortable. The welcome reception was due to last until quarter to seven and Bessie was suddenly sorry that Mark hadn't been even later than he had. She'd forgotten how much she disliked crowds.

She began to work her way around the room, sticking to the edge of the crowd that appeared to number somewhere near a hundred people. She could only hope that they weren't all planning to attend her talk on Sunday. While she'd been giving papers at these sorts of conferences for years and she loved sharing her research, she still wasn't totally comfortable in front of a large group of people.

Many of the faces she saw were familiar, but only in an "I know that person from somewhere" sort of way. Bessie knew that she ought to recognise some of the more important historians and archaeologists that were there, but at the moment she felt too overwhelmed by the noise and sheer number of people in the small space to start making sense of them all.

She headed towards the long table where food and drinks were being offered. That seemed the best place to station herself while she gathered her thoughts. She could get herself a drink and try out a few of the hors d'oeuvres without looking like she was avoiding talking to people. A few steps away from her goal, however, she was intercepted.

"Bessie? How wonderful to see you again." Helen Baxter sounded nervous and slightly desperate as she took Bessie's arm. "And thank goodness I found you. I was about to hide in the ladies' loo until time for the talk to begin."

Bessie laughed lightly. "Now don't do that," she told the woman. "Everyone is very friendly; you could have started a conversation with anyone."

Helen looked at Bessie sceptically. "I tried to start a chat with one guy and he was so insulted that I didn't know who he was that he scared me off doing anything more than nodding and smiling at the rest."

Bessie laughed again. Helen was a very pretty blonde in her mid-thirties; Bessie couldn't believe that any man wouldn't be happy to have her strike up a conversation. Helen was a nurse at Noble's Hospital with a special interest in the medical history of the island. She'd only recently started doing some of her own research and attending conferences and she wouldn't previously have had a chance to get to meet many of the people at this one.

"Which guy?" Bessie asked.

Helen wrinkled her nose and then looked around the room. "That's him, over there," she gestured towards the far corner of the room. "The man with the unnaturally dark hair. The one with the overinflated blonde hanging on his arm."

Bessie turned to see which man Helen was talking about. "Oh my," she replied. "His date doesn't look like the sort of person who usually attends these things."

"She must have been in the loo or something when I tried talking to him," Helen said. "He was standing on his own and so was I. I was just being friendly."

Bessie took another look at the mismatched couple. "That's Mack Dickson," she told Helen. "He's an archaeologist." Looking around to make sure she wouldn't be overheard, Bessie leaned in closer to Helen. "He likes to think he's more like Indiana Jones than a serious scholar, if you know what I mean?"

Helen grinned. "He's too old and fat to be Indiana Jones," she giggled.

Bessie smiled. "He's in his mid-forties and he only comes to these sorts of things when he thinks he has something shocking and terribly exciting to announce. I wonder what he's doing here?"

Helen shrugged. "I have no idea. I didn't see his name on the programme."

Bessie nodded. "He isn't on the programme. I'm sure of it."

"What about his sexy blonde girlfriend with the huge, um, assets? Does she usually come along?" Helen asked.

Bessie shook her head. "He always has a beautiful blonde woman on his arm, but I haven't seen this one before. Mind you, he hasn't been on the island in maybe five or six years. She was probably still in primary school then."

Helen laughed loudly at that. "She looks bored out of her mind," she whispered to Bessie. "I'm going to go and try to talk to her."

Bessie grinned. "Good luck," she told the other woman. Bessie felt much more relaxed now as she made her way to the refreshment table. She took a plate and piled a mini quiche and a couple of interesting-looking canapés onto it. After a bit of indecision, she selected a glass of white wine before turning her attention back to the room.

She watched as Helen made her way across the space. Bessie was gratified to see her get caught up in a conversation with Mark Blake from Manx National Heritage.

"Hello, Bessie." A quiet voice from behind her had Bessie spinning around. Liz Martin was standing next to the food table, clutching a half-full plate.

"Liz, how wonderful to see you here," she told the young and pretty blonde woman from her Manx language class. "Kys t'ou?"

Liz laughed. "Ta mee braew. Although actually, I'm feeling rather unsure of myself, but I've no idea how to say that in Manx."

"I should introduce you to Helen," Bessie told her young friend. "She's feeling rather out of place as well."

"I've never been to this sort of conference before," Liz confessed. "I'm only here to support Marjorie. I've had to leave Bill to get the kids to bed and you know that's usually a disaster."

Bessie laughed. "I would have thought, after all the classes you've been to, that Bill would have learned how to do it by now."

Liz shook her head. "He does better some weeks than others," she told Bessie. "Mostly, though, he's like a little kid himself. He would rather play with them then put them to bed. I feel bad, because he's at work all week, so he doesn't get anywhere near as much time with them as I do, but I do try to keep them to a routine at bedtime. It's almost getting harder as they get bigger, you know? They're getting to be a lot more fun to play with now that they can talk. Jackson is almost three; he's just about mastered 'hide and seek,' although he always insists on hiding in the exact same place."

Bessie laughed. "At least you don't have any trouble finding him."

"No," Liz agreed. "The problem is pretending not to find him. I have to say, Bill is much better at that than I am. He'll spend ages looking under sofa cushions and pillows and pretending to pull up the fitted carpets. All the while Jackson will be giggling madly from behind the door. Kylie doesn't understand that it's a game, of course, so if we say 'where's Jackson?' she'll run over and point to him." Liz shook her head. "Sometimes it's nice to get out among grownups for a few hours."

"Well, I'm sure Marjorie will be delighted that you came," Bessie told her.

Liz's handbag began to buzz insistently. She pulled her mobile from it and sighed when she looked at the tiny screen. "It's Bill. I just hope nothing's seriously wrong."

"It will be quieter down the corridor," Bessie suggested, pointing towards a short hallway that led to a few small classrooms and the loos.

"Thanks, I'll see you later." Liz dashed off before Bessie could reply. Bessie shook her head and then turned back towards the table to see what else was on offer.

"Oh, excuse me, do you happen to know what's in these?" Bessie turned towards the voice and smiled at the confused looking young man next to her.

"What's in what?" she asked.

"Well, all of this stuff," the man replied, waving an arm at the food table. "None of it looks the least bit familiar."

Bessie grinned. The poor man couldn't have been more than twenty-five. His green eyes looked tired and his thick brown hair needed combing. "From your accent, I'm guessing you're American," she said.

"Yes, I am," the man smiled back. "And I'm absolutely starving. I've been studying in London since the beginning of the year, but I went home for a few weeks and just flew back over yesterday, straight from Idaho to here with what felt like a dozen plane changes."

"That's quite a long journey," Bessie agreed. "Although I've only crossed the ocean by boat and that was quite a long time ago."

"By boat?" The man shook his head. "I thought flying was bad. The problem is, once I finally got to my hotel here, I pretty much just slept until about half an hour ago. I feel as if I haven't eaten in forever. But I'm, well, sort of a fussy eater," he shrugged apologetically. "I just want a nice plain ham sandwich, but I'd settle for bread and water."

"How about fish and chips?" Bessie asked, pointing to the tiny battered fish bites that were sitting on small slices of fried potato. "Or mini sausage rolls or Scotch eggs." Bessie led the man along the table, pointing out each item as she spoke. His face was a picture of concentration as she explained what was on each plate. Finally he selected a couple of things and took a hesitant bite of one.

"Hey, this isn't bad," he said, relief evident in his tone. He piled several more things onto his plate, shovelling another one into his mouth, before he finally turned back to Bessie.

"Oh my goodness, thank you ever so much," he said after he washed down his mouthful with a sip of wine. "I'm Joe Steele, by the way." He looked down at his hands and frowned. With a plate in one hand and a wine glass in the other, there was no way he could shake Bessie's hand, which he clearly felt he should.

"It's nice to meet you, Mr. Steele." Bessie grinned at his obvious confusion. "I'm Bessie Cubbon."

"Oh, it's nice to meet you as well, Mrs. Cubbon," the man replied. "Technically I'm Dr. Joseph Steele, but I've only had the title for about six months and I never think to introduce myself that way. Anyway, you can just call me Joe."

"Congratulations on earning your doctorate," Bessie replied. "Technically I'm Miss Cubbon, but everyone calls me Aunt Bessie, although I don't often introduce myself that way."

"Can I be rude and ask why people call you Aunt Bessie?" Joe asked.

Bessie nodded. "I was never lucky enough to have children," she explained. "But I very much enjoy their company. I have a little cottage by the sea in Laxey and over the last many years I've been happy to act as honourary aunt to just about every child in the village."

"What fun," Joe grinned. "So what brings you to the conference?"

"I've been doing research into Manx history for many years," Bessie replied. "I'm actually giving a paper on Sunday about nineteenth-century wills. What about you? What brings you here?"

Joe flushed. "I'm almost afraid to tell you," he told Bessie in a near whisper. "Everyone else I've spoken to has pretty much laughed at me."

"Oh dear," Bessie answered. "But why?"

"The thing is," Joe confided. "I'm a palaeontologist, or rather I was a palaeontologist. Just recently I found out that I have Manx ancestry and I started getting interested in the island. Now I want to do more research and some archaeology here, but some people seem to think that I should have just stayed at home, digging up dinosaurs."

"Who said that?" Bessie demanded, feeling angry that someone had upset the young man, who seemed to have nothing but good intentions.

"Oh, Dr. Dickson," Joe replied blushing. "I was so excited to meet him because he's so well known, even in the US, and I didn't know he was going to be here. Anyway, he seems to think that I'm nothing but an amateur who's sticking his trowel where it doesn't belong."

Bessie shook her head; that was two people the man had been rude to already and the conference hadn't even started yet.

"Don't pay any attention to him," Bessie told the young man. "Everyone here will be delighted if you want to undertake some research on the island. There are never enough trained and talented people to do the history of the island justice. Just ignore Mack Dickson and do what you want to do."

Joe smiled. "I can see why you're everyone's honourary aunt," he told Bessie.

The pair chatted amiably for several minutes as the room seemed to get increasingly crowded. Joe munched his way through several plates of snacks while Bessie limited herself to a few of her favourites. They both sipped their wine while Bessie filled Joe in on everyone that she recognised.

"That's Marjorie Stevens," she told the young man, gesturing to the pretty thirty-something blonde who had just entered the room. "She works in the archives here and was instrumental in organising the conference."

"She doesn't look happy," Joe remarked.

Bessie studied the woman who was something of a mentor to her, in spite of being substantially younger. Marjorie was frowning and her light blue eyes were puffy and red-rimmed. Bessie wondered what could possibly have upset her. She watched as Marjorie made her way through the crowd, heading straight for the table where Bessie was standing.

Marjorie stopped when she reached the table and Bessie watched as she grabbed a glass of wine. Bessie had never seen Marjorie drink anything stronger than tea, so she was surprised to see her down the wine in a single swallow. Marjorie had a second glass in her hand before she turned around and gave the room a quick once-over. Bessie smiled at her, but Marjorie didn't seem to notice.

"She's really pretty," Joe said. "But she looks really angry. Do you know what's going on?"

Bessie shook her head, trying to decide whether she should go and try talking to her friend or not. "I have no idea. When I talked to her yesterday, she was very excited about the conference. I can't imagine what's happened."

A snort of laughter from behind her had Bessie spinning around. "Harold," she cried in delight as she recognised the man who had obviously come up behind her while her attention was focussed on Marjorie. "How wonderful to see you again."

"Great to see you as well," the prematurely middle-aged and already grey-haired man replied gruffly. He was a well-known archaeologist and historian who had done a great deal of important work on the island, primarily attempting to find evidence that the Romans had either once lived on the island or at least visited it during their years of governing England.

"Have you met Dr. Joseph Steele?" Bessie asked, introducing the younger man. "Joe, this is Dr. Harold Smythe."

"Oh," Joe blushed. "What a great pleasure it is to meet you," he sputtered. "I'm a huge fan of yours and I was really hoping to get to talk to you about my research. But only if you have some time, I mean I don't want to impose."

Harold waved a hand. "Catch me over lunch or dinner tomorrow or we'll have drinks in the evening one night. Whatever works for you. I'm always happy to talk to anyone about their research. I'd be more enthusiastic if the circumstances were different."

"What on earth does that mean?" Bessie demanded. "This conference was your idea and you did all the groundwork. And now you've got a fabulous turnout for your opening lecture."

Harold laughed again. "If only," he muttered.

"What's going on?" Bessie asked, surprised by the angry look that flashed across Harold's face. It seemed to just about match the look that Marjorie was wearing.

Harold sighed deeply. "Mack Dickson is what's going on," he told Bessie with another sigh. "He arrived this afternoon and persuaded George Quayle that he should give the opening address."

"Pardon?" Bessie gasped. "But he can't do that," she insisted. "You spent months planning this conference and there was plenty of notice given for papers to be submitted. No one can just turn up on opening day and demand to speak."

"You can if you're Mack Dickson," Harold told her glumly. "Apparently he told George that what he has to say is so important that he has to go first."

"And George believes him?" Bessie asked.

"I guess so," Harold said. "I'm sure he told George more than he's telling anyone else." Harold shrugged. "All I know is that whatever he said, it was enough to persuade George to ask me to rearrange the schedule. Mack gets the opening talk and I get to scramble around and find someplace else to fit my talk into the programme."

Bessie frowned. "That is not fair," she said crossly.

"I'm sorry, but who is George?" Joe asked.

Harold shook his head. "George Quayle is the museum's main benefactor and also the very generous sponsor of this conference. I'm sure Mack knew that if he approached anyone on the conference committee and asked to give a talk we would all say 'no,' so he went behind our backs and appealed to George."

"And George is, um, persuadable," Bessie said with a rueful grin. "Mack obviously knew exactly how to put things to the man to get him to go along with his scheme. But what is Mack going to talk about?"

"That's the big question on everyone's lips," Harold replied. "He won't tell anyone anything except, 'It'll blow this conference out of the water,' and that's a direct quote."

Bessie frowned. "He always thinks whatever he's uncovered is the most interesting bit of history or archeology ever," she said. "I've never been terribly impressed with any of his 'big' announcements."

"No offense, my dear lady," Harold replied. "But you aren't the audience that Mack is trying to impress."

"I know the British university system is different," Joe interjected. "Like you don't have tenure and such, so is he trying to impress someone to get a better position?"

Harold shook his head. "Personally I think Mack is just the sort of person who's only happy if he feels superior to everyone. He always has to have the flashiest car, the prettiest blonde and the most shocking findings with his research. He's nowhere near as clever as he thinks he is, his work is nowhere near as carefully researched as it should be, he's...."

"On his way over," Bessie interrupted. A moment later the man in question joined their little group.

"Harold, my dear man, I do hope you aren't too disappointed to be giving up the opening to me. I can assure you that what I have to say will be of huge interest to you."

Harold smiled tightly. "Indeed, I'm very interested in hearing what you have to say."

"But Harold, you must introduce me to your friends." Mack gave Bessie an insincere smile. "Although you do look familiar," he told her. "I'm sure we've met."

"I'm Elizabeth Cubbon," she said as she offered a hand. "We met at the Celtic Scholars conference about six or seven years ago, when it was held in Port Erin."

Mack took her hand in both of his. "Ah yes, Bessie, isn't it? You research wills, don't you?"

Bessie nodded. "I've been focussed on the nineteenth century, but I'm starting to work my way backwards."

"How nice," the man answered vaguely as his attention turned to the rest of the group. "And you're that young American who's just given up dinosaurs in favour of digging into Manx history," he said as he nodded at Joe. "But you all have to meet Bambi."

Mack turned to the young woman who had accompanied him across the room. She was standing just behind him, staring blankly into space.

"This is Bambi Marks," Mack announced to them.

"Bambi?" Joe echoed quietly.

"She's American as well," Mack told him. "Maybe you've met?"

"Oh, well, I, that is, um, America's a big place, and I mean, um," Joe stammered as the beautiful blonde gave him a cool look.

"Just winding you up," Mack laughed, slapping the younger man on the back with false bonhomie. "Bambi, this is Joe Steele, Harold Smythe and Miss Elizabeth Cubbon. They're all deeply devoted Manx historians and researchers who work tirelessly to uncover the secrets of the past."

Bambi blinked. "Nice to meet ya," she drawled, looking past Bessie into the distance. The silence that followed her remark started to grow uncomfortable until Bambi suddenly spoke again.

"Mack, where's the ladies'?" she demanded in a loud voice.

Bessie sighed as Mack frowned at his date.

"It's just around the corner," she told the young woman. "Come along and I'll show you," she offered.

"Oh, fabulous," Bambi replied, still not looking directly at anyone.

Bessie led the much younger woman out of the foyer into the short hallway. Doors to smaller rooms that could be used as classrooms or for seminars and discussion groups opened off both sides of the hall. At the very end of the hall were the loos.

"Thanks, Mrs. Cubbon," Bambi remarked suddenly.

"Actually, it's Miss Cubbon," Bessie corrected her gently.

"Oh, okay," Bambi shrugged.

Bambi followed Bessie into the ladies' room, which was otherwise empty. Bessie decided that since she was there, she might as well take advantage of the facilities. The soft music that was piped into the room served to mask any noise within it. Moments later, as Bessie washed her hands, she realised that she was alone. Obviously Bambi had been quicker and had already left.

Bessie walked back towards the reception slowly. She wasn't in any rush to rejoin the crowd. In the doorway she paused and surveyed the room. A loud voice, booming over the low murmur, let her know that George Quayle had arrived even before she spotted him.

He wasn't hard to pick out in the crowd. He was at least six feet tall, which meant he was a good nine inches taller than Bessie. To Bessie's mind, he was at least as wide as he was tall, being generously padded all around. He was somewhere in his sixties with a still generous helping of white hair and bright green eyes that had never focussed on a stranger. Bessie watched as he greeted yet another person. She sighed and edged her way into the crowd, heading away from George. As soon as he spotted her, he'd be sure to join her, and she wasn't in any hurry for that to happen.

It wasn't that she disliked the man. It was impossible to dislike George Quayle; he was too kind and unfailingly generous. But he had made his fortune in sales, selling everything from encyclopedias to used cars to insurance, and whenever Bessie spoke with him she could just feel the salesman in him in every word. Even if his comment were as simple as "good morning," Bessie couldn't help but feel that he was working to convince her that she was having quite a pleasant start to her day, really.

He had grown up on the island, but made most of his fortune in the UK. He'd been back on Man for no more than a year, but he'd made a huge impact in that short time, donating generously to numerous causes and appearing at just about every event the island offered.

She worked her way through the crowd, nodding and smiling at many familiar faces, but not stopping to chat.

"Ah, Bessie, I was happy to see your name on the programme."

Bessie stopped and then smiled at the young man at her elbow. "William Corlett, how wonderful to see you here," she said with genuine enthusiasm.

"It's wonderful to see you as well," he replied in kind.

"Oh, but I should say 'Dr. Corlett' now, shouldn't I?" Bessie asked. "You've gone and earned your doctorate while I wasn't looking."

The man laughed. "You can call me anything you like," he told her. "We've known each other for far too long to stand on ceremony, surely."

"I saw your mother one day last week and she was trying very hard not to gush too much about your accomplishments," Bessie told the man. "She's ever so proud of you."

William flushed. "Mum and dad both seem pleased," he acknowledged. "And now it looks as if I might be able to find a position here on the island as well. They'd both like that."

"I didn't realise anyone was hiring archeologists," Bessie said. "Is MNH looking to expand their staff?"

"Haven't you seen the programme for this weekend?" William demanded. "I'm going to be talking about a proposal that being drawn up between MNH, a major university in Liverpool that I can't formally identify yet, and the Manx government. We're hoping to establish a research centre here on the island that would provide assistance to anyone and everyone that wants to study any aspect of the island."

"Really?" Bessie asked. "I just put all my registration paperwork in my bag and didn't even glance at the final programme. Marjorie showed me a draft copy last week, but I don't remember you being on it. Why haven't I heard anything about this before?"

William laughed. "It's been kept very quiet until now," he told her. "Only a handful of people have been involved up to this point, but now that we have the government on board, it's time to start fundraising. You know what that means. It won't be long before everyone is tired of hearing about the project."

Bessie laughed. "Fundraising is a tough job," she said. "I hope you have a lot of help."

"Oh, I do," William assured her. "In fact, I'm not even on that committee. MNH has their experts handling the bulk of it. I'm only involved inasmuch as they've offered me a job with the centre, if and when it actually happens."

"Well, I certainly hope it all works out," Bessie told him. "It sounds like just the sort of thing the island needs."

"And I'd love to be able to move back here for good," William said. "Then it will be time to start thinking about a wedding."

"You've asked Maggie to marry you?" Bessie asked. "Your mother didn't mention that."

"I haven't actually asked her yet," William shrugged. "But we've been together forever and everyone assumes we'll be getting married. I just need to make sure I have a good job in place and we'll be set."

It wasn't the most romantic declaration of love Bessie had ever heard, but it wasn't any of her business. "How's Finlo, then?" she asked, inquiring about William's cousin. The two were nearly as close as brothers, or at least had been growing up. "He did archeology at university as well, didn't he? Is he going to come and work at the centre as well or is he still flying?"

William laughed. "He's definitely still flying," he told Bessie. "He only got his degree to make his parents happy. They agreed to pay for his pilot's license if he got a good degree first. He loves flying. I suspect that's because there are a lot more pretty girls on planes than in muddy pits."

Bessie laughed. "He did always have an eye for a pretty girl."

"And a crazy get-rich-quick scheme," William added. "He's trying to persuade his parents to help him start a charter air service on the island."

"Surely that would be too expensive for the average traveller?" Bessie asked.

William laughed. "He's not interested in catering to the average traveller," he told her. "He's hoping to attract the very wealthiest of clients. He also figures that the entire Quayle family will have to use his service and goodness knows there are enough of us to keep him in business."

Bessie grinned. "Absolutely, you Quayle cousins are everywhere," she agreed. "But I'm still not sure a charter airline will fly, if you'll pardon the pun."

William laughed loudly. "I'm going to call Finlo later and tell him you said that," he told Bessie.

William disappeared into the crowd, while Bessie slipped over to a quiet corner where a few chairs had been placed. She sank into one. Maybe she could hide here until it was time for the lecture to start. Only a moment later, however, she was interrupted.

"Ah, Bessie, there you are," young Joe Steele grinned at her.

"No, don't get up," he insisted, even though Bessie hadn't moved an inch and had no intention of getting up. "Is it okay if I join you?"

Bessie shrugged. "You're more than welcome," she said politely.

The young man slid into a chair next to her and grinned. "I'm feeling positively exhausted," he confided. "I feel like I could sleep for a week. I don't suppose I can get any coffee anywhere?"

"There should be some on the table somewhere," Bessie replied. "I know there will be some available after Mack's speech. They're meant to be having an American-style 'dessert bar' with fairy cakes and brownies and the like. I'm sure there will be tea and coffee as well."

"So I just have to stay awake through Dr. Dickson's talk," Joe smiled. "That might be easier said than done."

Bessie smiled back at him. "It shouldn't be long now," she said as she glanced at her watch. "They should at least be opening the doors to the lecture hall soon so we can go in and get seats."

"I'm sorry, but may I join you?" The polite voice startled Bessie. She was quick to look over and smile at the newcomer.

"Of course you can," she said easily. "Anyone is welcome."

"Thanks," the young woman answered as she perched herself on the edge of the last remaining chair.

"I'm Elizabeth Cubbon," Bessie said as she studied the new arrival.

"Oh, I'm Claire Jamison," the woman replied.

"And I'm Joe Steele," the young man spoke from his seat as he leaned forward to offer his hand.

Bessie studied the woman as she gave Joe a hesitant handshake. Claire looked older than the young man who was now blushing as he sat back in his seat. Bessie would have guessed her to be around thirty. She had a great deal of dark brown hair piled messily on top of her head. Thick glasses made it impossible to determine her eye colour. She was slender and her business suit fit her perfectly.

"So what brings you here?" Joe asked.

"I'm doing some postdoctoral research into prehistoric island cultures," Claire explained. "I've been focussed on Anglesey for most of the year, but this conference gave me a chance to do some comparison work between Anglesey and the Isle of Man, and I loved every minute of it. I'll be talking about what I've found in tomorrow's evening session."

"Have you met Mack Dickson, then?" Bessie asked. "I know he did some work on Anglesey."

"I don't think so," Claire answered. "Is he here?"

"That's him," Bessie answered, pointing. "The dark-haired man standing next to the very young blonde."

Claire shook her head. "He doesn't look like anyone I've met," she told Bessie.

"What's Anglesey like, then?" Joe asked. Bessie sat back and relaxed, letting the conversation between the two young scholars carry on without her.

"Bessie? My goodness, but you were hard to find." The voice boomed across the room. Bessie sighed and got to her feet as George Quayle lumbered towards her quiet corner.

"Hello, George," she said softly.

"Bessie, I do hope you weren't hiding from me," he rumbled back.

"Now why would I do that?" Bessie asked. "It's always so nice to see you."

George grinned. "I could say the same about you," he told Bessie, pulling her into a bear hug. "You know I only agreed to sponsor this conference because Marjorie said you'd be taking part."

Bessie grinned. She knew no such thing and doubted there was any truth to it. "I'm just glad you agreed, for whatever reason. I've been so looking forward to this."

George smiled. "You know I'd do anything for you, Bessie, my love."

"Better not let Mary hear that," she joked.

"Aye, ah, yes, my lovely better half," he laughed. "She couldn't make it tonight, you know. So I'm all yours."

"I hope nothing's wrong," Bessie said with genuine concern. She didn't know Mary Quayle well, but she'd always admired the quiet and kind woman who was willing to be married to George.

"Oh, nothing's wrong," George assured her. "One of the grandkids is doing some play or something at school and she didn't want to miss it. You know we dragged the whole family back to the island when we moved back. Anyway, I'm sure she'll be here later in the weekend."

"Great, I'd love to see her," Bessie told him.

"Well now, it's just about time to go in." George took Bessie's arm. "You should come and sit up front with me. That way you won't have any trouble hearing."

Bessie bit her tongue. There was absolutely nothing wrong with her hearing, but she wasn't about to argue her way out of a front row seat. Especially not for this talk, which promised to be very interesting, indeed.

CHAPTER TWO

George escorted Bessie through the crowds towards the main lecture hall, formally called the A.W. Moore Lecture Theatre. He waved to one or two people over Bessie's head, but didn't stop to talk to anyone. Harold and Marjorie followed in their wake. Harold still looked angry and he seemed to be ignoring everyone as he stomped through the crowd, grimly focussed on the door to the hall. Bessie glanced at Marjorie. Her eyes were still puffy and red, but she gave Bessie a tight-lipped smile when Bessie caught her eye. Bessie wished that she'd been able to find time to talk with her friend earlier in the evening. Now their chat would have to wait until after Mack's lecture.

As George approached the door, Henry from Manx National Heritage quickly pulled it open for him. George and Bessie stepped into the room with Harold and Marjorie on their heels. Henry was quick to shut the door behind them, not allowing anyone else from the eager crowd into the space.

"I always like to sit right up front," George told the others, making his way down the narrow central aisle between the neat rows of folding chairs. "Come on, Bessie, you can sit with me and tell me if whatever Mack's talking about is any good."

Bessie sighed as she followed the man towards the front of the room. She hoped he wouldn't keep whispering to her during Mack's talk. She was eager to hear what Mack had to say.

Harold ignored George and Bessie and carefully chose a seat near the back door. Marjorie whispered something to him and slipped back out of the room. George, of course, sat in the very centre of the front row and waved Bessie into the seat next to his.

"Here you go, my dear," he told her. "Now you won't miss a thing."

He settled his considerable bulk into the seat, and that seemed to flip some unseen switch. Both sets of doors at the back of the room suddenly opened and the hall began to fill very rapidly with people. Bessie perched on her chair next to George and twisted around to face the back of the room. She watched as the space filled to capacity.

"I know that Harold Smythe is a smart guy," George told Bessie in a loud confiding tone. "But I don't think he would have packed them in tonight like Mack is doing."

Bessie couldn't help but agree. Mack was very good at generating interest in himself. She just hoped the talk would live up to his promises. She watched as Joe found seats for himself and Claire Jamison. The pair seemed to be having a great time talking together. Helen Baxter had found a seat as well, and she seemed to be talking earnestly with young Bambi, who looked bewildered. Bessie smiled and waved to a few friends and acquaintances she'd missed at the reception. She'd have to try to catch some of them during the "dessert bar" later.

A couple of members of the museum staff were kept busy bringing out additional chairs and for a while it looked as if some of the crowd might have to stand during the lecture, but eventually enough chairs were found and set up to accommodate everyone. The doors at the back of the hall were shut and an expectant silence descended on the room. Bessie settled back in her uncomfortable chair and turned her attention to the podium in front of her.

The pause that followed was just becoming awkward when Harold Smythe walked up from the back of the room.

"Ahem, um, good evening everyone," he began. "I've been asked to introduce our guest speaker tonight," he said. The expression on his face left no doubt in anyone's mind as to how he felt about being asked to perform the task. "I'm sure that you are all aware of our guest. Indeed, I'm certain that most of you are here at his invitation, but just in case you came expecting to hear a somewhat different speaker, ahem, let me set everything straight."

"They should have had me introduce Mack," George whispered to Bessie. "I've not got my knickers in a twist like Harold."

"Tonight we are, um, fortunate, to have Dr. Mack Dickson with us to present a paper about which I know nothing," Harold continued. "Mack is a well-known archaeologist and historian who always brings his own unique interpretations to everything he discovers. I know we're all waiting impatiently to hear about his latest findings, so without further ado, ladies and gentlemen, Mack Dickson."

Harold stomped back towards his seat at the back of the room without waiting for Mack to appear.

After what Bessie could only assume was meant to be a dramatic pause, Mack made his entrance through a small door at the front of the room. Bessie knew from experience that beyond the door was a tiny windowless space, known to everyone as the cuillee, where anxious speakers could gather their thoughts before they faced their audience.

Mack bounced up to the podium, seemingly immensely excited about something. "Good evening, everyone," he said almost breathlessly. "What I'm about to talk to you about is going to change Manx history forever."

"Well, that's some introduction," George muttered to Bessie.

Bessie heard a noise behind her and glanced back to see Marjorie slipping into the room. Henry quickly got up from his seat and waved Marjorie into it. No doubt, as one of the conference organisers, Marjorie had been checking on the arrangements for the rest of the evening.

Bessie turned back around. Mack was smiling at the crowd, waiting for them to settle after the minor interruption. He began his speech with a summary of the island's prehistory. It was likely that most members of the audience were already very familiar with the subject, but somehow Mack made it feel new and exciting.

"I'm not sure what he has coming up," George whispered to Bessie. "But this is all pretty interesting so far."

Bessie nodded her silent agreement. Mack had been talking for over twenty minutes and he hadn't said anything new, but Bessie still felt as if she was hanging on his every word. Whatever she thought of him as a person, he was an incredibly gifted speaker.

"The most interesting part of the island's prehistory, of course, is the lack of evidence for Roman occupation," Mack told them. "The Romans knew the island was here, and we have good reason to suspect that they traded with its residents, but we don't have any evidence for any Roman settlement. Until now."

He paused dramatically, taking a drink of water while a murmur went through the crowd. "I received a phone call a few months ago from a farmer I know here on the island. He'd decided to build a new barn in a field that hadn't been ploughed in many years. It was a field that has never, to the best of my knowledge, been excavated in any way. When the farmer began to dig the foundations for his new barn, he found an odd coin."

"Which he should have immediately reported to the proper authorities," George said to Bessie with a shake of his head.

"As he had no idea what he'd found, he called me and asked me to take a look. He didn't want to bother the good folks at Manx National Heritage if his bit of shiny metal turned out to be a bottle cap from the nineteen-fifties." Mack laughed, but that did little to diffuse the tension that was now building in the hall. Anyone on the island who found anything that could have serious historical value was meant to contact Manx National Heritage, not call Mack Dickson.

"Now I want to show you a few pictures," Mack continued, with something approaching a nervous grin.

The lights were dimmed and slides began to appear on the screen in the front of the room. Bessie watched as photo after photo flashed past, each picture showing different archaeological finds. Everything from small collections of coins to bits of broken pottery to pieces of glass appeared. Even to her untrained eye, all of the items, especially the coins, appeared to be Roman in origin.

After around a dozen slides had been shown, Mack stepped back to the podium and the lights were turned back on. "That's just a small sampling of what I discovered when I did a test dig in the farmer's field," he told his audience. "I haven't included any photographs of the handful of tesserae I found. I wanted to wait to show them to you after I've uncovered what I think will be an entire Roman mosaic floor."

He paused there and Bessie could hear the low buzz of excited conversation as it swept through the room. Mack hadn't exaggerated. If he was right and he'd uncovered evidence of a Roman settlement on the island, everything the historians thought they knew about the island's history would have to be re-evaluated.

"Well, that's certainly stirred things up," George whispered to Bessie. "Harold must be having fits in the back."

Bessie wondered how Harold was feeling. He'd spent most of his career looking for evidence of Roman occupation and it seemed like Mack had beaten him to the punch.

She sighed. "Poor Harold," she murmured to George. "He must be terribly upset."

"So where is it?" Harold let everyone know exactly how upset he was by shouting angrily from the back of the room.

Mack grinned. "I'm sorry, but I'm not taking questions right now," he said with a smirk. "After I've finished I would be happy to answer your questions, but for now I'd like to have a chance to conclude my remarks."

The whole room seemed to hold their collective breath as they waited to hear Harold's reply. He simply muttered "whatever," which felt somewhat anticlimactic.

Mack smiled a nasty smile and continued. "There is no doubt in my mind that what I've uncovered thus far should be counted as among the most significant archaeological finds in the history of the Isle of Man. What's even more exciting, though, is that I've barely scratched the surface. What I need now is funding and staff. I'd like to think that Manx National Heritage would be interested in funding a full-scale excavation at the site, and I hope they might have enough eager volunteers to help staff the undertaking. Of course MNH often struggles to find financing for their projects. I am, therefore, appealing to everyone in the audience tonight to consider assisting in some way with raising the necessary funds to make this dig a reality."

"I'll fund it," George announced from his seat. "You show me what you've found so far, and where, and I'll fund a proper dig of the whole site."

Mack flushed. "That's very kind of you, George," he said. "I can't tell you how delighted I am to hear that. On behalf of the entire Manx nation, I thank you most sincerely."

George snorted. "Sincerity isn't his strong suit," he muttered to Bessie quietly.

"I had planned on using the rest of my time to try to persuade you all to invest in the excavation. That's clearly no longer necessary, so I'll just wrap up there," Mack told the audience. "I need twenty minutes or so to gather my thoughts and go back over my notes before we have our question-and-answer session. I believe there's some sort of collection of puddings on offer in the lobby."

Before anyone could speak, Mack gathered up his notes and disappeared through the door to the cuillee.

As the cuillee door shut behind Mack, the room erupted. Bessie rose to her feet slowly, her mind racing.

"Well, that was certainly something," George said over the clamour.

"It was indeed," Bessie answered. "Poor Harold."

"Yes, rather," George glanced around the room. "I think he must have already escaped," he told Bessie. "I can't see him anywhere."

"Maybe he wanted to be first at the 'dessert bar,'" Bessie suggested wryly.

"That's probably it," George laughed. "Nothing like a chocolate biscuit to make you feel better after your entire life's work has just been snatched out from under you."

Bessie shook her head. "I think I'm going to go look for him, or maybe grab something sweet," she told George.

"I need to talk to a few people," George told her. "I'll catch you in a little while."

Bessie moved away, slowly ducking in and around the vocal

crowd.

"And I'll save your seat for the question-and-answer session," George shouted to Bessie.

Bessie grinned and waved her thanks just before the crowd swallowed her up. She made her way towards the open doors at the back of the room, noting that Marjorie had already left the room as well. She couldn't see Joe and Claire or Helen and Bambi either. Excited snippets of conversation washed over her as she travelled.

"No, there's never been any evidence...."

"Harold Smythe is the real expert, of course, but Mack's always happy to poke in...."

"...been cultivating relationships with the farmers here for the last ten years or more. I can't believe any of them would call Mack instead of Harold, but...."

At the door Bessie glanced back into the room. She didn't recognise any of the people who were now surrounding George. The room was slowly emptying as it became obvious that Mack was serious about taking a break. When she turned around, she didn't see anyone she knew in the foyer either.

When Bessie spotted the table laden down with puddings, she was glad she'd managed to beat the crowd, though. She grabbed a small plate and selected a delicious-looking chocolate brownie as well as a miniature Victoria sponge and a pair of chocolate éclairs. She picked up a hot cup of tea with her empty hand and looked around for somewhere to sit.

The foyer was now beginning to fill up as people streamed out of the lecture hall. An open door on the opposite wall caught Bessie's attention. She headed towards it. Inside the small lecture hall, the Kinvig Room, which would be used for other talks later in the weekend, tables and chairs had been set up in small groups that would lend themselves well to conversation. Bessie stepped gratefully into the room, eager to put her plate and drink down and then enjoy her treats.

Once inside the door, she realised that the room wasn't empty. Marjorie and Harold sat side by side in one corner having what looked like an intense conversation. Bessie coughed loudly as she took another step into the room. Two heads snapped in her direction. Bessie forced a smile onto her lips.

"I hope I'm not interrupting," she said. "The door was open."

"It really shouldn't have been," Harold said crossly. "Everyone will start coming in to eat their pudding if we don't shut it."

"That was kind of the point," Marjorie said on a sigh. "We wanted people to have a place to sit and chat with their 'dessert.'"

"Whose idea was this 'dessert bar' anyway?" Harold grumbled. "What's wrong with having a 'pudding bar,' that's what I want to know."

Marjorie laughed, but it sounded forced. "We invited the participants to make suggestions as to what they'd like to see at the conference. Our one American participant suggested a dessert bar and it sounded like a good idea. Who doesn't like cakes and biscuits, after all? 'Pudding bar' just didn't sound right somehow," Marjorie shrugged.

"I think it's lovely," Bessie said soothingly. She slid into a seat in a group of chairs near the others, close enough to talk with them, but far enough away that she hoped it didn't look as if she was intruding. She took a big bite of an éclair and grinned at the pair. "And it's delicious."

"Come and join us," Marjorie invited Bessie, as a few other people began to wander into the room. "We were just plotting how best to kill Mack and get away with it. I'm sure you'll have some useful suggestions."

Bessie moved over to join the pair, shaking her head as she did so. "You shouldn't even joke about such things," she told Marjorie. "I've been far too close to murder lately and it isn't funny, not in the slightest."

Marjorie flushed. "Sorry, Bessie," she murmured. "It's all just so awful."

"It is that," Bessie agreed. "How are you feeling?" she asked Harold.

"Totally destroyed," Harold told her. "I've spent my entire career chasing Roman remains and a lot of my time and energy has been devoted to establishing good working relationships with the various farmers on the island. I'm beyond devastated that one of them went to Mack instead of me with his find."

"Any idea who it was?" Bessie asked.

Harold shook his head. "I thought I was aware of everyone's plans for new construction through the end of the year," he told Bessie. "I wasn't aware of anyone planning a new barn on an old field."

"So how did Mack find this guy?" Marjorie demanded.

"The only thing I can figure is that he found some recent comeover who bought a farm and is making changes. I try to keep up with the new owners, but sometimes it takes me a little while to get in touch. I've been so busy with the conference lately that I must have missed something. Mack must have slipped in and caught the guy before I had a chance to talk to him."

"There can't be that many people from across buying up Manx farmland, can there?" Bessie asked.

"You'd be surprised," Harold answered her. "With the banks expanding so rapidly, lots of families are moving across. And at least some of them are considering small farms rather than life in a housing estate in Douglas. Lots of larger farms are being broken down into smaller plots. I doubt many of the new residents will even bother to farm the land; they just want the extra space. Maybe they want to keep a horse or two for their spoiled daughters, that sort of thing."

"I still don't understand why anyone would call Mack rather than you," Bessie said. "Everyone knows you're the expert on Roman finds on the island."

"What scant few there are," Harold grinned without humour. "I guess I might not be the expert any more, anyway."

Bessie sat back and watched the room slowly fill with people carrying plates full of treats. To her mind anyway, the 'dessert bar' was a huge success, whatever anyone wanted to call it. She smiled as Joe and Claire walked in, still deep in conversation. Helen strolled in by herself and quickly joined a small group of people that Bessie knew she'd met but couldn't instantly identify. After a while George came in, surrounded by a crowd of people who appeared to be hanging on his every word.

"They can't all be looking for funding, surely," Harold snarled.

"Don't be too sure," Marjorie replied. "I don't know many academics that aren't pretty much constantly on the lookout for new sponsors for their research. George only has himself to blame, announcing that he'd fund an entire excavation for Mack like that. I wonder if he has any idea what that's going to cost him?"

A few moments later Bambi wandered in, empty-handed and looking lost.

"Oh, for goodness sake," Marjorie said. "She looks like a lost puppy."

Bessie laughed. "I'll go rescue her," she offered. "I think someone ought to. She does look quite lost."

"By all means," Marjorie told her. "I haven't got the heart for it."

Harold laughed angrily. "Don't look at me," he said gruffly. "I'm still trying to work out how to kill her lover."

Bessie shook her head and then rose slowly. She'd emptied her plate and drunk her tea; it wouldn't hurt her to be nice to the young woman.

She smiled as she walked towards the pretty blonde. Bambi was looking around, as if trying to find someone. "Are you looking for someone special?" Bessie asked when she reached the woman.

"I thought maybe Mack had come in here," Bambi replied. "I knocked on the door to that little room where he went, but he didn't answer. I figured he must have gone to get a cookie or something, but I don't see him anywhere."

"I haven't seen him," Bessie told her. "I don't think he wants to come out and face questions at this point."

Bambi sighed. "I should just go back to the hotel," she said. "It isn't like all of this is my sort of thing anyway."

"I didn't think you looked like a historian," Bessie said. "So why are you here?"

Bambi sighed again. "Mack promised it would be fun," she told Bessie with a pout. "He made the island sound really cool and exciting as well, but so far all I've seen is the airport and the hotel."

"Mack's talk was certainly exciting," Bessie replied. "What he's found is hugely important for the island."

Bambi yawned. "History isn't really my thing," she shrugged.

"So what is your thing?" Even as the words left her mouth Bessie worried that she'd be sorry she asked.

"Fashion," Bambi answered, her eyes sparkling with sudden enthusiasm. "I'm hoping to study fashion design, marketing and merchandising soon. I'm planning to have my own label one day."

Bessie nodded. She knew nothing about fashion, but it seemed just possible that young Bambi was more than just a pretty face. "I'm sorry," Bessie blurted out before she could stop herself. "But is Bambi your real name?"

The young woman laughed. "You mustn't tell Mack," she said confidingly. "He thinks my parents are these wild, bohemian, counter-culture figures who named me after a Disney character or something. My real name is Margaret. I was named after that prime minister woman, but I hate it and I never use it."

"You were named after Margaret Thatcher?" Bessie asked.

Bambi laughed again. "That's the one. My dad's a huge fan of hers, but I don't do politics." She grinned at Bessie. "I absolutely refuse to remember the woman's name, mostly to annoy my father. I suppose I'll outgrow it some day."

Bessie laughed. She was starting to like young Bambi in spite of herself.

"But I thought you were American. I didn't know Americans followed British politics."

"My mother is American," Bambi replied. "Daddy is British. After they split up, when I was five, I got bounced back and forth between them every few months, so I've had a fairly peripatetic upbringing."

"That must have made attending school difficult," Bessie commented, fascinated by the woman who looked and acted like a dumb blonde, but used words like "peripatetic" in casual conversation.

"I bounced back and forth in school as well. I did boarding school for a few years, which was better, because it gave me some continuity, but then mum decided that she missed me too much and I was back to being dragged about by her whims." Bambi gave Bessie a wry smile. "She was between husbands, you see, and she hates being alone. I got dragged back to New York for a few months, until she met her next victim, er, I mean, love of her life. Then I was shipped back to daddy, who never knew what to do with me, either."

Bessie shook her head. "What a horrible way to grow up," she said with genuine sympathy.

Bambi shrugged. "It wasn't all bad. School wasn't any fun anyway, and I was well and truly spoiled by both of them. Really, it's just now that I'm an adult that they don't know what to do with me."

"I thought you said you wanted to go into fashion."

"I do, but daddy doesn't agree and won't pay for school. I've been doing some modeling, but it's unbelievably dull."

Bessie found herself glancing at the girl's ample frontage before she could stop herself.

Bambi laughed. "No, I haven't been doing topless stuff," she told Bessie. "Just a little bit of this and that. I haven't taken my top off yet. Daddy would go mad."

Bessie struggled to find the right reply to that. Before she could manage it, Bambi continued.

"Would you believe me if I said they were real?" she asked Bessie.

"No," Bessie blurted out.

Bambi laughed loudly. "Oh dear," she said. "Actually, they were an eighteenth-birthday present from my mum," she confided to Bessie.

"Pardon?" Bessie demanded.

The girl laughed again. "My mum thought I'd like them, and sometimes I do, but they do rather get in the way as well." The girl shrugged. "Daddy had just taken up with a nineteen-year-old page three model and mum thought getting me a boob job would be a hilarious way to embarrass him."

"Your mother has a strange sense of humour," Bessie commented.

Bambi grinned. "She does at that," she agreed.

"What on earth did your father think?" Bessie couldn't help but ask.

"I've no idea," the girl shrugged. "He's never said a word to me about it. Anyway, he's furious with me at the moment."

"Do I dare ask why or is that prying?"

"He hates Mack," Bambi replied. "Mack is about his age, you see, so daddy thinks he's only interested in me as a trophy girlfriend. Daddy knows all about that."

"You don't agree with your father about Mack?"

"I don't care," Bambi corrected her. "Mack's fun to be around, well, most of the time, and it isn't like I'm going to marry him or anything. We're just hanging out."

"And it's always fun to annoy your father, isn't it?" Bessie asked shrewdly.

Bambi blushed. "I'm hoping, if he gets annoyed enough, he'll give me some money to leave Mack," she whispered to Bessie. "Then I can head back to New York and start fashion school."

Bessie swallowed a dozen replies. She'd talked to a lot of children from dysfunctional families in her many years on the planet, but Bambi was in a league of her own.

"Anyway, you haven't seen Mack, then?" Bambi asked, dragging the conversation back to where it had started.

"Not since he left the podium," Bessie replied. "Did you say you knocked on the cuillee door? Maybe he didn't hear you knocking?"

"I banged pretty loudly," Bambi told her. "And I called his name. It's only a small room and anyway, I tried the door as well. It was locked." She sighed. "Maybe he was ignoring me."

"Surely not," Bessie said in surprise.

Bambi blushed. "We, um, haven't been getting along really well since we got here. I think he's sorry he brought me and I know I'm sorry I came."

"That's a shame," Bessie told her. "It's going to be a wonderful conference, but only if you're at least a little bit interested in the subject matter."

Bambi shook her head. "I'm sure it's all very interesting for some people, but Mack promised me a lot more excitement than it seems like he's going to be able to deliver. I think I might change my flight and head home tomorrow."

Bessie was torn between trying to persuade the girl to stay on the off chance that she might learn to enjoy history, and having sympathy for the girl's situation. Before she could decide how to respond, Harold Smythe interrupted them.

"I say, Bessie, would you mind terribly going and checking on Dr. Dickson? He said twenty minutes about half an hour ago and, um, everyone's getting restless."

Bessie grinned. Or rather, you're getting restless because you can't wait to ask a few pointed questions, she said to herself. She was nothing but polite out loud, though.

"I'd be happy to go and see if Mack is ready," she told Harold. "Pardon me, please." The last remark was directed towards Bambi, who nodded vaguely in Bessie's direction.

As Bessie crossed the room and walked back through the mostly empty foyer, she speculated that there wasn't really anyone else that Harold could have asked.

Mack would have been insulted if just anyone disturbed him, but as a fellow presenter at the conference, Bessie was at least quasi-official. And she was just about the only person involved in the conference who wasn't furious at the man.

She walked through the foyer and into the lecture hall. The room felt larger now that it was nearly empty. Henry and Doug were hard at work straightening the rows of chairs so that everything would be ready for the promised question-and-answer session.

"Kyst t'ou, Henry?" Bessie asked.

"Oh, um, ta mee braew," Henry replied, looking slightly flustered. "And I hope that's all the Manx you'll be wanting from me tonight," he told Bessie with a smile. "I'm too busy to think hard enough to remember my Manx."

Bessie laughed. "No worries," she told the man. "I don't want to do any more than that myself. But at least this way I can tell Marjorie I practiced when we get to class on Monday."

Henry laughed. "Oh, aye, every little bit helps, I suppose."

Henry was in the same beginning Manx language class that Liz and Bessie were taking. Marjorie Stevens was the instructor and they'd been meeting for several weeks already. Bessie's good friend, Doona, was also taking the class. With only a few weeks to go, Bessie knew she should have been able to say a lot more than 'how are you,' but even though this was her third attempt at the class, she didn't feel like she was retaining much of anything. Still, she found the class great fun and she enjoyed spending time with her classmates, even if she never mastered even the basics of the difficult Celtic language.

"I don't suppose Dr. Dickson has come out?" Bessie asked Henry now.

"I haven't seem him," Henry said, his tone apologetic. "But we've only been in here a minute or two. We were keeping track of the tea and coffee and the cakes until now."

"Everything was wonderful," Bessie told him with a smile. "The café bakers outdid themselves."

Henry grinned. "They had me in there all day yesterday mixing up stuff and hauling trays in and out of the oven. It's the first time I've ever helped in the café, but I think they were desperate."

Bessie laughed. "Well, you must have done a good job, because everything was delicious. They might want you to start working there full-time."

"Oh, I hope not," Henry answered. "It was fun in the kitchen for a change, but I love being outside at the different sites, meeting the tourists and the like. I'd really miss all of that."

"I'm sure they'd never move you where you didn't want to go," Bessie assured him. "You're too valuable to MNH."

Henry flushed at the praise and then turned back to rearranging chairs. Bessie took the final few steps to the small door at the front of the room. She tapped lightly on it.

"Mack?" she called softly. "Mack, are you in there?" Bessie increased the volume as she called his name again and then knocked a second time, more loudly. She waited a moment, straining to listen for a reply. She sighed and then rapped on the door quite hard. Henry and Doug had both stopped what they were doing to watch her with undisguised curiosity.

Bessie shrugged at the pair and then cautiously tried the door. Bambi had said the door was locked, but the knob turned easily in Bessie's hand. She pushed the door open and was surprised to find the room dark. Either Mack left or he was sitting in the dark gathering his thoughts. Bessie frowned, angry at Harold for putting her in this uncomfortable situation.

"Mack? Dr. Dickson?" She forced herself to speak firmly, feeling foolish as she suspected the room was empty. Pushing the door open the rest of the way, she reached around its frame to switch on the light. She was wrong. The room wasn't empty.

Mack was sitting on one of the small couches, facing towards the door. His face was red and it looked wrong, as if it were swollen or something. Bessie didn't take time to study it. She stepped backwards, nearly tripping over her own feet as she did so. With a shaking hand, she pulled the door shut behind her and spun around.

Henry took one look at her face and sighed. "Not another dead body?" he asked.

CHAPTER THREE

"Henry, you need to stay here and make sure no one goes in that room," Bessie instructed. "I need to go and talk to Harold."

"He's in there dead, isn't he?" Henry repeated himself. "I don't know what I've been doing wrong lately, but it seems like everywhere I go someone turns up dead."

"I know exactly what you mean," Bessie answered dryly. She left the room quickly and headed back towards the crowd that was still gathered in the Kinvig Room. Harold was standing near the door, presumably watching for Bessie.

"So, did you find him?" he asked as Bessie approached.

"Yes," Bessie said quietly. "But we need to call the police. Mack's dead."

"This isn't the time for jokes," Harold replied. "If Mack doesn't want to face the crowd, just tell me that and I'll make some sort of announcement."

"Harold, I really really wish I were joking," Bessie said earnestly. "But Mack is dead and the police will want to investigate."

"Show me," Harold demanded.

Bessie led him back across the foyer and into the lecture theatre. Henry hadn't moved from where Bessie had left him, in front of the door to the cuillee that held Mack's body.

Harold took a deep breath and then opened the door. He took a long look at the body and then shook his head. "You're not joking," he said in a choked voice. "All this time we were talking about killing him, he was in here dead?"

Bessie pulled him away from the door. "Henry, please shut the door," she said softly as she guided Harold to the nearest chair. The academic seemed to have aged ten years in the last ten seconds.

"Sit," Bessie demanded. Harold sank onto a chair and blinked at Bessie.

"What do we do now?" he asked.

"I'm going to call the police," Bessie told him. "They'll have to come and investigate. We just have to hope whatever happened had natural causes."

"You can't be suggesting that someone murdered him?" Harold said in a shocked voice. "That simply isn't possible."

"I'm suggesting we call the police and let them handle things," Bessie said soothingly. "It isn't our job to worry about what happened. They're the experts."

Harold was staring at the door that Henry was standing in front of with a blank look on his face, so Bessie dug her mobile out of her handbag and dialled 999.

Bessie limited herself to the facts and kept the call as short as possible. She just hoped that the police would arrived before the conference crowd got tired of their "dessert bar" and headed back to the lecture theatre to see why there was such a long delay.

She needn't have worried. Within a very few minutes the first uniformed constables had arrived to secure the scene. Bessie and Harold were asked, very politely, to remain where they were until the Criminal Investigation Division Inspector arrived.

"Bessie, what exactly is going to happen next?" Harold asked as the two uniformed men ushered Doug and Henry into chairs towards the back of the lecture hall.

"I'm not sure," Bessie replied. "I think...."

"Sorry, but we have to ask you to not talk to one another," one of the uniformed men said. "It's just a precaution."

Harold opened his mouth and then snapped it shut. Bessie sighed and slid back in her seat, wishing that it was going to be Inspector John Rockwell from the Ramsey CID coming in to investigate. There was no chance of that, however, in downtown Douglas.

Sure enough, a few minutes later an angry-looking middle-aged man whom Bessie had never seen before stomped into view. Something about him said both "important" and "official" and Bessie smiled to herself as the two young constables snapped to attention when they spotted him.

The man spoke quietly with the two uniformed men and then opened the door to the small room where Mack's body remained. He spent no more than a moment or two looking into the space before he turned towards Bessie and Harold. A seemingly permanent frown was etched on his face, as he crossed to them.

Bessie studied him as he took the half-dozen or so steps necessary to cross the room. His dark brown hair had more than a smattering of grey mixed into it. From where she was sitting it was difficult to determine his exact height, but Bessie would have guessed that he was a few inches shy of six feet tall. When he was close enough to speak, she noted that his brown eyes already looked tired.

While the new arrival was probably of a similar age to Bessie's friend, Inspector Rockwell, Bessie had never noticed any grey hair on her friend's head. She couldn't help but feel that Rockwell was in far better shape and was much better looking than the man who now spoke.

"Who found the body?" he demanded without preamble.

"I did," Bessie answered in a clipped voice.

"And you are?"

"Miss Elizabeth Cubbon."

"And how did you happen to find the body, Ms. Cubbon?"

"Dr. Smythe," Bessie waved a hand toward Harold, "asked me to find Mack and ask him if he was ready for the question-and-answer session. I was looking for him, and I guess I found him."

"Rather," the man sighed. "Can you formally identify the dead man?"

Bessie gulped. "I don't know," she prevaricated. "What does that entail? I mean, I knew who he was, but we weren't related, or really even friends."

The man sighed again. "Is there anyone here who was related to the deceased?"

"Not that I know of." Bessie looked at Harold who simply shrugged. "His girlfriend is here. Does she qualify?"

"Never mind," the man said impatiently. "Who was he?"

"Dr. Mack Dickson," Bessie replied. "I think his first name was actually Malcolm, but everyone called him Mack. He was an archaeologist and historian who came to talk about his research at the conference that started tonight."

"Who's in charge of the conference?"

"I suppose that would be me," Harold spoke with obvious reluctance. "I mean I organised it, with help from a few others, mainly Marjorie Stevens. Mr. George Quayle is our conference sponsor."

The inspector rolled his eyes. "As if it weren't bad enough," he muttered.

Movement at the back of the room caught everyone's attention as the man himself strolled in.

"Ah, Inspector Corkill, what brings you here?" George demanded as he looked around the room.

"It seems your honoured guest ended up dead," the policeman replied.

"Mack? Well, he was asking for it," was George's unexpected reply.

"Really?" the inspector asked. "What makes you say that?"

"Well," George said as he joined the inspector and the others. "He came in here and made all sorts of unreasonable demands about giving the first talk of the conference. Then he turned up with a girlfriend just out of school who was guaranteed to make all his exes unhappy. And finally he made an announcement about his findings that had to be designed to upset everyone. I bet whoever killed him had a queue behind him to help finish the job."

"I don't believe I said it was murder." The inspector was staring at George. "But I'm intrigued by the idea that you assumed it was."

George waved a hand. "He was young and reasonably fit and healthy," he argued. "There's no good reason for him to just drop dead. Someone had to have killed him."

"It looks to me like anaphylaxis," the inspector said. "It could just be a tragic accident. I don't suppose any of you know what he might have been allergic to?"

"Peanuts." A voice from the doorway at the rear had them all jumping and turning to see who had come in.

Bambi spoke again as she walked towards them. "Mack was very allergic to peanuts. But he was super careful about them. He never would have eaten anything that he wasn't sure about. And anyway, he always had at least two adrenaline injectors with him. He knew the warning signs and how to deal with them. He would have given himself an injection and called 999 if he thought he was having a reaction."

The inspector shrugged. "We haven't searched the scene yet. Maybe he panicked or something."

Bambi turned to him. "We haven't been introduced. I'm Bambi Marks," she told him.

"I'm Inspector Peter Corkill from the Douglas branch of the CID. I assume you were well acquainted with the deceased?"

Bambi flushed. "We were, that is, we started dating about a month ago. This conference was Mack's idea of a romantic weekend getaway."

Inspector Corkill nodded. "I'm sure I'll have many questions for you once the coroner has inspected the body."

"Anyway, someone needs to let everyone know what's going on," Bambi told them all. "It's getting late and people are starting to wonder what's gone wrong."

"The whole bloody conference has gone wrong," Harold muttered from his seat, dropping his head into his hands.

"I'll make an announcement," the inspector said. "I'll get my men to start taking people's information and then letting them go. Until I hear otherwise, I'm assuming that this was just an unfortunate accident."

"But where did Mack get his hands on something with peanuts in it?" Bambi demanded. "He never would have eaten anything he wasn't sure about."

"There's a plate on the table next to him with a half-eaten brownie on it," the inspector replied. "I saw a table full of brownies and cakes when I came in. Presumably he thought the brownie was safe and, sadly, he was wrong."

"He never went anywhere near the dessert bar," Bambi argued. "Someone must have taken the brownie in to him. He was murdered."

Peter Corkill shook his head. "You've quite the imagination," he told Bambi. "But it isn't murder unless I say it's murder. And at the moment I'm saying tragic accident."

Bambi opened her mouth to argue further, but Bessie interrupted before she could speak.

"My dear child," she said as she stood up and took Bambi's arm. "You're obviously tremendously upset at your heartbreaking loss. Right now the best thing we can do is get out of the inspector's way and let him get on with his work." She began to guide Bambi out of the room, muttering soothing nothings to her as they went.

They were nearly at the door before the inspector spoke. "Just let me make that announcement before you go out there," he told Bessie. "Otherwise you'll get overrun with questions."

Bessie nodded and stepped aside to let the inspector leave the room ahead of herself and Bambi. She followed him quickly, though, not wanting to miss what he was going to tell the crowd.

Back in the foyer, it appeared that almost everyone had made their way out of the Kinvig Room. People stood in small clusters and most of them were now casting anxious looks at the inspector.

"Good evening, everyone," Inspector Corkill said loudly. The last of the auxiliary chatter died out and everyone looked curiously at him. He cleared his throat.

"I know that it's getting late, but I'm going to have to ask you to bear with me for a short time longer. There's been an unfortunate accident and I'm sorry to inform you that Dr. Dickson appears to have suffered a fatal allergic reaction to something."

The loud gasp interrupted whatever the inspector was going to say next. All heads turned and watched as the colour drained from Marjorie Stevens' face. The teacup she was holding fell to the ground, mercifully bouncing on the thick carpet rather than breaking. A man standing near her reacted instinctively in reaching out to catch her as she swooned.

"Who's that?" Corkill barked at Bessie.

"Marjorie Stevens. She works here at the museum and helped organise the conference," Bessie replied without thinking.

"Interesting," the inspector said.

Across the room, two men were now helping Marjorie into a chair that someone quickly dragged out of the Kinvig Room. The inspector cleared his throat again.

"I'm going to ask you all to be patient while the constables interview each of you in turn. At this point I'm really only gathering names and contact information. It's late and we all need our sleep. You'll be allowed to leave as soon as you've spoken to one of my men."

"What about my conference?" Harold demanded, from the doorway behind the inspector.

Corkill swung around and Bessie caught the angry look that flashed across his face before he gave Harold a tight smile. "Assuming I don't find anything suspicious in my investigation, the conference can carry on as scheduled," he replied. "I can't promise you access to the lecture theatre, but I'm sure the museum can find space for things elsewhere."

For a moment it looked as if Harold was going to argue, but finally he shrugged and moved into the foyer, heading towards Marjorie.

"I'd like to ask you all to remain silent as you wait for your turn to be interviewed," the inspector announced.

The lift doors opened and several more uniformed officers emerged. Bessie led Bambi towards the Kinvig Room. If they had to wait, they might as well sit down. An uncomfortable silence descended on the foyer as people fought the urge to talk under the watchful eye of the inspector and his staff.

Corkill had a quick conversation with the newly arrived officers and then he headed back into the Moore Lecture Theatre. The uniformed men and women spread out and began herding small groups of people into larger clusters in separate sections of the room. Bessie saw Henry moving through the crowd with a large set of keys on a ring. He opened the doors to several of the small classrooms that opened off the short hallway. Within minutes each uniformed officer had gathered up a collection of people and ushered them towards a classroom.

Bessie watched the groups as they formed orderly queues outside each classroom door. The silence was uneasy, but unbroken aside from the quiet murmur that came from the classrooms themselves. Marjorie remained seated in one corner of the foyer and Bessie and Bambi joined her now, as Harold pulled chairs from the Kinvig Room for them all. They could do little more than exchange sympathetic looks as they waited for their turn to speak to someone.

To pass the time, Bessie recited the times tables in her head. She'd done them through twice, from one to twelve, and was at three sevens are twenty-one for the third time when Inspector Corkill emerged from the lecture hall.

"Ah, just the people I wanted to see," he exclaimed, as if surprised to find them all waiting for him. He looked them all over for a moment and then sighed. "Ms. Cubbon, wasn't it? I suppose I should take you first. I'm sure it's well past your bedtime, isn't it?"

Bessie counted to ten before she said something she'd regret. She hated having special privileges accorded to her simply because of her age, but the inspector was right. She was tired, and it was well past her usual bedtime. As she rose to follow the man she reasoned that everyone else was staying in Douglas and could be in bed only a few minutes after their interview. She still had to call and reschedule her taxi; the one she had previously arranged would have come and gone by now. Once she finally found one to pick her up, it still had to drive her back to Laxey.

The inspector led Bessie back into the Moore Lecture Theatre, steering her towards a small table that had been placed in one corner. Two chairs were pulled up to the table and Corkill held one out for Bessie. Once she was settled, he took the other chair.

"I know it's late and I'm sure you're tired," he told Bessie as he pulled a notebook out of his pocket. "I'll try to keep this brief."

"Obviously, I want to help as much as I can," Bessie replied.

"The lateness of the hour and my level of comfort are far less important than figuring out what happened to Mack."

"Now, now, my dear Ms. Cubbon," the inspector said patronisingly as he patted Bessie's arm. "It's my job to figure out what happened to Dr. Dickson. You don't need to worry yourself with that. I just need you to answer a few questions."

"It's Miss Cubbon, actually," Bessie told him, her voice cool.

"Pardon?" Corkill looked confused.

"You called me Ms. Cubbon," Bessie said patiently. "I'm actually Miss Cubbon."

"Oh, well, I hardly think we need to worry about that, do we?" The inspector gave her an ingratiating smile. "Let me rattle through my questions and then you can go."

Bessie nodded, already annoyed with the man. He was clearly nowhere near as smart as John Rockwell, and Bessie couldn't help but compare the two, which did nothing to improve her opinion of Inspector Corkill.

"First, can I get your address, please?"

"Treoghe Bwaaue, in Laxey," she replied.

Corkill gave her a look she couldn't read. "I did wonder," he said after a moment. "You're Rockwell's Miss Marple, aren't you?"

Bessie flushed. "I wouldn't consider myself anything of the kind," she replied.

"But you have been heavily involved in a couple of very high-profile murder cases in Laxey lately, haven't you?"

Bessie nodded reluctantly.

"Let me make my position clear, then," he told Bessie in a stern voice. "Civilians have no place, no place at all, in a police investigation. And that goes for any police investigation, from parking tickets through to murder. Rockwell came over here from Manchester with his own ideas about how to do things, and he can run his little station in Laxey however he likes until the Chief Constable gets tired of his antics, but his way isn't my way. Have I made myself clear?"

Bessie swallowed half a dozen replies that she wanted to give before she finally answered. "Perfectly," she said tightly.

"So then, Ms. Cubbon, how well did you know the deceased?"

Bessie sighed silently. "How well does anyone know anyone?" she asked in return. "I've no idea how to quantify the extent of our relationship. He was an acquaintance that I'd run into at several of these sorts of conferences. I wouldn't call him a friend, but we'd spoken several times and once had a very lively debate on the role of women at prehistoric Ronaldsway."

She forced herself to smile at the man. "And it's Miss Cubbon," she reminded him.

"You knew his Christian name," the inspector commented.

"We'd discussed nicknames once," Bessie replied. "He asked me if Bessie was my real name or just a nickname. I told him that no one has ever really called me Elizabeth, except my mother when I was in trouble. He said something similar about his own name."

"So who might have wanted him dead?" the inspector asked. "Who benefits from his death?"

Bessie shrugged. I've no idea who might have wanted him dead or who might benefit," she answered. "As far as I knew, he was just another archeologist."

"One with a proclivity for young, pretty blondes," Corkill suggested. "And one who was stepping on a lot of toes with his new research."

Bessie nodded. "Both of those things are true," she agreed. "But neither of them necessarily leads to murder."

"I didn't say it was murder," Corkill replied coolly. "I suppose Inspector Rockwell prefers chasing murderers to the more ordinary police work that needs doing on a daily basis, but I look at something like this and see nothing but an unfortunate accident."

"Bambi seems convinced that it was murder," Bessie suggested.

"And I'll talk to Ms. Marks later and then thoroughly investigate her claims," Corkill replied. "It isn't your concern."

Bessie nodded, not trusting herself to speak.

"Are you staying somewhere locally at the moment?" Corkill asked.

"No," Bessie answered. "I couldn't see the point. Laxey isn't far away."

"No, I suppose not," he replied. "When are you planning to be back here?"

"I expect to be here all day tomorrow," Bessie assured him. "There's a full programme of events and I don't want to miss any of the wonderful speakers. That is, assuming the conference continues as scheduled."

"I don't see any reason to cancel anything, at least not at the moment," the inspector told her. "You won't be able to use this room, but beyond that, the conference can go ahead as planned."

"Well, that is good news," Bessie smiled. "I just hope I'm not too tired to enjoy myself tomorrow."

"I guess that's my cue," the inspector muttered. "I don't have any further questions for tonight," he told Bessie. "I may want to ask you more tomorrow."

Bessie sat still for a moment, thinking about all the things that the inspector should have asked her. She sighed. "I guess I'll get out of your way, then." She got to her feet and made her way slowly out of the room. Inspector Corkill followed, presumably planning to collect someone else to question.

Bessie pulled open the door into the foyer and walked through it. She was surprised to see John Rockwell from the Laxey Constabulary pacing back and forth in the foyer.

"Inspector Rockwell?" she said tentatively.

He had been marching away from her when she spoke, now he spun around and quickly crossed to Bessie's side. "Bessie, how are you?" he asked, his stunning green eyes staring hard into her tired grey ones.

Bessie was immediately touched by the concern in his voice. "I'm just fine," she assured him with a tired smile.

"Rockwell? What brings you here?" Inspector Corkill didn't bother to hide the annoyance in his voice as he confronted his fellow policeman.

"Someone let me know that Bessie had found a body," Rockwell said easily. "I thought maybe she could use a bit of moral support and a ride home."

Corkill frowned and walked closer to Bessie and the other

inspector. He leaned in towards Inspector Rockwell and spoke quietly, but with intensity. "Just make sure you don't find yourself interfering with my investigation," he hissed. "You can do what you like in Laxey, but this is my jurisdiction and if I find out you're trying to push in on my case I'll file a formal complaint with the Chief Constable. Have I made myself clear?"

"Just giving a friend a ride home, Pete," Rockwell grinned at the other man. "You have a good night." With that, Rockwell took Bessie's arm and led her to the lifts. Neither spoke as they waited for the car to arrive. A uniformed constable joined them just before the lift doors closed, so the ride down was equally silent.

Bessie waved a quick farewell to the two Manx National Heritage workers who were stationed at the museum's front door as she left. They both looked bored and tired and she wondered how long they would be stuck there. It had already been a long night and it didn't look like the police were wrapping things up, at least not yet.

The inspector had managed to park very close to the museum's entrance and Bessie sank gratefully into the comfortable seat in his nondescript saloon car. It wasn't until they had negotiated their way out of the tiny car park and were headed through downtown Douglas that Bessie found enough energy to speak.

"Thank you ever so much for coming to collect me," she said. "I'm sure a taxi would have taken ages to arrive and I'm completely done in."

Rockwell glanced over at her and smiled. "I was happy to do it," he assured her. "Once I heard what was happening, I called your taxi service and told them to leave you to me. I knew there was no way you were going to be able to get your scheduled ride home."

"But how did you know what had happened?" Bessie asked.

"When you called 999, the operator noted your name in the computer system. Doona has an automatic flag on your name so that if it gets entered into the system anywhere, a window pops up and requests that someone call her and let her know what's going on."

"Oh really?" Bessie said sharply. "That seems a bit, well, intrusive."

Rockwell patted her arm. "Please don't be too hard on her," he asked Bessie. "She's only done it because she cares for you. If she hadn't done it, I would have, especially after the last few months."

Bessie shook her head. "I don't need looking after like I'm old and senile and incapable of taking care of myself," she complained.

Rockwell laughed. "No one that knows you would ever suggest any such thing," he told her. "If it makes you feel any better, I have the same sort of flags on my wife and my kids, and nearly everyone in the police has at least one or two people that they've flagged. It isn't like you get any special treatment or anything. It's just a request for information."

"Well, if I can't get special treatment, I really don't see the point at all," Bessie said, forcing a smile. She was not happy with the situation, but there was little point in continuing to argue the point with the inspector. She'd discuss things with Doona at a later date.

"Anyway, Sam, the 999 dispatcher, called Doona to tell her what was going on and then Doona called me. She wanted to come down and get you herself, but I overruled her. I figured if anyone was going to incur Inspector Corkill's wrath, I would rather it was me."

Bessie shook her head. "He wasn't very nice, and he asked stupid questions," she complained. "And he didn't bother to ask any important ones, either."

Rockwell sighed. "He's actually a very competent investigator," he told Bessie. "I stepped on his toes a bit last month with Anne Caine's car crash. It was technically his jurisdiction and I not only got involved in the investigation, but I requisitioned his department for the staff to protect her." He sighed. "The later events at the Sea Terminal didn't help, either."

"He didn't strike me as competent," Bessie replied. "He bumbled around asking me why I knew the dead man's Christian name and not bothering to ask whether or not I knew about his life-threatening allergies. He asked who might benefit from Mack's death, but refused to admit that it could be murder." She sighed deeply. "It was all very frustrating, and he insisted on calling me Ms. Cubbon the whole time."

Rockwell laughed again. "Ah, Bessie, only some of us can be taught," he told her. "I believe I only made that mistake once."

"Indeed," Bessie grinned. "And you were smart enough to learn from your mistake."

The pair settled into a comfortable silence as Rockwell drove out of Douglas and along the coast. It was too dark to enjoy the scenery and Bessie found herself nodding off in spite of her best intentions. She woke up with a start when the car came to a stop in the small parking area outside her cottage.

"Oh, my goodness," Bessie exclaimed. "I can't believe I fell asleep. I'm so sorry." She could feel herself blushing in the dark car.

"No worries," Rockwell assured her. "I hope you don't mind, though, if I take up a bit of your time with a few questions now that you're home?"

"Of course not," Bessie told him. "Come in and I'll make a pot of tea. You can ask whatever you like."

The inspector followed Bessie into her cottage. Bessie flipped the switch on the kitchen lights and they both blinked rapidly as the room was flooded with light. It only took a moment for Bessie to fill the kettle with fresh water, and while they waited for it come to a boil, Bessie dug out a box of chocolate biscuits that she'd been saving for a special occasion.

"What did you want to ask me?" she asked Rockwell as the pair settled in at the small kitchen table with their biscuits and tea.

"Just tell me what happened tonight," he suggested.

Bessie nodded. "I'm sure I've mentioned this conference at least a dozen times to you," she laughed. "Tonight was finally the opening night. When I got there, though, everything was in a bit of mess." She paused for a drink of tea.

"Why?"

"Dr. Mack Dickson had turned up. Apparently he appealed directly to George Quayle to be allowed to give the opening lecture of the conference and George gave it to him."

"George Quayle, everyone's favourite lately-returned-home millionaire?" Rockwell checked.

"That's the one," Bessie agreed. "He's the main sponsor for the conference, which gives him a lot of influence."

"What do you mean by 'main sponsor'?" Rockwell asked.

"Basically, he's paying for it all. Or rather, he's paying for whatever the registration fees won't cover, which will probably be most of the conference."

"Okay, so that gives him enough authority to make big changes to the programme at the last minute. Does he usually take that sort of advantage of his influence?"

Bessie shook her head. "Actually, he's usually the perfect sponsor. He usually comes along and at least pretends to be interested in whatever the event is. He often brings some of his wealthy friends to events and gets them to make generous donations as well. He's sometimes been known to make requests for certain things like early entry or special behind-the-scenes tours or whatever, but this is the first time I've ever known him to make changes to a programme."

"That's interesting," Rockwell remarked. "Any guesses as to why he asked for the change?"

Bessie shook her head. "Apparently Mack just knew what buttons to push to get his way. Honestly, Mack was an expert at finding people's buttons and pushing them."

"Even yours?"

Bessie laughed. "He wasn't interested in me. I'm an amateur historian who is too old to appeal to his libido, totally without influence in academic circles and nowhere near wealthy enough to underwrite his schemes. He was willing to talk to me if there was no one else more useful around and he was even sometimes polite to me, but mostly he ignored me."

Rockwell nodded. "So who was upset about Mack's sudden appearance?"

Bessie shrugged. "Mostly Harold Smythe. He'd organised the conference and was meant to be giving the opening talk. He and Mack have a professional rivalry going back many years anyway. Marjorie Stevens seemed quite upset as well. I guess because she was the official Manx National Heritage staff member tasked with working with Harold on the conference, she may have seen George's interference as an insult of some sort."

"Anyone else unhappy with Mack?"

"He was rude to Joe Steele, an American paleontologist that I just met tonight, but Mack could be very rude when he was in the mood. Mack's girlfriend was bored to tears, but I don't see that as much of a motive for murder."

"And you think it was murder?" Rockwell asked.

Bessie shrugged again. "Bambi, that's Mack's girlfriend, thinks it was murder. She insisted to Inspector Corkill that Mack never would have eaten something unless he was sure it was safe. And she thought he had his adrenaline injector with him as well. I know I didn't see anything like that when I found the body, but I suppose he might not have been able to get it out in time or something."

Now the inspector shrugged. "Eventually, I'll be able to get access to the official crime scene photos and notes," he said. "But in the meantime, we'll just have to go on what you saw."

"Well, I didn't see any evidence of any injector," Bessie replied.

"Did you know that he had severe allergies?"

"Oh yes," Bessie nodded. "And before you ask, anyone who has ever been to a conference with the man knew about them. Obviously, his allergies were very serious, but he was something of a bore about them. At every meal and every tea break he would make an elaborate show of talking with the catering staff about ingredients, and shaking his head over every answer. Most of the time whoever arranged the conference would order in special food just for him, but he usually wouldn't eat it. More than once I watched him sniff at something and poke at it, and then sigh and shake his head and mutter something like 'mustn't risk it,' and throw it away."

"So pretty much everyone in the room knew how to kill him," Rockwell sighed.

"I guess so," Bessie replied. "But honestly, I think most of us thought he was overdramatising his condition. I guess we were wrong."

Rockwell sighed. "I'm too tired to think anymore," he confessed. "What's happening next with your conference?"

"According to Inspector Corkill, everything can go ahead as planned. The museum will have to find us another space to use for lectures, but otherwise, we should be back on as scheduled tomorrow morning at eight."

"What time do you wrap up tomorrow night?"

"The last talks begin at half seven. They should finish by nine, even with lots of questions. There will be some sort of food and drink after that. I think it's just tea and coffee tomorrow night."

"So if I were to arrive sometime around nine, you would be ready for a ride home?"

Bessie flushed. "I don't like dragging you back into Douglas again," she protested. "I can get a taxi. It isn't a problem."

"I'm sure you are perfectly capable of getting a taxi," Rockwell grinned. "But you're on the inside of what might be another murder investigation and I can't help but be intrigued. I'll give you a ride home and you can give me all the skeet from the scene of the crime."

Bessie laughed. "I guess that's a fair deal," she told her friend.

CHAPTER FOUR

It only took Bessie a few minutes to tidy up the kitchen after the inspector left. She made a quick telephone call to her taxi service, reaching their answering machine as expected. After leaving a message asking for an earlier pickup the next day than originally scheduled and cancelling the ride back home that she would no longer need, she finally headed for bed. She was feeling physically exhausted but mentally energised. In spite of the way her mind was racing, she managed to fall asleep quickly and slept well.

Six o'clock came far too soon, however, after the unusually late night. Bessie sighed as she slid out of bed and headed for the shower. She wasn't going to be able to get properly caught up on her sleep until the conference was over. This morning called for coffee, rather than tea, but she'd have to wait until she got to the conference to get it.

Her day improved when Dave, her favourite driver, appeared in front of her cottage at exactly the time she'd requested in her late-night message.

"Good morning, my dear," he greeted Bessie with a huge smile, climbing out of the car to open the passenger door for her. He waited until she was safely tucked up inside the vehicle before he closed the door behind her and returned to the driver's seat.

"How's my favourite passenger?" he asked as he fastened his seatbelt and started the engine.

"I'm fine, Dave. How are you?"

The pair chatted amiably as Dave drove into Douglas. If he'd heard anything about Dr. Dickson's untimely death, he was kind enough not to mention it to Bessie. She wasn't about to bring the matter up, either.

Dave didn't ask Bessie where she wanted dropping off. He simply pulled into the museum car park and parked as close as he could to the building's front door.

"Here we are then." He grinned at her after he'd climbed out of the car and opened her door for her.

"Thank you so much." Bessie smiled back at him. She took the two small steps to the front door, but it was locked. Bessie frowned. It was only half seven and the museum didn't open until ten, but the conference schedule showed registration and breakfast from eight. She had assumed, when she'd ordered the earlier taxi, that someone would be there working out the changes that Mack's death had necessitated. She'd hoped she could be helpful, but first she had to get inside.

"Do you want to try the back door?" Dave asked her.

"I suppose," Bessie replied.

"Hop in."

Bessie laughed. "I think I can walk to the back door," she told the man. "It's only a few steps, for goodness sake. I didn't get my walk this morning, so I need the exercise."

Dave smiled. "I'll just wait here, then, until I'm sure you can get in."

"You don't have to," Bessie assured him. "If I can't get in now, I can just wait. I'm sure it won't be long before someone turns up."

Dave shrugged and looked at the sky. It was overcast and it did look as if it might rain at any moment. Bessie hurried along the short distance to the back entrance and pulled hard on the heavy door. It opened easily.

"I'm all set," she called back to Dave.

He waved and climbed back into his car. Bessie smiled as he drove past her slowly, heading for the tiny turning-around space at the back of the car park.

There were only a few security lights on inside the museum and Bessie waited a moment to let her eyes adjust. Once she was fairly confident that she could see well enough to move through the building safely, she headed towards the front door, glancing at the displays as she moved past them.

"Hello?" she called cautiously when she heard a noise somewhere in front of her. The silence that followed made her heart beat faster. She increased her pace, eager to reach the front of the building with its glass doors and windows. Another noise had her jumping again.

"Hello? Is anyone there?" she called as loudly as she could, stopping and pulling her mobile phone from her handbag as she did so. She wanted to be ready to dial 999, just in case.

"Hello?" a voice called back. "Who's there?"

"It's Bessie Cubbon," Bessie called, feeling as if she almost recognised the voice.

"Oh, Bessie, how did you get in?" the voice shouted to her. A moment later Bessie sighed in relief as Henry Costain came around the corner into view.

"The back door was unlocked," Bessie told him.

Henry frowned. "It really shouldn't be," he said. "I better check on it."

"Is anyone else here?" Bessie asked. "I came in early to see if Harold or Marjorie needed any help with rearranging things."

"They're both upstairs drinking coffee by the gallon and arguing about the schedule." Henry replied.

"I'll head up there, then," Bessie laughed. Henry nodded and headed towards the back, presumably to lock it up. Bessie turned and continued on her way to the front, feeling less nervous knowing that the museum wasn't empty.

She passed through the front foyer, glancing through the windows into the car park. A car turned in as she passed and she grimaced as she recognised the driver. It looked like Inspector Corkill was getting an early start, too.

Bessie slipped down the corridor to the lifts quickly, before he spotted her and tried to get her to let him in. She didn't have keys to the building and had no idea how to unlock the doors. The inspector would simply have to press the door buzzer and wait for Henry to answer.

AUNT BESSIE CONSIDERS

As Bessie emerged from the lift on the education level, she could hear voices, but she couldn't make out what either speaker was saying. She headed towards the noise. In the Kinvig Room, she found Harold and Marjorie having an animated discussion.

"I'm only keeping the secrets I have to keep," Marjorie said to Harold as Bessie crossed the threshold.

Bessie coughed loudly, her fake cough causing a minor uncontrollable coughing fit. "Goodness," she laughed as she caught her breath. "That was unexpected."

Harold and Marjorie were both looking at her with concerned expressions on their faces. Bessie couldn't help but wonder if the concern was for her or came out of worry that she'd heard their conversation.

"I'm fine, really," she said heartily. "I could use a drink of water, that's all."

Marjorie jumped up and quickly handed Bessie a bottle of water from the table at the front of the room that was already set up for breakfast. Bessie opened it and drank a sip, smiling her thanks to Marjorie.

"I thought I would come in early and see if you needed any help with anything," she told the pair after she'd swallowed and then joined them at a table in the middle of the space.

"I think we're okay," Harold replied. "We've moved the talks that were scheduled for the Moore Theatre down to the Ellan Vannin Theatre downstairs. That means the museum won't be able to show tourists the introductory movie whenever we're using the space, but the museum has kindly agreed to accommodate us anyway."

Bessie nodded. "That was nice of them," she said.

Harold and Marjorie exchanged looks that left Bessie wondering just how "kindly" the museum had agreed to the change.

"Anyway, I think everything is sorted out and we'll be ready to open the doors at eight for breakfast and registration."

"I hope I don't have to change your plans." The voice from the doorway startled them all.

Bessie turned around and forced herself to smile at Inspector

Corkill as he walked into the room.

"Good morning," Bessie said politely.

"Good morning," the inspector muttered, looking past Bessie to focus on Harold. "Dr. Smythe, I hate to bother you, but I need to ask you a few more questions"

Harold frowned. "I've told you everything that I know," he said, too loudly. "Hem, er, that is, I'm happy to help in any way I can," he said, in a carefully modulated tone. "But I can't think that there's anything I can usefully add."

"I'll have to be the judge of that, won't I?" Corkill smiled humourlessly.

"I suppose so," Harold shrugged.

"Bessie, why don't we go down to my office for a few minutes?" Marjorie suggested. "I have those documents we were talking about last night and we can get out of the inspector's way."

"That sounds great," Bessie smiled. She took the arm Marjorie offered and the pair made their way out of the room. Bessie spent the ride down in the lift wondering what Marjorie wanted to talk to her about. She'd played along in front of the inspector, but she hadn't talked to Marjorie about any documents in months.

The pair were silent as they walked through the dimly lit corridors in the still-closed museum. Marjorie unlocked her office door and flipped on the lights. Bessie blinked at the sudden brightness.

"Please, have a seat," Marjorie told her. Bessie dropped into one of the two visitor's chairs in front of Marjorie's desk. As ever, the desk was covered in papers, books and a few odd artifacts. Marjorie slid into her padded desk chair and sighed deeply.

Bessie gave her a sympathetic smile. "This conference isn't going at all like you planned, is it?" she asked gently.

Marjorie laughed harshly. "It's all so awful," she told Bessie. "I almost packed my bags and headed for the Sea Terminal last night when I got out of here. If I thought I could just disappear and never be found, I might have tried it." She sighed again. "The only thing that stopped me is knowing that, if I left, I would definitely jump to the top of the suspect list."

"I know Mack's death is upsetting, and so was his forcing himself into the conference programme, but I'm not sure why those things would make you want to run away. Besides which, Inspector Corkill seems to think it was just an accident. He probably doesn't even have a suspect list." Bessie leaned forward to pat her friend's hand. "Even if he does have a list, there's no real reason for you to be on it, is there?"

To Bessie surprise, the usually calm and collected Marjorie burst into tears. Bessie pulled a pack of tissues from her bag and handed tissue after tissue to the woman, waiting patiently as Marjorie sobbed. After several minutes, Marjorie gave her a watery smile.

"I'm so sorry," she said softly.

"And that's my last tissue, so you need to stop now," Bessie told her with a wry smile.

Marjorie managed a weak chuckle and then sat up straighter. "I am sorry," she repeated herself. "But I really needed that. I've been holding it in since yesterday afternoon."

Bessie nodded. "You looked upset last night, but I never got the chance to ask you what was wrong."

"I need to make some tea," Marjorie told Bessie. There was a small table in the corner of the office with everything necessary. Bessie sat silently as Marjorie filled the kettle from a large bottle of water and then switched it on. While they waited, Marjorie found some custard cream biscuits in a drawer and dumped them unceremoniously onto a paper plate.

Bessie grinned and grabbed one when Marjorie offered the plate. Marjorie fixed cups of tea for them both and Bessie was relieved to see that Marjorie was much calmer when she sat back down with her drink.

She gave Bessie what looked like a genuine smile and then sighed. "I'm sure you heard the rumours when I first moved to the island," she began. "I came here because I was running away. I'd had my heart comprehensively broken and I wanted a completely new start."

Bessie nodded. The heritage community on the island was small and close-knit. Every new MNH staff member was discussed and when someone from the UK who was highly qualified but had no real background in the island's history applied for a position, his or her possible motives for moving to the island were dissected endlessly. Bessie had heard tell that Marjorie was fleeing from a failed romance and she had a sinking feeling she knew what was coming next.

"The man who broke my heart was Mack Dickson," Marjorie continued, confirming Bessie's fears.

"Marjorie, I'm so sorry," Bessie said quietly.

Marjorie's eyes filled with tears again. "Don't be nice to me," she told Bessie. "I don't have time to cry again."

Bessie laughed. "And I really don't have any more tissues." Marjorie managed a shaky laugh before she downed her tea and quickly fixed herself another drink.

Bessie waited patiently while her friend composed herself. "You don't have to tell me anything," she said softly, after Marjorie returned to her seat with her drink.

"I know I don't have to," Marjorie replied, "but I need to tell someone and I can't think of anyone I'd rather talk to about it than you."

Bessie smiled. "I'm flattered, and I'm happy to listen. Hopefully, I'll be able to help as well."

Marjorie shrugged. "It isn't much of a story anyway," she said. "We met, I fell hard, he cheated, and I left. That's pretty much the whole thing in a nutshell." Marjorie flushed as she realized what she'd said.

"No pun intended, I'm sure," Bessie remarked, hoping to defuse the awkward choice of words.

Marjorie shook her head. "The thing is, I'm just as sure as Bambi is that it was murder, whatever Inspector Corkill seems to think."

"Why?" Bessie asked the obvious question.

"Mack was too careful. He would never have even so much as sniffed food that he wasn't totally sure about. He'd had a terrible reaction once as a teenager and it scared him enough to make him extremely cautious. Apparently before that he never really paid much attention to his allergy and just thought his parents were being overprotective. When he nearly died, he learned that they were right. He was just lucky that someone else in the group he was with also had an allergy. His friend recognised the warning signs and jabbed him with his own adrenaline injector before he called 999."

"That was lucky," Bessie remarked. "Too bad his friend wasn't around last night."

"He didn't need to be," Marjorie said intently. "Mack knew what to look out for now and he would have realised what was happening. He would have called 999 and jabbed himself as soon as he started to feel the reaction start."

"Maybe he did," Bessie suggested. "Well, not calling 999, but maybe he gave himself a injection, but it didn't work. Is that possible?"

"It's very possible," Marjorie told her. "That's why Mack always carried at least three injectors with him at all times. If the first one doesn't do enough to stop the attack, it's safe to use a second one. Mack always said the third one was 'for a friend.'"

"With his history, that makes sense," Bessie said. "But maybe the attack was just too quick for him to do anything. Maybe the police found his injectors in his pocket where he could have grabbed them if he'd only had a little bit more time?"

Marjorie shrugged. "Okay then, here's a question for you. Where did the brownie come from?"

"There was a whole table of them in the foyer," Bessie reminded her.

"Did you see Mack in the foyer?" Marjorie demanded.

Bessie frowned. "No, I didn't," she admitted after a moment. "He went into the cuillee after his talk and I didn't see him after that."

"That's because he never left the cuillee," Marjorie told her. "He would have been swamped by people throwing questions at him. He was quite happy tucked away, letting the tension build up until he was ready for the question-and-answer session. He wouldn't have left the room. Someone took the brownie to him."

"Maybe he grabbed one before he started his talk?" Bessie suggested.

"They didn't start putting them out until after Mack started speaking," Marjorie told her. "I was standing in the foyer until I heard Mack begin and then I slipped in, after I told the catering staff to clear away the food and start putting out the dessert bar."

Bessie sighed. "We could quiz the catering staff. Maybe someone saw Mack grab one just before they started putting things out?"

Marjorie shook her head. "I've already done that," she told Bessie. "Everything for the dessert bar was kept in the café downstairs until after they cleared away the canapés. The brownies weren't even cut until they were ready to put them out, because they didn't want them to get stale."

"So someone was kind enough to take Mack a brownie," Bessie replied. "That still doesn't make it murder."

"Except that the brownies that were supplied by the café definitely didn't have any nuts in them," Marjorie said triumphantly.

"Are you sure?"

"Absolutely. I talked to the head chef myself and he confirmed it. There aren't even any peanuts in the café at any time. The chef doesn't like them."

"What did Inspector Corkill say about all of this?"

Marjorie flushed. "I haven't exactly told him," she mumbled.

"What?" Bessie demanded. "But you have to tell him everything you've told me."

Marjorie shook her head. "I'll end up as his main suspect," she argued. "He'll soon find out that our brownies didn't have nuts and then he can work the rest out himself. If I tell him that we used to date, he's bound to think I had something to do with Mack's death."

"If he finds out later, from some other source, you're going to look more guilty than if you go and tell him yourself," Bessie suggested.

"I don't know." Marjorie's eyes filled with tears again. "I'm not sure I can bear to talk about Mack with anyone else, least of all with Inspector Corkill. Can't you just solve the murder and then I won't have to tell anyone about my past?"

Bessie frowned. "Finding murderers is a job for the police," she said. "And Inspector Corkill made it very clear when he interviewed me that he wasn't going to let me interfere with his investigation. I really think you should have a talk with him."

"I'll think about it," was all Marjorie said in reply.

"So if you're sure it was murder," Bessie said thoughtfully, "who could possibly have done it?"

"Everyone who ever met him?" Marjorie suggested with a wry smile.

Bessie grinned. "He wasn't that bad."

"You didn't date him," Marjorie retorted.

"Neither did Harold, but Inspector Corkill seems to think he had a motive."

Marjorie nodded. "Mack's talk just about destroyed poor Harold. All these years he's been looking for Roman remains and Mack is the one that actually finds them? Harold could have killed him. You know, Mack would have done serious damage to Harold's career if he hadn't died."

"This wasn't the first time Mack had done something like this," Bessie recalled.

"No, he made a habit of it," Marjorie said. "I'm sure there are other people here who had their careers negatively impacted by the man."

"Do you think you can get me more details on exactly who?" Bessie asked.

"Without Inspector Corkill noticing that I'm asking, I assume."

Bessie laughed. "Well, yes."

"I'll see what I can find out," Marjorie promised.

"Marjorie, I know you didn't kill him," Bessie assured her friend. "Are there other women here who used to date him and might have done it?"

Marjorie shrugged. "Every blonde under forty should be a suspect," she replied.

"Oh dear," Bessie frowned.

"Obviously, I didn't keep track of his love life after we split up," Marjorie told Bessie. "But when we met he already had a girlfriend."

Bessie frowned. "Did he now?" she asked, trying not to

sound judgmental.

"He did. Unfortunately, he didn't think to mention it to me until months later. When we met, I was living in London and he was working on an excavation in Leeds. We met at a conference in York and started dating, but we only saw each other on odd weekends for about four months. When his dig finished, he casually mentioned that he'd be moving back in with his girlfriend in Birmingham for a short time."

"And that's when you dumped him," Bessie suggested.

Marjorie laughed humourlessly. "If only I had been that smart," she replied. "Oh, we had a huge fight and I told him I never wanted to see him again. He showed up on my doorstep a week later with a suitcase and moved in. I was stupid enough to be thrilled when he told me he'd picked me over her, whoever she was, and naïve enough to think that he'd be faithful to me."

"But he wasn't?"

"Mack didn't even understand the concept of monogamy," Marjorie said with a sigh. "But he wasn't running around sleeping with every woman he met, either. I don't know exactly how to explain it. He always had a girlfriend that everyone knew about, that he took to events and that sort of thing. But he also always had another girlfriend on the side."

"How nice," Bessie said sarcastically.

Marjorie managed a small grin. "Yeah, well, the thing is, I didn't even realise that I was in the 'on the side' category until I'd already fallen head over heels. Once he moved in with me, I got, well, promoted, I guess. I became the woman that everyone saw him with and got to meet his friends and whatever. What I didn't expect was that he'd find a new woman to replace me as the 'other woman' or whatever you want to call it."

Bessie shook her head. "I'm sure going over all of this has to be painful," she told Marjorie. "I'm sorry."

Marjorie shook her head. "It's been enough years. I should be over it," she said. "I actually thought I was over it until he suddenly appeared. Seeing him again brought back a whole load of emotions I thought I'd firmly squashed."

Bessie frowned. "So if Mack brought Bambi with him as his

girlfriend, does that mean he was seeing someone else behind her back?"

"Probably," Marjorie answered. "I suppose he might have changed, but I doubt it. He and Bambi didn't seem to be getting along all that well, anyway. Maybe she found out about the other woman?"

"I don't think so," Bessie said slowly. "Bambi told me that they were fighting. I think she would have mentioned if she'd found out that he was cheating on her."

"So maybe she hadn't found out yet."

"Why would Mack's secret girlfriend be here, though?" Bessie asked. "I mean, surely he wouldn't have brought both Bambi and his mistress to the conference?"

Marjorie shrugged. "He might not have invited her specifically, but she could be here anyway. He liked to get involved with other academics. Usually he could get them to help him with his research. He hated doing research."

Bessie frowned. "So the important question now is, who is she?"

CHAPTER FIVE

Marjorie and Bessie chatted until it was nearly time for the day's talks to begin. They discussed everyone at the conference, but Bessie didn't feel like they got any closer to discovering either the murderer or the identity of Mack's secret girlfriend. She felt frustrated, because they had no evidence that he was seeing someone behind Bambi's back, and even if he was, they didn't know for sure that the woman was even on the island. Somehow, both those things just felt highly plausible to Bessie, so she was going to assume that they were true, at least for the time being.

Back upstairs, the foyer had filled up with a combination of eager historians and archeologists, a handful of reporters who were hoping to question people about the murder, and a few members of the general public who had a sudden macabre interest in the conference. Bessie stopped to check the notice board where a neatly typed note had been pinned up.

"*Please note the following changes to today's schedule:*

At 10:00 a.m. Dr. Harold Smythe will be giving his lecture in the Ellan Vannin Theatre (ground floor).

Dr. Joseph Steele's lecture will be held in the Kinvig Room.

Dr. Michael Brown's lecture will be held in the Blundell Room.

At 2:00 p.m. Marjorie Stevens will be giving her

lecture in the Ellan Vannin Theatre (ground floor).

All bus excursions have been cancelled due to circumstances beyond our control.

At 4:00 p.m. the Round Table Discussion will take place as scheduled, at a location as yet to be confirmed.

At 7:30 p.m. Paul Roberts will be giving his lecture in the Ellan Vannin Theatre (ground floor).

Dr. Claire Jamison will be giving her lecture in the Kinvig Room as originally scheduled."

Bessie wondered why the bus excursion had been cancelled. Poor Marjorie and Harold. They'd worked very hard for so many months to arrange everything. She walked through the room, waving and nodding at some of the people she knew, but she didn't stop to talk to anyone. She headed straight for the Kinvig Room and the first lecture of the day. The doors were still shut when she arrived, and she was just wondering what they were waiting for when a loud voice called for attention.

"If I could just have everyone's attention for a moment? Please, can you all quiet down?"

Bessie turned and spotted Harold at the far end of the room. He really needed a microphone to make his voice loud enough to be heard over the general babble. Slowly, people began to stop talking and turned to face him.

"Ah, um, thank you," he said, looking flustered. "I just wanted, that is, I think it's only appropriate if we have a minute of silence in honour of Mack?"

A quiet murmur went through the crowd, but no one objected.

"Okay, well, then, um, let's have a minute of silence, shall we?" Harold asked, and the room fell quiet.

Bessie felt as if she could hear the large clock on the wall behind her ticking off the seconds as she tried, but failed, to think about Mack and his untimely death. They were only about halfway through their minute when the lift doors suddenly opened with an accompanying "ping" that sent a nervous giggle through the crowd. Inspector Corkill and two uniformed constables stepped out of the lift and stopped short as every person in the room stared at them in the heavy silence.

The inspector cleared his throat and glanced around the space. "Should I ask what's going on?" he asked eventually.

"We were, um, having a minute of silence for Mack," Harold replied. "It seemed like the appropriate thing to do."

"Indeed," Inspector Corkill nodded. "I'm sorry I interrupted, then."

"No problem," Harold assured him. "We were just about finished anyway. It's time for our first session of the day to begin. I hope that's okay with you?"

The inspector frowned, but nodded. "That's fine. My men and I are here to spend some time going back through the room where the body was found. What did you call it again?"

"The cuillee," Harold answered. "It's Manx for back room."

"Yeah, well, that's where we'll be. We'll try to stay out of the way of the conference," Corkill said.

"Obviously, we all want to help as much as we can," Harold replied, too loudly. "If there's anything that I can do, please don't hesitate to ask."

A perfunctory nod was the only reply he received as the inspector and the other officers turned and headed into the Moore Theatre. The inspector used a key to open the door and then, once they were all inside, he shut the door tightly behind them. Another moment of awkward silence descended on the foyer.

"Well then, right, um, I guess we should get started with the day's events," Harold said finally.

Henry was only a few paces away from Bessie and he quickly used his keys to open up the Kinvig Room.

"My lecture will be taking place in the main theatre downstairs," Harold told the crowd. "Dr. Joseph Steele will be talking in the Kinvig Room about applying the techniques he's learned as a paleontologist to Manx archeology. Dr. Michael Brown will be discussing seventeenth-century pottery in the Blundell Room, which is just down the hall."

Bessie watched as the bulk of the crowd headed towards the lifts and the stairs. Harold, as one of the main speakers at the conference, was sure to be popular. That was why she had decided to attend Joe's talk. She didn't want him to end up talking to an empty room. She barely knew Michael Brown, and had very little interest in old pottery, anyway.

Bessie smiled as she took a seat near the front. The small space began to fill slowly, with several familiar faces from the previous evening. Liz Martin was back, presumably having a day away from the demands of motherhood. Bessie waved to Claire Jamison and Helen Baxter as they took seats near the front. She was surprised to see Bambi wander into the room just moments before Joe was due to begin speaking.

An hour later, Bessie felt like she'd learned far more than she'd ever wanted to know about digging for dinosaurs. She wasn't completely clear on exactly how that applied to Manx archeology, but archeology wasn't her field, so she gave Joe the benefit of the doubt on that score. The question-and-answer session that followed the talk was, luckily, short, as it was of no interest whatsoever to Bessie.

When the audience had run out of questions and the room began to clear, Bessie checked her copy of the schedule. The next thing scheduled was a catered lunch at noon. That gave Bessie an hour to chat with some of the other conference-goers.

She made her way out of the room and surveyed the lobby. Bambi was standing along one wall, holding a steaming cup. Bessie headed straight for her.

"I really didn't expect to see you here today," she said as a greeting.

Bambi laughed. "I can't figure out why I came," she told Bessie. "I barely slept last night and when I got up this morning I couldn't figure out what to do with myself. The police won't let me go home yet and the hotel room got claustrophobic in about three minutes. I finally decided that hanging out here was better than sitting around feeling sorry for myself." She grinned at Bessie.

"Having said that," she continued, "if that last talk is anything to go by, I might just go back to the hotel after lunch."

Bessie laughed. "Dr. Steele isn't the most gifted speaker I've ever heard," she told the young woman quietly. "But Marjorie is giving a talk this afternoon about the archives, and that should be excellent."

Bambi made a face. "I'm not sure I feel right going to her talk," she confided in Bessie. "I know she and Mack used to date, and I feel sort of weird about it."

"Did Mack tell you that?" Bessie questioned.

"Yeah," Bambi shrugged. "When we first arrived, he was talking about how his talk was going to be so explosive and important. He said he was going to put Harold Smythe in his place and teach Marjorie Stevens a lesson all at one time. I asked him about them and he said Harold was an academic rival and Marjorie was a romantic one." She waved a hand. "It was something like that, anyway."

Bessie frowned. "He called her a rival?" she asked.

Bambi shrugged again. "I can't remember exactly what he said. It didn't really seem important at the time, you know? I was trying to get him to agree to let me skip his talk and he was trying to persuade me that I would want to be here for the 'fireworks,' as he put it."

"Did you tell the police about the conversation?" Bessie asked, wondering if Marjorie was going to have to talk to Inspector Corkill about her relationship with Mack whether she wanted to or not.

Bambi shook her head. "No, it didn't seem important. That stupid inspector is convinced that it was all just a horrible accident. He won't listen to me, anyway. I answered all of his questions, but I didn't volunteer any more information that I had to."

"But you still think it was murder?"

"Of course it was," Bambi sighed. "But no one else seems to agree."

Bessie was going to argue, but their conversation was interrupted by Joe Steele, who was eager to find out what Bessie had thought of his talk. Bessie gave him the sort of polite feedback that was required of her, and by the time she'd finished, Bambi had disappeared.

Bessie made her way around the foyer, smiling and nodding at friends and acquaintances as she went. Liz was sitting on her own, sipping a drink, as Bessie skirted the crowd.

"I didn't know you were planning on coming again today," Bessie said, after the pair had exchanged polite hellos.

"This conference is all that Marjorie has been talking about for weeks," Liz said with a laugh. "I figured that it was only neighbourly of me to come."

Bessie grinned. "My neighbours don't seem to feel the same way," she said jokingly.

"Ah, you know me," Liz said. "Any excuse to get away from my little darlings for a few hours. I thought they should have some quality time with hubby. He can deal with the nappies and finding something for them for lunch and try to keep them entertained all day. Maybe he'll actually start to appreciate everything I do for a change."

Bessie laughed. "He'll be worn out when you get home," she predicted.

"No doubt," Liz laughed again.

"Do you know anyone here other than Marjorie?" Bessie asked.

"Besides you and Henry, you mean?" Liz replied. "Not a soul." She gave Bessie a long look. "You aren't investigating that man's death last night, are you?" she asked in a dramatic whisper. "I mean, I know you've helped find murderers in the past, and his dying like that was terrible and all, but I thought the police said it was an accident."

Bessie shook her head. "Inspector Corkill made it clear that he's not going to tolerate any interference in his investigation," she told Liz. "And as far as I know, they still think it was just an accident. I was just wondering if you'd ever come across any of the others when you were at school or anything."

Liz frowned and then leaned over, close to Bessie's ear. "I actually met the guy who died once," she whispered. "But I haven't told the police, and I hope you won't either."

"Why haven't you told them?" Bessie demanded.

Liz sighed. "I kind of went out with Mack once or twice when I was at university. He was a lot older and he was just there as a visiting professor for a few weeks. He seemed so sophisticated that I felt a bit overwhelmed by his attention. But I was already dating Bill, and he doesn't know about Mack. It would break his heart if he found out that I dated another man while we were already a couple. It was only a few dates anyway. It never got serious or anything. Mack was just looking for a good time and I wasn't willing to provide it for him."

Bessie shook her head. "You really should tell the police everything," she counselled the young woman. "It could be important."

"It was ages ago," Liz replied airily. "Mack didn't even recognise me when I came in. Besides, his death was an accident, right?"

Bessie shook her head. "I still think you should tell the police. There's no reason why they should mention anything about it to your husband."

Liz shook her head. "I don't trust that Inspector Corkill," she told Bessie. "He seems like the type who would tell Bill just because he could. If it turns out that it was murder, maybe I'll say something."

That was the best promise that Bessie could get from Liz, even though she kept trying for a few more minutes. Bessie was ready to give up anyway when Liz's mobile rang.

"It's hubby. He probably can't figure out what to do about lunch," Liz sighed. "I need to take this."

Bessie sighed as well and then turned her attention back to the crowd. She spotted Helen Baxter grabbing herself a cup of coffee and headed towards her. "So did you ever get a chance to chat with Bambi last night?" she asked Helen after they'd exchanged greetings.

Helen laughed. "She's actually really fun," she replied. "We had a great conversation about expectations versus reality and I was really enjoying getting to know her. Unfortunately, her boyfriend didn't seem to like watching her have fun and he dragged her away to talk to some group of researchers he knew from across."

"That's a shame. I think Bambi could really use a friend right now," Bessie replied.

"Is she here?" Helen sounded surprised. "I didn't think she'd bother coming back, now that Mack is, er, isn't, um, well, you know."

Bessie sighed. "She is here, somewhere, or at least she was. I hope if you see her you'll lend her a sympathetic ear."

"Of course," Helen answered. "I can't imagine what she's going through. She and Mack weren't getting along very well, but she did care about him."

"And you'd never met Mack before last night?" Bessie double-checked.

Helen shook her head. "No, I'd never had that particular pleasure before," she commented dryly.

"I know you said he was rather rude to you," Bessie grinned. "But that was just Mack. He was a brilliant speaker."

"He was indeed," Helen agreed. "I thoroughly enjoyed his talk, even if I didn't quite get what all the fuss was about."

Bessie smiled. "Roman remains are the most sought-after archeological finds on the island. We know the Romans knew the island was here and we have evidence that they traded with people on the island, but what everyone wants to know is whether they ever settled here or not, and if not, why not? It seems, after last night, that Mack found proof that they did, indeed, have a settlement on the island."

Helen shrugged. "It was all such a long time ago. I just don't see what difference it makes."

Bessie laughed out loud. "I'll be honest with you, but you mustn't tell anyone," she said in a whisper. "I'm not sure I see what difference it makes either. I'm much more interested in our more recent ancestors. But a lot of people here would argue otherwise."

Helen laughed and then looked around. "As long as we're telling secrets, I have to tell someone about last night or I'll just burst."

"What happened last night?" Bessie said curiously.

"You know I said that Mack was rude to me when I tried to start a conversation?" she reminded Bessie.

"Yes."

"Well, later, when I went back over and started chatting to Bambi, he kept giving me strange looks. After he dragged Bambi away, he left her with a group of people and came back over to me and started talking."

"What did he want?" Bessie asked.

"Basically, he wanted me to go to bed with him," Helen said bluntly.

Bessie gasped. "Pardon?"

Helen giggled. "He didn't put it quite that way," she said. "But that was what he meant. He actually apologised for being rude to me at first and then suggested that he could make it up to me over drinks later. Everything he said was carefully polite, but there was definitely a lot of innuendo and whatnot."

Bessie shook her head. "What a horrible man, though I suppose I mustn't speak ill of the dead."

Helen smiled. "He was rude and very conceited," she told Bessie. "But I wouldn't have called him horrible. I think in his own, admittedly arrogant, mind, he thought he was paying me a compliment."

Bessie bit back a dozen different retorts and then sighed. "Men."

Helen grinned. "That just about sums it up," she agreed.

The pair chatted about this and that until it was time for lunch. Helen had made arrangements with a friend from town to meet for lunch elsewhere, so Bessie headed down to the café on her own. She grinned at the man at the door, who was checking everyone's conference tickets as well as trying to explain to an elderly couple why they couldn't go in and get a cup of tea in the café because the conference was using the entire facility for the weekend.

Inside, she grabbed a plate and filled it from the generous buffet. Joe Steele was at a table with Claire Jamison and he waved Bessie over to join them.

Bessie sank down at the empty seat at their table and smiled at the pair. "Thanks for letting me join you," she said. "It's filling up fast in here."

Joe grinned back at her. "You're more than welcome. I really appreciated your help with the food last night. Today poor Claire had to try to identify what I might like for me."

Claire laughed. "I can't believe that the food here is that different from what you can get in the US," she said. "What do they serve at conferences there?"

Joe shrugged. "I haven't been to that many conferences," he replied. "And a lot of the ones I went to weren't very well-funded. Lunch was usually a plate of lunchmeat and a loaf of bread. If we were very lucky, there might be mayonnaise. Sometimes, actually just once, there were small bags of potato chips and chocolate chip cookies as well." He sighed. "That was an excellent conference."

"What was it about?" Bessie asked with a grin.

"I've no idea, but the food was fabulous," Joe laughed.

The trio talked briefly about various conferences and events that they had attended, and then discussed their research.

"I've just about convinced Joe that he should come and do some digging around Anglesey," Claire told Bessie. "He could do some interesting comparisons between Anglesey and the island."

"I'm thinking about it," Joe replied. "I've never been to Anglesey, and you make it sound very tempting."

Bessie studied the young man's face. He looked more than a little smitten with the attractive, if somewhat older, woman.

"Now that you're taking a break from dinosaurs, do you have an area that you're especially interested in?" Bessie asked him.

"After last night?" Joe asked. "I want to work on Mack's Roman site, but then, so does every other archeologist here."

Bessie shook her head. "First you have to find it," she said.

Joe shrugged. "I figure someone else must know where it is, mustn't they? A find this big and important can't stay a secret for long."

"I guess we'll find out in time," Bessie answered.

After they'd all stuffed themselves with the delicious lunch, pudding was served. Bessie helped herself to a few of the miniature pastries.

"American-style desserts last night and French-style pastries today," Joe remarked. "Don't the British do desserts?"

"We do puddings," Claire told him. "Lots of lovely hot

puddings that are best served dripping with hot custard or cream. Maybe we'll get to sample something tonight after dinner, but if not, I make a terrific bread and butter pudding, and if you come and study on Anglesey I'll whip one up for you."

Joe laughed. "As if I needed any more temptations to get me there?"

After they finished their pastries and the tea that went with them, it was time for Marjorie's talk. Joe and Claire were going to take a tour of the museum, a hastily arranged alternative to the bus excursion that had been cancelled. Bessie wandered down to the main theatre by herself. She was happy to find that Henry had saved her a seat in the front row.

"I thought I'd save you one at the front so you could hear everything," he explained to Bessie in a loud whisper.

Again, she thought about arguing that there was nothing wrong with her hearing, but she didn't. Instead, she settled into her seat and thanked Henry politely.

A few moments later George Quayle bounded in, with his wife, Mary, in tow. Bessie had never quite figured out what the lovely woman saw in George. The pair was surely evidence that opposites attract, as Mary was no more than five feet tall and was slender. She was quiet, and Bessie had known her for several months before Mary had begun to really talk with her. Bessie had eventually realised that Mary was terribly shy and, with George around, she rarely needed to exert herself.

Bessie watched as George waved to various people and shouted greetings towards them from the doorway. After a few minutes, he and Mary headed towards the seats marked "reserved" that were next to Bessie.

"Bessie, my dear, I'm so glad you came back," George said in his booming voice.

"Why on earth wouldn't I have come back?" Bessie asked.

"Well, after last night's tragic accident...." George trailed off and looked around the room.

"Oh, hush, George." Mary Quayle shook her head and then took Bessie's hand and pulled her to her feet for a hug. "Pay no attention to George," she suggested. "No one is going to miss this wonderful conference just because of one unfortunate incident."

"I don't know," George argued. "I suspect attendance will be down today. That's why we came, you know," he said to Bessie. "We wanted to make sure that everyone had a good turnout for their talks. Especially Marjorie."

"That was kind of you," Bessie murmured as she settled back into her seat.

Mary slid into the seat next to Bessie. "What's Marjorie going to be talking about?" she asked her.

"The archives," Bessie replied. "It should be an excellent presentation. She's going to talk about what they actually have in there, what they are trying to get, and what they'd love to get their hands on. She told me that she's got a few surprises for everyone as well. Apparently, she's come across a few very interesting documents lately that no one knew they had."

"That sounds wonderful," Mary said with a smile.

"I certainly hope so," Bessie grinned.

Marjorie looked upset and nervous after Harold's introduction, but once she got into her talk, she visibly relaxed. Bessie thought she knew quite a bit about the museum archives, but she was amazed to learn more about the important items that the museum was looking after on behalf of the nation.

The forty-minute talk went quickly and the question-and-answer session was lively and informative. Marjorie seemed much more like her normal self as she answered questions about her beloved documents and papers.

"That was fascinating," Mary said to Bessie when the question-and-answer session was over.

"Definitely one of the highlights of conference," Bessie agreed.

"She was wonderful," George interjected. "I didn't realise how much wonderful material they had in those boxes and files down there."

Bessie grinned. "I didn't either, and I've spent a lot of time poking around in them myself."

George waved at someone and shouted "hello" across the still crowded space. After a moment he shook his head. "I'm going to have go and say something to Jack," he told his wife. "I'll leave you with Bessie, shall I?"

"Oh, yes, please," Mary said anxiously.

George walked away, pushing through the crowd as he climbed up the shallow stairs that the staggered seating in the room required.

Mary sighed deeply as the throng swallowed him up. "I do wish he wouldn't insist on dragging me to these things," she said quietly, almost to herself.

"Aren't you enjoying yourself?" Bessie asked.

Mary flushed. "Oh, no, I'm having a wonderful time," she replied too quickly. "It's all just a little overwhelming, all these people and well, everything."

Bessie nodded, feeling a pang of sympathy for the shy woman. "It was kind of you to come," she told her. "I'm sure Marjorie appreciated it."

"George insisted," Mary replied. "I was going to stay home and I think, if that man hadn't died last night, George wouldn't have minded. But he was really afraid that no one would be here today."

"I think the opposite is true," Bessie said, glancing around. She hadn't realised just how much the room had filled up after she'd taken her seat. It looked as if every seat had been full and no one seemed to be in any hurry to leave, even though the talk was over.

"It does seem a very good turnout," Mary said.

"I don't think I recognise more than half of them," Bessie said. "I wonder where they've all come from?"

"As long as they've paid their conference fees, I don't care where they've come from," Mary said stoutly.

"I hope everything's okay for you and George," Bessie replied cautiously.

Mary flushed. "Oh, everything's fine," she said. "I just worry...." she trailed off and looked down at the ground.

"Worry about what?" Bessie asked in her kindliest voice.

"Nothing," Mary shook her head. "Nothing at all, really."

"You know I'm always happy to lend an ear if something is

troubling you," Bessie told the other woman.

Mary smiled faintly. "Troubling me, yes, that's a good way to put it. But I was raised that you didn't bother other people with your troubles."

"I was as well," Bessie grinned. "But sometimes you need your friends."

"Thank you for being a friend," Mary told Bessie. "I've always wanted to ask you to come around for tea one day," she said softly. "But I'm sure you're much too busy."

Bessie laughed lightly. "I'm never too busy for my friends," she said firmly. "Let's set a date now, before we both get back to our busy lives."

The other woman smiled brightly and the two quickly compared their schedules, finally settling on a date that was only a little over a week away.

A moment later George reappeared, dragging what seemed like half the room with him. He pulled Mary into the group, shouting introductions at her while Bessie gratefully slipped away.

Bessie headed towards the back of the room, carefully skirting the crowd. She had about half an hour to fill before the start of the round table discussion that she was meant to be taking part in. The discussion had originally been scheduled for the Moore Theatre, and she wanted to try to catch Harold to find out its new location. It wasn't the sort of thing that would work well on the stage in the main theatre, but they might not have a choice.

As she made her way towards the group that Harold was talking with, Bessie gave some thought to her conversation with Mary. The other woman seemed to be worried about money. Bessie wondered if she knew that her husband had offered to fund Mack's excavations at the Roman site. In spite of the tragedy of Mack's untimely death, Mary Quayle had good reason to be relieved that he wouldn't be around to take George up on his generous offer.

Bessie had just reached Harold's side when a sudden silence fell across the room. She turned around and saw that Inspector Corkill had just walked in.

"Ah, good afternoon, everyone," the inspector said loudly. "I was just looking for Harold Smythe and Marjorie Stevens. I'd like a few minutes of your time, both of you, please?"

Marjorie had been chatting with Harold and his group of friends, and now Bessie watched as she turned as white as a sheet.

"I can't talk to him," she whispered to Bessie, grabbing her arm. "You've got to sneak me out of here."

"Don't be silly," Bessie hissed back at her. "You've got to talk to him. You've no idea what he wants. Maybe he just wants to talk about the archives."

Marjorie shuddered and Bessie watched tears begin to fill her eyes. "I simply can't do it," she said again.

Bessie stared hard into her friend's eyes. "You have to do it," she said resolutely. "And you can do it. You just need to pull yourself together. Take two deep breaths and focus on getting yourself under control."

The inspector hadn't moved. Instead he was watching Bessie and Marjorie with an interested look on his face. "Is there something wrong?" he asked politely.

"I'm sorry, but Marjorie isn't feeling well," Bessie replied. "She was too nervous to eat lunch before her talk and now she's feeling a bit lightheaded."

"Perhaps you could take her and find her a snack while I talk with Dr. Smythe?" the inspector suggested.

"That's a wonderful idea," Bessie replied. She took Marjorie's arm and began to lead her out of the room.

"You won't mind if I send a constable with you," Corkill continued. "Just to make sure she's ready when I need her."

"Of course we don't mind," Bessie said. Now she was worried about her friend. If the inspector was putting a police guard on Marjorie, he had to suspect her of something.

Marjorie said nothing as Bessie escorted her from the room. Corkill's uniformed constable was only a step or two behind. Bessie glanced back and saw that Harold had made his way down to where the inspector was standing, and the two seemed to be having an intense conversation.

Bessie nearly had to drag Marjorie into the corridor and then through the museum to the café. The last remnants of lunch were still being cleared away and Bessie quickly fixed her friend a plate of food. She also piled a bunch of pastries onto a plate and handed them to the uniformed officer.

"We don't have to mention this to Inspector Corkill," she told him.

"Gosh, thanks," he said with a huge grin.

Marjorie ate silently and mechanically, while Bessie patted her arm and kept her teacup full. It wasn't much more than ten minutes before their uniformed companion received a call to let him know that Corkill was ready for Marjorie.

"There, you see? He only needed ten minutes with Harold. I'm sure you'll be fine," Bessie assured Marjorie.

Marjorie didn't answer; she simply gave Bessie's hand a squeeze and then followed the constable down the hall. Bessie sighed and grabbed herself another pastry as she left the room. It was getting closer to time for the round table discussion and not only did she not know where it was being held, she wasn't sure if Harold and Marjorie were even going to be able to take part.

CHAPTER SIX

In the end, someone made the decision to hold the round table talk in the upstairs foyer. While that meant that they might be frequently interrupted by people coming and going, it was felt that the foyer setting was more conducive to the sort of group discussion that the organisers wanted to encourage. By the time Bessie reached the foyer, the area had already been set up for the talk.

Bessie smiled to herself as she took her seat at the end of the long rectangular table. Of course, if they had actually used a round table, some of the participants would have to have their backs to the audience, but it amused her that the event was so obviously misnamed. Harold was already sitting in his seat at the middle of the table, with Joe Steele to his left between Harold and Bessie. Marjorie's name was on the name card to Harold's right. William Corlett and Claire Jamison finished that side of the table, and Bessie saw that Paul Roberts was meant be to be sitting between her and Joe. Paul arrived only a moment later, saying a polite "hello" to Bessie as he slid into his seat. He immediately opened a notebook and began to write furiously.

This gave Bessie time to reflect on what she knew about the man. Somewhere in his mid-sixties, he still looked like the hippy he had once been. His grey hair was long and untidy and his clothes were brightly coloured but in bad repair. He was something of an amateur archaeologist, in that he'd never taken a degree in the subject. Instead, he'd learned by doing at sites all across the British Isles. His many years of experience had made him an expert in Roman finds, which consequently meant he rarely visited the Isle of Man. Bessie had met him at a handful of conferences over the years and she had come to like the grumpy and somewhat prickly man. There were some that felt that his lack of a formal degree meant that he shouldn't be taken seriously, but Bessie didn't fall into that camp.

Marjorie slipped into the room looking as if she was still close to tears. She made her way to the table as quickly and unobtrusively as she could, pausing when she reached Bessie's end of the table.

"They just wanted to know if I knew where Mack's slides had ended up," she whispered to Bessie.

"What slides?" Bessie asked. "The ones from last night?"

"Yes, it seems they've gone missing," Marjorie replied.

"But how could that happen?" Bessie asked. "Did Mack have them with him in the cuillee or were they still in the projector at the back?"

Harold frowned down the table at Bessie and Marjorie. "If we're all here, we should probably get started," he said loudly.

"Later," Marjorie said as she slid past Bessie towards her seat.

"I wanted to see those slides," Paul said in Bessie's ear as Harold stood up slowly.

"I'm sure you're not the only one who wanted a look," Bessie said in response.

Paul frowned and looked as if he wanted to say more, but he was interrupted.

"Well now, good afternoon," Harold said loudly to the small crowd that had gathered. "Welcome to our round table discussion on archaeological and historical research methods. Every one of the speakers on the panel has given, or will be giving, a talk here at the conference this weekend. For now, they're going to talk about their own work and their own individual research methods." He paused, and after a moment a few people clapped politely.

"Yes, well, then, as I was saying, everyone is here to share their best ideas. Each of our speakers will give themselves a short introduction and talk for a few minutes about their research methods. After everyone has had a chance to speak, we'll open the floor to questions from the audience. I'm hoping that this will be one of the weekend's best opportunities for us all to learn from one another."

Another courteous round of applause followed as Harold sat back down in his seat. The introductions started at the opposite end of the table, so Bessie sat back and listened as Claire gave a short biography of herself and then discussed the day's topic. By the time the other five speakers had had their turn, Bessie was feeling quite drowsy and she worried, as she began her own introduction, that the audience was as bored as she was.

"Good afternoon, I'm Elizabeth Cubbon and I'm an amateur historian. I have been specialising in studying wills from the nineteenth century, and I'll be talking more about that tomorrow afternoon during my presentation." Bessie kept her remarks as brief as she could, eager to get to the questions from the floor. She could only hope that they would liven things up a bit.

Half an hour later, Bessie was starting to worry that she was going to fall asleep right there at the table. Harold was relating yet another long story about an archaeological dig that had found absolutely nothing and Bessie mind was wandering all over the place.

"Okay, time to make this interesting," Paul muttered under his breath as Harold finally wound up his tale. "I have a question," he said loudly. "What happened to the slides from Mack's talk last night? I want to have a good look at them to see what exactly he found."

Harold flushed and shook his head. "The police are investigating that very thing," he told Paul. "At the moment no one seems be certain where the slides disappeared to during the confusion last night."

"Well, that's rather convenient for you, isn't it?" Paul asked.

"Whatever do you mean by that?" Harold demanded, his face bright red.

"If Mack really did find what he claimed to have found, your career is in trouble, isn't it?" Paul shook his head. "I didn't like

Mack and he didn't give me any respect because I didn't have the right piece of paper to show folks, but if he did find Roman remains on the island, he deserves proper credit for that."

"I hope you're not suggesting that I would do anything to interfere with Dr. Dickson getting full credit for his work?" Harold was nearly incandescent with rage.

Paul shrugged. "I just think it's weird that the slides have disappeared, that's all," he said. "I didn't arrive on the island until this morning, so I missed the big announcement and the slide show last night. I was really looking forward to examining the finds in detail. Does anyone know where Mack was keeping the things he discovered?"

Harold glanced at Marjorie, who shrugged, and then shook his head. "Mack showed us a handful of slides of what he said were Roman remains," he told Paul in a tense voice. "He didn't say anything about where he found the remains or what he'd done with them. I suppose we would have tried to get that information during the question-and-answer session if it hadn't been for Mack's unfortunate accident."

A burst of laughter from the back of the room captured everyone's attention. Bambi waved as all eyes were suddenly on her. "I just love how you described Mack's death as an 'unfortunate accident,'" she said loudly. "He was murdered and everyone in here knows that. It's only the police that want to think otherwise."

"Now, now, Ms. Marks," Harold said anxiously. "I'm sure the police are doing a thorough job of investigating Mack's, um, untimely passing. It certainly isn't my place to offer any opinion about what happened to him. I'm sure we shouldn't even be speculating at this point. Not about poor Mack and not about the slides, either." The last remark was directed at Paul, who shook his head.

"Shouldn't be speculating?" Bambi repeated. "Surely it isn't speculating when you know something absolutely. Mack would never have eaten anything he wasn't one hundred percent positive was safe. He must have trusted whoever gave him that brownie. There's no other possible explanation."

"And I'm sure the police are giving that idea their full attention," Harold said, in what Bessie could only assume was meant to be a reassuring tone. "Figuring out what happened to Mack is their job. I'm an archeologist and a historian, not a police detective. I didn't think you worked for the police, either?" he challenged Bambi.

"If it wasn't murder, where are Mack's adrenaline injectors?" Bambi countered Harold's question with her own. "You must know that he always had at least three with him at all times. I hope you've told the police that fact."

"I knew Mack had a nut allergy," Harold answered. "Anyone who ever organised a conference that he attended knew about his food allergies. But what he did about ensuring his safety with regard to that allergy was his own business, not mine. I vaguely remember him pulling out an injector once at some other conference when he was worried about something he'd eaten, but I certainly couldn't tell the police that he always carried three of them with him. I had no idea."

"But where did the...." Bambi kept going, but Harold interrupted.

"Young lady," he said loudly over her words. "I understand that you are very upset about your loss. But we are trying to run an academic conference here, not a police investigation. I suggest you take your concerns and your accusations to Inspector Corkill. I'm sure they will be far more welcome there than they are here. Now, where were we?"

"We were talking about the missing slides," Paul reminded him with a nasty grin.

"Ah, yes, well, as I said, the police are investigating that and, again, I think we need to leave them to do their job. Let's open the floor to other questions, shall we?" Harold sighed and then looked out over the small group that was listening intently now. A hand shot up from the audience. Harold smiled gratefully at the young man who stood up as Harold acknowledged him.

"Um, hi, I'm Dan Ross, from the *Isle of Man Times*. I was wondering whose farm it was where Dr. Dickson found those remains that everyone is so worked up about."

Harold frowned. "As of right now, we don't have an answer to that," he told the reporter.

"But surely after everything that's happened, someone must have come forward and identified themselves?" the man said incredulously. "I mean, this is the biggest find in years, possibly the biggest find ever on this island. I understand that Dr. Dickson wanted to keep it quiet until his talk, but now that it's public knowledge, surely the farmer will want to talk to other archeologists about what's on his land and, hopefully, he'll have a few words for the press as well."

"As I said," Harold repeated himself stiffly. "The last I knew, no one has come forward to admit to owning the land that Mack excavated."

"Surely between you all, you must have a guess as to who it is, though?" Dan argued. "You've been digging on the island for something like fifteen years, and William Corlett was born and raised here besides. Between the two of you, you must know every farmer and every possible field location that Mack could have used."

Harold flushed. "I have made a point, during my long career, to get to know every farmer on this island whenever possible. As far as I know, no one made their land available to Mack for an excavation in the last year or more. William, do you have any thoughts on the subject?"

William Corlett looked up from his notes and frowned. "I'm still really new to archeology, but, as Dan points out, I grew up here and I have family scattered just about everywhere from the Point of Ayre to Port Erin. Last night was the first I'd heard about Mack doing any digging on the island. I called a few people I know this morning and no one seems to have any idea where he might have been excavating."

"Are you suggesting that he fabricated his finds?" Dan demanded aggressively.

William flushed. "I'm not suggesting anything," he said defensively. "I'm just trying to answer the question. As yet, and it has only been what, less than twenty-four hours since Mack spoke, I haven't had any luck in finding the farmer that Mack claims called him and invited him to excavate his field. I'm sure Harold has been doing his fair share of contacting people as well, but obviously he hasn't found the right person yet, either."

"I have indeed, been making phone calls," Harold replied. "And I've met with the same results that young William discussed. No one will admit to being the farmer in question and no one seems to have heard anything about any archeological sites being dug in the past year. Obviously, farms and parcels of land are being sold all the time and, equally obviously, I haven't had a chance to talk to everyone I know. At this point it is impossible to draw any conclusions. As with Mack's death and, um, the missing slides, I must suggest that we need to rely on the police to sort everything out. Now I think we need to move on to another topic."

"Why would Dr. Dickson fabricate such a thing?" Dan threw out, obviously not ready to accept a change of subject just yet.

"As I said," Harold replied testily, "we don't know that he did. At this point, anything is possible."

"If he did make it all up, he couldn't possibly have expected to get away with it," Paul interjected from his seat next to Bessie. "Harold is an expert on this island and I know a thing or two about Roman remains. Mack knew that I was coming; we talked about it last week on the phone. There's no way he would risk his career with made-up evidence. Whatever is going on, I have to believe that Mack found exactly what he claimed he'd found."

"Well, at least someone has faith in the man," Harold muttered. "If he hadn't been so secretive, maybe we'd have more answers."

"He always wanted to surprise everyone with his big announcements." Bessie wasn't sure why she felt the need to defend the man, but she spoke up on his behalf. "It was all just part of Mack being Mack. I knew the man for many years and I never saw him at a conference when he didn't have some important bit of new research to announce. Admittedly, this one was the biggest of them all, but he loved surprising his audience and he enjoyed feeling like he'd done something really amazing."

"Do you think that's what got him killed?" Dan demanded of Bessie from where he was still standing in the audience.

"I've no idea," Bessie said, slightly flustered by the sudden question. "As far as I know at this point, Mack's death was an unfortunate accident."

"And yet, you seem to have a knack for stumbling over murders, don't you, Aunt Bessie?" Dan smiled at her. "I've been wanting to talk to you for months about all the dead bodies that seem to be stacking up around you. You never return my phone calls."

"And I certainly won't after today, either," Bessie replied sharply. "I've had the extreme misfortune to find myself on the periphery of a couple of murder investigations in the last few months," she admitted. "But that's hardly relevant to anything that is currently happening."

"On the contrary," Dan grinned. "I know Inspector Rockwell in Laxey regards you as a valuable asset to his investigations. Apparently there isn't anything that happens in Laxey that you don't know about. Is Inspector Corkill showing you the same courtesy? Is he having long chats with you about the various suspects and using you for the latest skeet?"

Bessie pressed her lips together and counted to ten before she replied carefully. "Inspector Rockwell is a nice man and a very smart policeman. I do know a lot about happenings in Laxey because I've lived there for many many years. I'm sure that Inspector Corkill is also a very smart policeman and I'm more than happy to stay well clear of his investigation. I'm sure there is nothing useful that I could contribute to it."

"So you're happy with the idea that it was all just an unfortunate accident?" Dan asked Bessie. "Because that seems to be the line that the police are taking."

"It isn't any of my business," Bessie said sternly.

"Well, it is my business," Bambi interrupted. "And I'm happy to go on record that I'm not satisfied with the police investigation up to this point."

"Indeed?" Dan turned eagerly to Bambi. "I know you think it was murder. Where do you think the police have gone wrong?"

Bambi grinned, seemingly pleased to have a chance to air her grievances. "For a start, they won't listen to me," she replied. "I keep telling Inspector Corkill that it was murder and giving him all my reasons why I'm so certain that it was, but he just pats me on the arm and says that they'll investigate. But so far they don't seem to have done a whole lot of that. I'm sure I've found out more than they have, just from chatting with people."

"What have you found out?" Dan asked, scribbling excitedly in a notebook.

"I've found out that Harold was furious that Mack took his place as the first speaker at the conference and that Mack's findings just might mean that Harold loses his job."

"That isn't true," Harold exploded. "My job is perfectly safe and secure, thank you very much."

"But Mack's findings weren't good for you professionally," Paul suggested. "Surely you can't deny that."

Harold sighed. "Mack's findings were like a smack in the face," he said sadly. "Both personally and professionally. I thought I had a good working relationship with the men and women who own the farms around the island. The thought that one of them went to Mack instead of me would have been heartbreaking, even if all Mack found was a pile of nineteenth-century rubbish. That he found evidence of a Roman settlement was devastating." Harold took off his glasses and rubbed a hand over his face. "And yes, it will have repercussions in my professional life. Only time will tell how bad those will be."

Bambi nodded. "One could argue, therefore, that Dr. Smythe had a convincing motive for murder," she said.

Harold shook his head. "If I could have had a few minutes alone with Mack right after his speech, I might have strangled him to death on the spot, but I never got near him. As soon as Mack finished speaking, he locked himself up in the cuillee and I never saw him again, at least not alive."

"What else have you learned?" Dan pressed Bambi for more information.

Bambi shrugged. "I learned that Mack was trying to cheat on me, chatting up some blonde and trying to get her to meet him later. I suppose that gives me a motive for murder as well, but like Harold, I never spoke to him after his talk."

Dan looked up from his rapid note-taking. "What blonde?" he asked.

Bambi laughed. "You're meant to be an investigative reporter. Time for you to do some of the work."

"Anything else to add?" Dan asked hopefully.

"I know that Mack used to be involved with someone on the panel," Bambi said, gazing at Marjorie. "The way I heard it, he broke her heart into a million tiny pieces. I'm not sure if that's a motive for murder or not, but if I were Inspector Corkill, I'd be checking it out."

"And you had better believe that I will be," Inspector Corkill said loudly, coming out from behind a small divider that had been left near the back wall of the foyer. "While this has all been very interesting indeed, I think it's time to put a stop to all of the accusations and arguments," he remarked, as he strolled towards Bambi.

"I didn't know you were there," she said faintly, as he reached her side.

"But I'm sure you expected all of your comments to reach my ears eventually," the inspector countered. "I think you and I need to have a nice long talk, don't you?"

Bambi shrugged. "I guess," she muttered.

Inspector Corkill turned back towards the panel at the table. "I'll be wanting to talk to everyone on the panel once I'm done with Ms. Marks. I'd be grateful if you could remain in the foyer until you're called for."

He took a few steps towards the door with Bambi in tow. "Oh," he called back over his shoulder, "and Mr. Ross, if I were you I would be very, very careful about what I put in the paper. A lot of what was said here today was simply the result of angry and unhappy people speculating wildly. I'd hate to see any of that speculation in a respected newspaper like the *Times*."

Bessie watched as Dan frowned and slumped back into his seat. There was no doubt he'd get a good story from today's events, but it seemed that perhaps he wouldn't be able to use everything he'd heard.

Harold cleared his throat. "Did anyone else have any

questions about the actual subject of this round table discussion?" he asked tiredly.

The long silence that followed seemed to answer the question. "Okay, well, then, I guess that concludes our round table," Harold said with a sigh. "Thank you all for coming."

Bessie sighed and slid back in her chair. The conference was certainly not going the way everyone had hoped. For a minute or two it seemed as if everyone was determined to remain in the foyer, presumably anxious to see the next act in the continuing drama that the conference had become, but eventually a few people began to straggle out and after several minutes only a handful of people remained in the foyer with the round table participants.

"So now we all have to just sit here and wait for the police to question us again?" Harold demanded. "That Bambi has a lot to answer for."

Bessie got up and went to Marjorie's side. "Are you okay?" she asked her friend anxiously.

Marjorie gave her a tentative smile. "I'm actually relieved," she told Bessie. "I was so worried about my secret coming out that I couldn't think straight. I'm sure talking to the police will be uncomfortable, but at least I can just tell them everything and not worry about it."

Bessie smiled at her, but the back door swung open before she had a chance to reply. "Ms. Cubbon? I'd like a word with you now, please."

After giving Marjorie's arm a quick pat, Bessie gave the inspector a small smile and followed him wordlessly into the conference room he was now using for interviews.

CHAPTER SEVEN

Bessie took the seat that the inspector indicated at the small table in the corner of the room. She glanced out the window. It looked like a nice afternoon outside and she hoped she might sneak a short walk in before the end of the day. She'd been up too early to walk this morning and had been too busy with the conference ever since.

"Now then, Ms. Cubbon, I'd just like your thoughts about what was said at the discussion group out there," the inspector told her.

"It's Miss Cubbon," Bessie said patiently. "And I haven't really had time for any thoughts. It was all a little bit overwhelming."

"Of course," the inspector frowned. "Let me ask more specific questions, then."

Bessie braced herself for what she suspected was going to be an unpleasant interview.

"Let's start with Harold Smythe," Inspector Corkill suggested. "I assume you were aware that his research centred on Roman history and that Mack's findings were upsetting to him?"

Bessie shook her head. "I was, of course, aware of Harold's work. I've known him for many years and I've always enjoyed hearing him speak about his research. But how upset Mack's talk made him I could only guess. It was obvious earlier in the evening that he was disappointed that Mack was giving the opening talk rather than the schedule going ahead as planned, but it seemed to me that he was blaming George Quayle rather than Mack for that turn of events."

The inspector frowned. "I haven't had a chance to speak at

length with Mr. Quayle as yet," he told Bessie. "But getting back to Harold, what about the damage that Mack's finding are going to do to his career?"

"I don't know anything about that," Bessie replied. "As far as I know, Harold is a highly respected professor. Whatever Mack found, I can't believe it could do all that much damage. Harold was disappointed, but the find will give many archeologists and historians lots of work for many years to come. Being the first to find the evidence is exciting, but it isn't the only thing that matters."

Inspector Corkill shook his head. "I realise you're determined to protect your friend," he told Bessie. "If we do decide that Dr. Dickson was murdered, I'm going to have to look a lot more closely at Dr. Smythe."

Bessie simply nodded, not wanting to argue with the man. She watched as he flipped through the notebook on the desk.

"So did you know that Dr. Dickson and Marjorie Stevens used to date?" the inspector asked in a casual tone.

"Marjorie mentioned it to me this morning, when we were talking about Mack," Bessie admitted.

"Can you repeat the conversation for me, please?" Corkill asked.

"I could," Bessie said with a sigh. "But there's very little point. I can summarise it in a few sentences. They dated several years ago and it ended badly when Marjorie discovered that he was cheating. After it ended, she moved to the island to get away, and yesterday was the first time she saw him again since they broke up."

The inspector frowned again. "As I said, it's obvious that you're doing your best to protect your friends," he said. "I'm going to let it go for now, but I may have to ask you again for a more complete account of that conversation with Ms. Stevens."

Bessie nodded again, wishing that she could be having this conversation with Inspector Rockwell instead. She knew she could trust Rockwell with every last detail that she knew. He would carry out a proper investigation into Mack's death. In spite of this different line of questioning, Bessie still felt as if Inspector Corkill was convinced the death was an accident.

"Tell me about Bambi," Corkill invited Bessie. "She volunteered that she'd discovered that Mack was chatting up other women. Was she angry enough about that to kill him?"

Bessie shook her head. "I just met the woman last night," she pointed out. "We've barely spoken."

"You're meant to be an astute judge of character," the inspector told Bessie. "I'm just looking for your opinion."

Who has he been taking to, Bessie wondered as she considered the question. "She seems like a smart young woman," Bessie said after a moment. "I think if she did do it, she would be smart enough to keep her mouth shut now and let everyone think it was an accident. Instead, she's running around telling anyone who will listen that Mack was murdered."

"Unless it's an elaborate double bluff," Corkill suggested.

Bessie raised an eyebrow and pressed her lips together. The idea seemed ludicrous to her, but telling the inspector that wouldn't make him like her any better.

Corkill made a few notes in his notebook and then gave Bessie what looked to her like a fake smile. "I think that's all my questions for today," he told her. "Or at least for now. I assume you'll be here for the rest of the day?"

Bessie shrugged. "I might try and get away for an hour or so and take a short walk," she answered. "I didn't have a chance to get any exercise this morning and I'd like to stretch my legs before the rest of today's talks."

The inspector nodded. "That's fine. I know where you live, anyway, so I can always find you if I need you."

"Indeed," Bessie smiled faintly.

"I'll walk you out," he told her as she stood up. "I need to collect the next person on my list."

The pair made their way back into the foyer where the inspector asked Claire Jamison to join him. She gave Bessie a grin as she strolled past her. No one else seemed to have moved from their spots at the conference table, but the museum staff were busily refreshing the tea and coffee that were laid out on long tables along the wall.

Bessie filled a plate with biscuits from the table and then fixed a cup of milky tea. She took them over to the panel members, who were all wearing uneasy looks.

"Have some biscuits," she suggested as she put the plate in the middle of the table. She handed the cup of tea to Marjorie. "You look like you could use this," she told the younger woman.

Marjorie smiled. "Thank you, I really can. I don't know why I didn't think to get up and get something myself."

Bessie watched as the plate of biscuits was passed down the table. Everyone managed to find something palatable from the selection she'd gathered and she was relieved to see some of the tension lifting from her friends' faces as they nibbled their sugary treats.

"That's done the job," Harold announced. "I'm going to grab a coffee. Does anyone want anything?"

Joe and William both muttered affirmatives and got up and followed Harold across the room.

Paul grinned at Bessie. "Was it awful in there?" he asked.

"Not at all," Bessie assured him. "Inspector Corkill just asked me a few questions about everyone, that's all."

"I'm not sure why he even wants to talk to me," Paul said. "I wasn't even on the island last night."

"I guess he's looking for background information," Bessie suggested. "You know all of the key players, at least a little bit."

Paul shrugged. "I guess."

"Do you think the inspector thinks I killed Mack?" Marjorie asked timidly.

"I don't think the inspector thinks anyone killed Mack," Bessie replied. "From what he said to me, I think he still thinks it was an accident. Anyway, I know you didn't kill Mack, so you don't have to worry about answering the inspector's questions."

"I didn't kill Mack," Marjorie agreed. "But I still don't want to talk to the inspector."

"You'll be fine." Bessie patted her arm. "I'll stay with you until he's ready for you, shall I?"

"If you wouldn't mind, I'd appreciate it." Marjorie gave her a huge smile that looked almost genuine.

"The round table discussion broke up early and there isn't

anything else on the schedule before dinner," Bessie said. "I think, after you've gone in to talk to Inspector Corkill, I might take a short walk."

"It's a lovely day for it," Paul told her. "I almost hated coming inside after I got off my flight."

"It would have been a great day for touring Castle Rushen and the Abbey," Bessie remarked. "What happened to the planned excursions?" she asked Marjorie.

Marjorie shrugged. "The inspector asked us to cancel them," she told Bessie. "He wanted people close by just in case he had any further questions for them."

"I suppose that's just as well, considering," Bessie said with a sigh. "Is anything going to happen as scheduled at this conference?"

"On that note, Harold and I were just talking, and we've decided to ask the café staff to push dinner back an hour," Marjorie told her. "The round table was supposed to take about ninety minutes, and then dinner was meant to start at six, but with the police here questioning everyone again we can't be sure about the timing. Harold suggested we move dinner back to seven to be on the safe side. Of course, as it's not even five yet, that should give you plenty of time for a walk before dinner."

"What's happened to tonight's talks then?" Bessie asked.

"They've been pushed back an hour as well." Marjorie sighed. "It means a late night for everyone, but it seemed like the best solution to a difficult situation."

Bessie grinned. "As unhappy as I am with the way the conference has been going," she told her friend, "I am glad that I'll be able to get a walk in. I'm so used to walking whenever I feel like it."

Paul smiled at her. "And at home you get to walk on the beach as well. Your cottage is lovely, and in such a perfect location."

Bessie smiled back. She'd invited Paul and a handful of others to her cottage one evening many years earlier when they were in the middle of an excavation at Rushen Abbey. She'd been visiting the site when a huge rainstorm put a stop to the day's work. The original plan had been for a picnic dinner on site, but that changed to takeaway pizza in Bessie's small cottage as the rain continued to fall.

"I'm glad you enjoyed your visit to my cottage," she said now. "I love having access to the beach all the time and I start to feel quite cooped up when I can't get out and about for a day."

The trio chatted about nothing much and before long the others rejoined them, hot drinks in hand. Bessie had to keep fighting the urge to watch the clock; she was feeling so anxious to get away. It was certainly no more than fifteen minutes later, though, when Inspector Corkill reappeared.

"Ms. Stevens? I'm ready for you now," he announced.

Marjorie gave Bessie a worried look and then drained her teacup. "Wish me luck," she whispered as she stood up.

Bessie gave her a sympathetic smile and then watched as she joined the inspector.

"I guess Claire must have slipped out the back after her talk with the inspector," Joe said in a disappointed tone.

"She seems quite nice," Bessie said with a smile.

"She's lovely and very smart," Joe answered. "I really think I'm going to take her up on her offer and do some research in Anglesey. She makes it sound very tempting."

"Mack did some work in Anglesey, didn't he?" Bessie asked Harold. "I'm sure I remember reading a paper he wrote about his research there in some conference proceedings or something."

"He did work in Anglesey," Harold confirmed. "It was probably two or three years ago and I don't think he was there for long. I think he stepped on a few toes and ended up leaving under something of a shadow." Harold sighed deeply. "Of course, those sorts of things never stuck to Mack for long. Somehow, he always managed to come back stronger than ever."

"He was such a gifted speaker," Bessie replied. "I'm sure his students loved him."

"They did," Harold admitted. "And he was very good at raising funds, so his administration loved him. Look at how he won George over. Mack was an expert at finding ways to fund his projects, which always seemed to find dramatic and exciting things. I hate to admit it, but the world of archeology will be less rich for losing him."

A few minutes later a pair of uniformed constables arrived. They apparently had orders to keep the panel members company while their boss questioned them in turn. The awkward silence that descended on the room made Bessie even more anxious to leave.

"I think I'll head out for that walk," she told the others. "I'll be back before seven so I don't miss dinner."

One of the policemen checked her name off the list he had been given and gave her a tight smile. "You've been cleared for now," he said. "But the inspector may well have more questions for you later."

"Fair enough," Bessie grinned. "I won't go far."

She took the lift down to the lobby and felt a huge sigh of relief rush out of her as she pushed open the huge glass door at the front of the museum. Outside, the sun felt warm and the world felt brighter than normal to Bessie. She grinned at her own foolishness. She was as giddy as a small child given an unexpected day off school.

The car park extended along the side of the building and Bessie followed it now towards the long path that led into downtown Douglas. She walked slowly, enjoying the stunning view out over Douglas Bay. With no clear idea of where she was going, she headed for the promenade that stretched almost the entire length of Douglas Beach.

Twenty minutes later, she reached it and sank down onto a convenient bench. She watched the gentle waves as they lapped up on the sand and sighed with contentment. While she wanted to get more walking done, she didn't want to overdo it, either. She still had the long walk back up the hill to get back to the museum.

She studied the small crowd of people on the beach, wondering whether a walk in the sand would be more enjoyable than a stroll through the city centre. In the end, she didn't have to decide.

"Bessie? Bessie Cubbon? Is that you?"

Bessie looked up in surprise and then smiled broadly. "Bahey

Corlett? What are you doing here?" she asked her old friend. Bessie had first met Bahey many years earlier, shortly after she returned to the island from her childhood in America. Bessie hadn't yet turned twenty, and Bahey had been a child. The pair had little in common in those days, but now that Bahey was retired, the age gap felt insignificant.

Bahey grinned. "Surely I should be asking you that question," she told Bessie. "Seeing as how I live down here and you don't."

Bessie laughed. "Fair enough," she replied. "Are we not far from your new flat, then?"

"Not far at all," Bahey told her. "I'm just up there, down that alley."

Bessie stood up and looked where Bahey was pointing. She could see a neat row of recently built flats that disappeared along a narrow road behind the row of hotels that stood along the promenade.

"I have a great view of the sea from my bedroom," Bahey told Bessie.

"How wonderful," Bessie replied. She had her own spectacular and uninterrupted sea views from nearly every room of her cottage, but she didn't feel it was polite to mention that.

"Oh, I know you've got better views," Bahey laughed, clearly reading Bessie's mind. "But I never imagined I'd retire and have my own place, so I feel pretty good about where I've ended up."

"I'm so glad that you're enjoying your retirement," Bessie smiled.

"Yes, well, after all that unpleasantness in March, it's nice to get back to my simple life."

Bessie wasn't sure she'd call the two murders, coupled with the two attempts on her life, simply "unpleasantness," but she didn't argue. "I'm glad things are back to normal," she said instead. "How's your sister?"

"Oh, she's dandy," Bahey told her. "Her William has finally started to take a bit of notice of his old mum. I'm sure it's his new girlfriend that he's really trying to impress, but he's paying for someone to come in once a week and clean and tidy for Joney. He's having some necessary work done around the house as well.

A bit of painting and decorating and just a general spruce up. You know it needed it."

"It did indeed," Bessie agreed. "I'm glad that William can help her out."

"Well, it's harder for us women on our own, isn't it?" Bahey asked. "I'm lucky that Mr. Pierce looked out for me so well, but when I need some painting done I've got to just do it myself or pay someone to do it for me. Sometimes I do think it would have been handy to have a kid or two around."

Bessie laughed. "They don't always turn out the way you want them to, though," she reminded her friend.

"Oh, aye, I guess we've both seen plenty of that, not just recently, but over the years as well."

"Indeed," Bessie agreed.

"Well, I was just off to do some shopping," Bahey told Bessie. "You doing the same or did something else bring you into Douglas?"

"I'm attending the conference at the museum," Bessie answered. "We had a short break, so I snuck away for some fresh air and to stretch my legs."

"Oh, my," Bahey said. "I heard that someone died. Is that true?"

Bessie frowned. "Unfortunately, yes," she told her friend. "Dr. Mack Dickson was a very talented archeologist and, sadly, he had an allergic reaction to something he ate and passed away."

"Those allergies are something, aren't they?" Bahey asked rhetorically. "I mean, in my day no one was allergic to anything. We just ate what we were given. Now it seems like everyone I know is complaining about not being able to eat this, that, and the other. One of the women down the hall from me daren't eat anything but white rice and fruit. Everything else makes her itchy and what not."

"I do seem to know a lot more people with allergies now than I used to," Bessie said. "I'm sure the medical profession is working on trying to find out why that is."

Bahey shrugged. "It's a shame about your friend, though. I hope you wasn't close friends."

"We weren't close," Bessie replied. "But it is still very sad."

"Anyway, I'm going to do some shopping. I don't suppose you want to tag along? I need a new dress for tomorrow night." Bahey looked up and down the promenade and then leaned in close to Bessie. "I've got a date, you see."

Bessie hoped that she managed to keep her face from showing the shock she felt. She had to bite her tongue to keep from blurting out something that would have been rude. After a moment, she smiled and managed a reply. "How nice," she said, somewhat lamely.

Bahey looked sheepish. "I know, it's kinda weird, like, me dating at my age and all, but he's a neighbour in the building. I don't know if he really likes me or if he's just being polite, like, and taking me to dinner because he's new to the building, but I want to look nice anyways."

"Of course you do," Bessie replied, feeling slightly more composed. "I'd love to come with you to find something," she said impulsively. Bessie hadn't been shopping with a friend for "date" clothes since she was a young teen in America. Of course, in those days, some fifty or sixty years earlier, money was much tighter and she and her friends usually just window-shopped for things they'd have bought if only they could have afforded them.

As the pair made their way back across the road towards the shops, Bessie remembered a long-forgotten shopping trip she had taken only a week or two after she'd met Matthew, the man she'd come to fall madly in love with. She had taken every penny of her savings with her and had just enough money to buy herself a new skirt. She'd been so excited when she'd put it on the next day, heading to a friend's house where she was sure Matthew would also be.

Bessie sighed to herself. Those had been almost magical days and she wondered what she might have done differently if she could have seen the tragedy that was to come. She shook her head. There was no use dwelling on the past. She was a very happy woman now and if she went back and made changes along the way, she might not have ended up where she was. She couldn't imagine being any happier anywhere else at this point in her life.

The pair had great fun for the next half hour, with Bahey trying on several dresses and checking for Bessie's opinion on each one.

"Too short," they both agreed about one.

"Too young," Bessie said about another.

"Don't want to look like mutton," Bahey had agreed with a sigh. "It is a lovely dress, though."

Finally they agreed on a pretty but sensible black dress.

"At least I know I have shoes that will go with it," Bahey said as they waited for the clerk to ring up the sale. "I have enough pairs of black shoes to open my own shop."

Bessie laughed. "I'd better get back up the museum," she told her friend. "It was great seeing you. I'll call you next week and we'll make plans to have lunch or something."

"That sounds good," Bahey told her. "I'll tell you all about my date."

Bessie grinned. "I'd like that."

There was a lot on Bessie's mind as she made her way back to the museum. Her interlude with Bahey had been fun, and she wasn't looking forward to getting back to the conference. After months of looking forward to it, there was no doubt that Mack's death and the subsequent police investigation had cast a long and dark shadow over what should have been a very enjoyable weekend.

She got back to the museum just minutes before seven.

"Hey, Aunt Bessie. Everyone's on their way to the café for dinner," Henry told her as a greeting from his post behind the front desk.

"I guess I'd better head there, then," she replied. "Thanks."

"Dr. Smythe is still with Inspector Corkill," Henry told her in a whisper. "He's been in there for almost an hour now. Everyone else was in and out in like ten or fifteen minutes."

Bessie shrugged. "I guess the inspector has found a lot to discuss with Harold," she said in a neutral tone, while her mind was racing. What on earth could the two be talking about for this long?

Henry shrugged as well. "I just thought it was interesting," he told Bessie.

"It certainly is that," she agreed. "But there's probably a perfectly good explanation."

"I guess." Henry seemed disappointed.

"What's on the menu for dinner?" Bessie changed the subject.

"It's an Italian feast," Henry told her. "Pasta and that sort of thing."

"I love Italian food," Bessie said happily.

Henry nodded. "They originally planned to have a Manx buffet, but apparently George Quayle doesn't like kippers or queenies."

"I guess, if he's paying for a lot of it, he can have a say in the menu."

"Yeah, and don't tell anyone, but I rather agree," Henry laughed. "I'm really looking forward to when my replacement gets here and I can get in and get something to eat myself."

"I'll see you later, then," she told the man. She could smell the delicious aromas of garlic and tomatoes as she neared the café.

Marjorie was standing near the door as Bessie arrived and Bessie could see that her friend was glad to see her.

"Did you enjoy your walk?" Marjorie asked.

"It was very nice," Bessie told her. "I hope your session with Inspector Corkill wasn't too hard on you?"

Marjorie shook her head. "I think you may be right about him still thinking it was an accident," she told Bessie. "He only asked me a few questions and he didn't really seem interested in my answers. I think I only spent ten or fifteen minutes with him, although it felt longer."

Bessie smiled. "I'm sure it did, but at least it's over now and you're not keeping any secrets from the police anymore."

Marjorie smiled uneasily and muttered something under her breath. "I guess we should get something to eat," she said to Bessie in an artificially bright voice.

Bessie stared at her friend for a moment, wondering what had just gone unsaid. But this wasn't the time or the place for asking.

Instead, the pair joined the short queue waiting to fill plates from the buffet. Bessie glanced around, noting who was there and who was missing. When she'd reached the front of the queue she decided that she'd spotted everyone she'd expected to see, except for Harold, who was presumably still talking with the inspector.

The food looked even better than Bessie had anticipated and the fresh sea air had stimulated her appetite, so she loaded her plate with pasta smothered in tomato sauce, crunchy-looking garlic bread that was dripping butter and had big chunks of garlic studded across it, and a large scoop of grilled vegetables. She had to set her plate down to fill a bowl with mixed salad greens that she topped with dressing and a few croutons. With both hands full, she surveyed the room, looking for somewhere she and Marjorie could sit.

Liz Martin waved to her from a nearly empty table in one corner of the room. Bessie gratefully moved towards her after telling Marjorie, who was still building her salad, where she was headed.

"I didn't know you were still here," Bessie remarked to Liz after she'd taken her seat.

"I went home for a little while and fed everyone dinner, but since I paid for the full conference, I figured I should come back and have my dinner here. If they hadn't changed the time, I would have missed it, but I'm really glad I didn't, because everything is delicious."

Bessie smiled. While Liz had been talking, she'd tried the food. "It is really good," she agreed.

Liz laughed. "Actually, anything I don't have to cook is good for me," she told Bessie. "I was ridiculously pleased to be making food for hubby and the kids knowing that I wouldn't be eating it."

"Why didn't you just have hubby cook?" Bessie asked, perhaps a bit nosily.

"Bill's actually a good cook," she told Bessie. "But when he cooks he goes all out and does fancy dishes. The kids don't usually like it and it isn't worth the effort for just him." She shrugged. "If there had been something else going on here that

I'd wanted to attend, he would have handled it, but I wasn't that interested in the discussion group anyway, so I was happy to pop home. We're only just around the corner from here."

"I remember Marjorie saying you were neighbours," Bessie replied. "And I know she doesn't live far away."

"Did I hear my name?" Marjorie asked as she arrived at the table with a very full plate of food.

"We were just talking about how you and Liz live close by," Bessie answered.

"We do, indeed," Marjorie said. "And mostly I love living close to work."

The threesome kept their dinner conversation light and inconsequential. Dessert was tiramisu and Bessie felt as if she couldn't possibly ever eat another bite once she'd finished it. "Everything was excellent," she told Marjorie. "My compliments to whoever arranged for it all."

Marjorie smiled. "I arranged this one," she replied. "Harold was in charge of lunches and I said I'd sort out dinner tonight."

"Who arranged for yesterday's dessert bar, then?" Bessie couldn't help but ask.

Marjorie shrugged. "The idea came from Joe Steele. I guess Harold must have set it all up, though. I know I didn't do it."

"Maybe that's why the inspector is spending so much time with him?" Bessie suggested.

There were two different talks on the schedule that evening. Originally intended to begin at half seven, the revised start time was an hour later.

Not long before eight, Harold rushed into the café, a scowl on his face. He fixed himself a plate of food and carried it to an empty table near the door. Bessie finished the last of the cup of tea she'd been nursing while chatting with the others and stood up.

"I'm going to go see how Harold's doing," she told her companions.

"If he needs me for any conference business, let me know," Marjorie requested.

"Will do," Bessie promised.

Harold was busily shoveling his dinner away as Bessie approached. "Mind if I join you?" Bessie asked him as she slipped into the seat next to him.

Bessie watched his face, as politeness fought with his desire to be alone. In the end, courtesy won out. "Of course not," he muttered unconvincingly.

Bessie grinned to herself. She was too nosy to let the unenthusiastic welcome deter her. "I hope Inspector Corkill didn't annoy you too much," she said. "I guess he's just doing his job."

"Ha! He's witch-hunting is what he's doing," Harold said forcefully. "This is all that stupid Bambi woman's fault. I swear I could kill her." Bessie could tell from his expression that as soon as the words were out of his mouth, Harold realised how unfortunate they were.

"You know what I mean," he muttered, looking down at his now nearly empty plate.

"I do," Bessie agreed. "But I don't think you should be too hard on Bambi. Her logic seems perfectly sound to me."

Harold made a face and pushed his empty plate away. "Inspector Corkill is the expert," he argued. "If he thinks Mack's death was an accident, then I'm inclined to believe him."

"But does he think it was an accident?" Bessie asked. "After all the time he spent with everyone this afternoon, I'm wondering if he's changing his mind."

Harold shrugged. "I wasn't asking the man any questions," he told Bessie. "I was simply answering them. I've no idea what the inspector thinks happened to Mack."

"What sort of questions was he asking?"

"You'd be better off asking me what he didn't ask," Harold replied bitterly. "He wanted to know all about the planning we did for the conference, how we selected the speakers, who made everyone's travel arrangements, when I found out Mack was coming, et cetera, ad nauseam."

"I would have thought he'd have asked all of those questions last night," Bessie remarked.

"Maybe he is changing his mind about what happened, then," Harold said. "Whatever he's thinking, he's definitely ruining the conference."

"It certainly hasn't gone to plan," Bessie agreed.

"Not even close," Harold said miserably. "I can't help but blame George Quayle for a lot of what's gone wrong. If he had told Mack he couldn't speak, Mack wouldn't have even been here."

"Where is George?" Bessie asked, refusing to be drawn into that particular discussion.

"He had a dinner meeting, but he'll be back for tonight's talks. He said he was planning to go to Paul's presentation."

"I was as well," Bessie replied. "I wonder if George will bring Mary with him again."

"I doubt it," Harold said. "George loves this sort of thing, but Mary only comes when she has to. She's actually painfully shy, you know."

"I did know that," Bessie grinned.

People were starting to trickle out of the café now, heading for home or back upstairs for the final talks of the day. Harold stood up abruptly.

"I need to get back upstairs and make sure everything's ready for the last of today's speakers," he told Bessie. He was walking away before Bessie managed a reply.

"Well, okay, then," she muttered at his departing back. She glanced around and then decided to head upstairs herself.

In the foyer the long tables had been set with tea and coffee again, and bottles of water and trays of biscuits filled every inch. Bessie couldn't resist grabbing a custard cream as she walked past. She helped herself to a bottle of water as well, feeling as if she'd had more than enough tea with dinner.

Bessie looked over her schedule again. She was now having trouble deciding which lecture she wanted to attend. Paul Roberts was a nice guy and usually an interesting speaker, but she was enjoying getting to know Claire Jamison and her talk sounded intriguing. Bessie knew little about Anglesey and she thought it might do her some good to learn more.

George was leaning against the back wall, deep in conversation with Harold. Bessie decided to let George make the decision for her. Whichever talk he decided to attend, she'd go to the other. She had no doubt that many of those present would follow George wherever he went; she'd try to help make up the crowd at the other presentation.

"Have you finished with your water?" Bessie jumped as someone spoke from behind her. She spun around and blinked at Joe Steele. "I'm sorry, were you talking to me?" she asked.

Joe laughed. "I guess I sort of snuck up on you, sorry. I told Claire I would help her collect all of the empty water bottles," he explained. "She's very keen on recycling and she was getting upset that so many bottles were just being thrown away."

Bessie smiled at the man. He was holding a large black bin bag that seemed to be about half full of bottles. "That's a great idea," she told him. "But I haven't finished with mine yet. I'll make sure I get it to you or Claire when I'm done, okay?"

"Great," Joe grinned. "Claire went through the trash and managed to collect two bags full when we first came up after dinner. Now we're trying to make sure to let people know what we're doing, so no one else throws their bottles away." He gestured to the other side of the room where Claire was chatting with Bambi. Bambi was shaking her head and holding on to a nearly full water bottle. Claire nodded and then moved on to tackle her next unsuspecting water drinker.

"She needs to get ready for her talk, doesn't she?" Bessie asked Joe.

"Yeah, you're right, I'd better go remind her." Joe dashed off and Bessie grinned as she watched him catch Claire's arm. The two had a whispered conversation that resulted in Claire heading towards the Kinvig Room with Joe on her heels.

"I wonder where that's going to end up," Marjorie said in Bessie's ear as she joined her.

"Claire and Joe?" Bessie asked. "They are very cute together, aren't they?"

"She's a little bit older, but maybe he needs that little bit of maturity. He's almost like an overgrown puppy."

Bessie laughed at the accurate description. "I think she's just about convinced him to do some work on Anglesey," she told

Marjorie.

"Ah, how romantic," Marjorie replied. "Can't you just see them snuggled up together in a trench full of mud and water, digging to their hearts' content in spite of the rain?"

Bessie laughed again. "I can indeed."

Harold called for attention now, asking everyone to make his or her way to either the Kinvig Room or the Ellan Vannin Theatre. Marjorie followed the bulk of the crowd down the stairs for Paul's talk, but Bessie hung back, her eyes on George Quayle.

"Ah, Bessie, will you be joining me for Paul's talk?" he asked as he and his entourage swept past her.

"You know, I think I'd rather hear what Claire has to say," she told him. "It doesn't look like she's going to have as much of a crowd as Paul and I want to make sure she feels welcome here."

"Very sensible," George replied. "Maybe I should try her talk as well?"

"Oh, I don't think so," Bessie answered hastily. "I mean, you and Paul are old friends. You don't want to let him down."

George frowned. "I suppose you're right."

Bessie grinned to herself as she watched the man head towards the lift. She really did like him, but a little bit of George Quayle went a long way. She'd just about had her fill of his company for this weekend.

She took a few quick steps towards the Kinvig Room, not wanting to be late. The foyer was nearly empty now, but Bessie noticed that Bambi was still in her chair in the corner. For a moment Bessie thought about just ignoring the young woman in favour of getting a decent seat at Claire's talk, but that seemed too rude. She'd drag Bambi along to the talk and see if that helped change the woman's mind about how interesting history could be, she decided.

Bessie crossed the room quickly, hoping that Claire would turn out to be a more gifted speaker than Joe had been, for her own sake as much as for Bambi's. When she reached Bambi, she was shocked to find that the young woman was asleep. Presumably, she hadn't been sleeping well with all the stress from Mack's death, but still, it was only half eight. Bessie was tired, but she'd never let herself fall asleep in a public place like that.

Pausing a step away from the girl, Bessie coughed loudly. She hoped she could wake Bambi without embarrassing her. Bambi didn't move. Bessie coughed again, which brought on a genuine coughing fit. Glad she had kept her drink, Bessie uncapped it and took a sip. When she had composed herself, she was surprised to see that Bambi still hadn't moved.

An uneasy feeling settled in Bessie's stomach. She stepped over to Bambi and put a hand on her arm. Relief flooded through her when Bambi's skin was warm to her touch. She shook the other woman gently, but got no reply.

"Bambi? Bambi, are you okay?" Bessie said, her volume increasing with every word. She pulled on Bambi's arm and Bambi's head fell backwards. While Bessie could see that the woman was still breathing, Bambi was clearly not just sleeping. She was completely unconscious.

CHAPTER EIGHT

As Bessie dialled 999 she wondered what Doona would make of the call she was going to get shortly. Bessie requested an ambulance for Bambi, giving the operator all of the information that she had, which wasn't much. She had no idea what Bambi had eaten that day, whether or not the woman had any allergies or what sort of medications she might be on. The operator asked Bessie about illegal drugs as well, but Bessie was equally clueless.

"She often seemed to not be paying attention," Bessie told her. "But whether she was under the influence of something or just bored out of her mind, I don't know."

Bessie was trying to keep her voice down, but in the empty foyer the sound obviously carried into the Kinvig Room. Joe Steele stuck his head out and frowned deeply at Bessie. He began to pull the door closed, but then stopped and left the lecture room to cross to Bessie's side, closing the door to the Kinvig Room behind him as he exited.

"What's going on?" he whispered.

"Something's wrong with Bambi," Bessie hissed back. "I'm on the phone with the emergency services now."

Joe frowned and picked up Bambi's wrist. "Her pulse is very weak," he told Bessie. "I'd guess she's overdosed on something."

"That was my guess as well," Bessie said. "But why?"

Joe shrugged. "Maybe it was an accident, or maybe she was really upset about losing Mack?" he speculated.

"Or maybe someone wanted to make her stop insisting to

everyone that Mack was murdered."

Joe looked surprised. "You think someone tried to kill her?" he asked.

"I don't know," Bessie answered. "But I think the police should investigate."

"And we will," Inspector Corkill assured her as he crossed the room. He'd obviously just come out of the Moore Lecture Theatre, but Bessie and Joe had been so intent on Bambi that they hadn't noticed him.

"I didn't know you were still here," Bessie said.

"Obviously," the inspector replied in a cold voice. "That would be why I had to get a call from dispatch telling me that there's been an attempted murder in the same bloody building where I'm working."

"If I had known you were still here, I would have shouted for you," Bessie said, trying to soothe his clearly ruffled feathers.

"Yes, well, it's a bit late for that, isn't it?" The inspector checked Bambi's pulse and then shook his head. "I just hope it isn't too late for the ambulance."

Bessie watched over Bambi anxiously for several minutes as Inspector Corkill made what seemed to be an endless number of phone calls. Joe paced back and forth, debating loudly to himself as to whether he should interrupt Claire's talk or not.

"For goodness sake," Bessie finally erupted. "Either go back in and listen to Claire or sit down and be quiet."

Joe looked at her sheepishly. "I'm sorry, I just don't quite know what to do."

The "ping" of the lift cut short that conversation, and Bessie watched wordlessly as the ambulance men raced in and began to work on Bambi. The inspector headed back inside the Moore Theatre, still talking on his mobile. Within minutes they had Bambi on their stretcher, heading for the lift and Noble's Hospital.

"Any of you next of kin?" one of the men asked.

"No, her family is all across, I think," Bessie replied.

"Any of you able to come along and fill out the paperwork, then?"

Bessie exchanged glances with Joe, who shook his head. "I

don't think I exchanged more than three words with the woman," he said anxiously.

"I'll go," Bessie sighed. "She shouldn't be left on her own, the poor girl."

As Bessie boarded the lift with the stretcher, she glanced back towards the Kinvig Room. She doubted that Claire had finished her talk, but presumably the noise and commotion caused by the ambulance crew had interrupted. The door now stood open and several people were crowded in the doorway, staring after Bessie and Bambi.

Downstairs, things weren't any better. As Bessie followed the stretcher from the building, she saw that dozens of people were clustered around the museum entrance, their worried faces bathed in the flashing red lights.

"What's going on?" Harold demanded of Bessie as she hurried past the crowd.

"Something's happened to Bambi. I'm going with her to hospital, unless you'd rather go as the conference chair?"

Bessie knew what his answer was going to be by the look that flashed over his face. "Um, no, you go," he stammered out. "I didn't even know the girl."

There was no time for Bessie to point out that she didn't actually know the girl either. The stretcher was slid into place and one of the medics helped Bessie climb in after it. She was directed to a small seat along the side wall of the vehicle and she'd only just sat down when the ambulance pulled away, sirens blaring and lights flashing.

Bessie did her best to stay out of everyone's way as they worked to keep Bambi alive on the short journey to Noble's. When they arrived, Bessie was asked to go to the admitting desk while Bambi was whisked away.

Bambi's handbag had been on the chair next to her and someone had handed it to Bessie after Bambi had been loaded on to the stretcher. Now, Bessie held it tightly, hoping it would contain contact information for Bambi's next of kin.

At the admitting desk, the pile of paperwork that Bessie was asked to complete had her shaking her head. "I'm sorry, but I simply can't answer ninety-nine percent of these questions," she told the not terribly sympathetic woman behind the desk. "I only talked to the woman a few times and I certainly don't know her National Insurance number or even her home address. I'm not even sure where she lives, although I'd guess London."

"That's pretty vague, isn't it?" the clerk asked. "Wasn't there anyone at the museum that knew more about her? Why was she even there?"

"She was dating the man who passed away yesterday," Bessie replied. "My goodness, was that only last night? It seems a lot longer ago than that."

"I heard about that," the woman behind the desk said. "Anaphylactic shock, nasty that is. Guess your young friend took losing her boyfriend pretty badly if she's gone and tried to top herself, no?"

"There's no evidence to suggest that she tried to commit suicide," Bessie said tartly. "It could have been an accident or...." she trailed off, unwilling to discuss attempted murder with a stranger.

"Bessie? What's going on?"

Bessie spun around and smiled with relief as she met Helen Baxter's blue eyes.

"I was happily listening to Paul's talk and then the ambulance arrived and everything went crazy. I figured I might be more help here than I would be there."

"I'm surprised that Inspector Corkill let you go," Bessie said.

Helen flushed. "I'm not sure that he noticed," she muttered. "Anyway, what's going on?"

"I was going to go to Claire's talk, but then I noticed that Bambi was still sitting in the foyer. I went over to talk to her, but I couldn't wake her up." Bessie frowned at herself as she heard her voice quaver.

Helen quickly enveloped her in a hug. "You poor dear," she said soothingly. "But who on earth suggested your coming with the ambulance? Surely Harold or Marjorie could have done that. You look completely done in."

"I guess I was just in the wrong place at the wrong time,"

Bessie said with a shrug. "But now I have all this paperwork to fill out and I can't answer any of the questions."

Helen smiled. "Carole," she said to woman behind the desk. "Bessie and I are going to head to the café and get as much of this done as we can. I'll get it back to you as soon as I can."

Carole nodded and then went back to reading her magazine. Helen led Bessie to the café, which was empty except for one man who was sitting, reading a newspaper and sipping a hot drink at the counter. The pair slid into seats in the corner and Helen went up the counter and had a quick conversation with the man behind it. A moment later she returned with a tray containing tea and biscuits for Bessie and herself.

"Put extra sugar in your tea," she instructed Bessie. "You've had a shock."

Bessie did as she was told, nibbling a digestive in between sips. "Ah, that's better," she said after a few minutes.

"Then let's see what we can do with this paperwork," Helen suggested. "Do we know Bambi's surname?"

"It's Marks," Bessie recalled. "But her name isn't really Bambi. Her real name is Margaret."

Helen raised an eyebrow and then shrugged and filled in the form in front of her. "Don't suppose you know Margaret's address?" she asked.

"I don't," Bessie told her. "But I have her handbag."

"That's a bonus," Helen grinned. "Let's hope her driving licence and a list of emergency contacts are in there."

Bessie put the small handbag on the table and then sighed. "I hate to open it. Handbags are such personal things."

"I'll do it if you want," Helen offered. "I've had to do this dozens for times for patients who, for whatever reason, can't do their own paperwork. It isn't a big deal."

Bessie shrugged. "It feels like a big deal."

Helen reached across and took the bag from Bessie. "You can be my witness that I've not taken anything I shouldn't," she told Bessie.

The bag was fairly empty, at any rate, containing only a small wallet and Bambi's mobile phone. Helen opened the wallet and grinned.

"That's what we need," she said, holding it up to show Bessie that Bambi's licence was in a clear pocket right in the front of the wallet.

Helen quickly copied down the woman's address information, and then she slid everything out of the wallet and flipped through it with professional detachment.

"Nothing else useful," she said with a sigh as she replaced credit cards and store loyalty cards into their slots.

Bessie checked the handbag again and then smiled. "Her passport is here, too," she said, as she dug it out of the bag.

"No one ever fills out the emergency contact information in those things, though," Helen laughed.

But Bambi was an exception. Bessie handed the passport to Helen, who copied the information that Bambi had provided.

"Now we just have to get in touch with Mr. Marks and let him know that Bambi's in hospital," Helen said. "For now, let's find out how she's doing."

"For now, you both have a few questions to answer."

The voice from the doorway sounded angry, and Bessie couldn't stop the sigh that she felt came from her toes as she turned in her chair to face Inspector Corkill. She opened her mouth to speak, but was interrupted.

"Ms. Cubbon, I'm sure you can't begin to imagine how I felt when I got a call from our dispatch centre telling me that someone had called for an ambulance only a few feet away from me. Perhaps you'd like to consider what went through my mind when the ambulance crew left with Ms. Marks and I discovered that not just one, but two witnesses had left while my back was turned?"

"I was asked to accompany Ms. Marks here, to take care of her paperwork," Bessie replied, keeping her voice calm.

"Indeed? I shall have words with the ambulance team about proper protocol, in that case. Ms. Baxter, did someone ask you to come along or was that your own initiative?"

Helen flushed. "I was worried about Bessie," she said. "She was terribly pale when she left the museum and I thought she might need a bit of looking after."

Corkill frowned. "Which one of you grabbed the evidence on your way out?" he demanded.

"What evidence?" Bessie asked.

"Ms. Marks's handbag is missing," he replied. "I'm guessing that's it on the table in front of you. It certainly matches the description I was given."

"One of the medics handed it to me when they moved Bambi," Bessie told him. "I thought I'd better bring it so I would have her address and things like that."

"Thus destroying any chance of our getting any evidence from it to prove attempted murder." The inspector sighed. "I suppose I need to have several long talks with the ambulance crew."

"They were just worried about Bambi," Bessie said. "I'm sure attempted murder never crossed their minds."

"I don't need you to make excuses for them," Corkill growled. "No doubt they'll have plenty of their own."

Bessie bit her tongue and exchanged glances with Helen. It was all she could do not to giggle at the absurdity of the situation. Helen winked, and then smiled at the inspector.

"I'm awfully sorry," Helen said, standing up and walking towards the officer. "I didn't mean to cause any trouble or anything. It's just that Aunt Bessie is such a special lady and I was worried about her. She's had a rough couple of days, with finding Mack's body last night and now Bambi today. I didn't want her to be all alone in Noble's with no one to turn to."

She stopped right in front of the man and Bessie bit back another laugh as she watched Helen lick her lips and toss her hair. "I'm sorry we took the things out of Bambi's wallet to get the information the hospital needs, but I didn't know what else to do. Anyway, I'm happy to answer any questions, really I am."

Corkill flushed and glanced over at Bessie. "I'd like you both to answer a few questions," he replied. "But first I need to check on Ms. Marks. Please wait here." He stomped out of the room and once he was out of sight, Bessie let herself relax.

"You were flirting with him," she said to Helen.

"He isn't bad looking," Helen replied. "Any idea if he's single or not?"

Bessie shook her head. "I don't know anything about him."

"Maybe I should try to find out," Helen said with a mischievous grin.

Before Bessie could reply, two uniformed constables came into the café. "I'm supposed to get Ms. Marks's handbag from you," one of them said nervously.

Bessie quickly dumped everything they had taken out back into the bag and handed it to the young man. He took it by the strap and dropped it into a large plastic bag. "Thanks," he muttered as he turned and left the room.

The second young man smiled at them. "I'm just here to keep you two company for a short while," he said.

Bessie looked at Helen and then sighed. She could understand why the inspector had sent him, but she didn't welcome the man's intrusion.

"Tell me," Helen said to the man, "is Inspector Corkill single?"

Bessie finally let herself laugh out loud as the young man gave Helen a bewildered look. Half an hour later, she felt far less like laughing. Helen had asked the young constable a long list of questions about the inspector but the man had refused to tell her anything at all. Bessie was bored, tired and getting grumpy when the inspector finally returned.

"Ms. Cubbon, if you could just tell me what happened tonight as clearly and concisely as possible, we might all get out of here before midnight," the inspector said in lieu of a proper greeting.

"Can you please tell me how Bambi is doing, first?" Bessie asked plaintively.

The long silence that followed Bessie's request had her convinced that he was going to refuse. Eventually, however, he cleared his throat.

"The doctors seem to think she's going to be okay," he told Bessie.

"Oh, thank heavens," Bessie replied.

"Hurrah," Helen said.

"That fact doesn't leave this room," Inspector Corkill said sternly. "I've no idea if I'm dealing with an accidental overdose, a suicide attempt, or attempted murder, but whatever happened, I don't want anyone sharing any information about Bambi's condition, understood?"

Bessie and Helen both quickly agreed. "Right then, Mrs. Baxter, I'll be with you in a moment," he told Helen. "I hope you'll excuse Ms. Cubbon and myself."

"No problem, but it's Ms. Baxter. I'm single." Helen gave him a dazzling smile. "Here, you sit here," she offered, getting to her feet. "I'll go sit at the counter out of the way."

Bessie couldn't help but notice how the inspector's eyes followed Helen as she walked across the café. The uniformed constable followed after her, perhaps to keep her from telling the counter staff any secrets.

With Helen safely out of the way, Inspector Corkill sank down into the chair she had just vacated. "What happened tonight?" he asked in a tired voice.

Bessie found herself feeling sorry for the man, even though she still didn't like him or the way he was conducting his investigation.

"I'm not sure where you want me to start," Bessie replied. She knew Inspector Rockwell would have asked her to start with what time she woke up that morning and taken her through her whole day, but Inspector Corkill shrugged.

"I talked to Bambi after the scene at the discussion group this afternoon," he told Bessie. "She said she was going to go back to her hotel to lie down for a little while after our talk. When did you next see her?"

Bessie frowned as she tried to think. She remembered standing in the buffet queue and looking around the room to see who was there. She didn't remember seeing Bambi.

"I don't think she was at dinner," she told the inspector uncertainly. "I don't recall seeing her, but I wasn't looking for her, either."

Corkill made a note. "After dinner, when you came back up to the foyer, was she already there?"

Bessie nodded. "She was sitting in the same chair where I found her," she told the man.

"Was she alone?"

Bessie thought hard. "I think the chairs on either side of her were occupied," she said hesitantly. "But I wasn't close enough to recognise the occupants."

"But you're sure it was Bambi?"

"She's pretty unmistakable," Bessie laughed. "Especially in that crowd. With all that blonde hair and that amazing figure, even sitting down on the other side of the room there was no mistaking her. Middle-aged historians, on the other hand, all kind of run together."

Corkill nodded. "Did you see anyone talking to her?"

Bessie shook her head. "I'm afraid I was focussed on the biscuits and on getting a bottle of water." She frowned. "I did see Claire Jamison talking to her," she recalled. "Claire and Joe were collecting empty water bottles for recycling and I saw Claire asking Bambi for hers."

"Oh, wonderful, I bet she's collected hundreds of them, and I'm going to have to have them all checked to make sure they only had water in them. My budget doesn't stretch to that." The inspector sighed deeply.

"I could sit here asking you questions all night," he told Bessie. "But we're both tired and I still have to talk to Ms. Baxter, and then I have to go back to the museum and find all those da..., er, darn water bottles."

"I'm sorry if I've complicated things for you," Bessie said sincerely.

"I'm more unhappy with Claire Jamison than you at the moment," he admitted. "Anyway, one more quick question. I don't suppose you've heard anything about the missing slides?"

Bessie shook her head. "No one I've talked to seems to have any idea what happened to them," she told him.

The inspector sighed. "I'm going to let you go. I assume you'll be at the conference again tomorrow if I want to talk to you."

"I'll be there. Breakfast starts at eight and I'm giving my talk at two."

"Oh, I know," he sighed. "I have the whole schedule memorised now."

Bessie stood up and took a few steps away from the table.

"Oh, and Miss Cubbon? I've had you listed as a permitted contact for Ms. Marks, at least until her family gets here. You'll be able to call and get information about her condition if you want to do so. I'll ask you to keep anything you learn to yourself, though."

Bessie was so surprised she couldn't think of a suitable reply for a long minute. "Thank you," she finally said.

"No problem," Inspector Corkill said gruffly.

Now Bessie headed for the door, wondering how she was going to get home. She hadn't even had a chance to let Inspector Rockwell know what was going on. She hoped he hadn't driven to the museum to collect her.

"Ah, Bessie, there you are," Inspector Rockwell's voice came from behind her as Bessie emerged from the short hallway that led to the café. She turned around and smiled at the man who was leaning against the corridor wall.

"Inspector Rockwell, I'm sorry I didn't get a chance to call you and tell you what was happening," she said. "Everything happened so fast and I was so worried about Bambi."

The inspector held up a hand. "Please don't apologise and please call me John," he told Bessie.

She grinned at the repeated request. Somehow she still couldn't bring herself to call the man by his first name, in spite of their growing friendship.

"Dispatch called Doona to let her know what was happening and she called me," the inspector informed her.

"Oh, good. I was worried that you'd turn up at the museum and wonder where I'd gone."

"I hope you're ready for home now," the inspector said. "It's getting late and we have a lot to talk about."

"We do indeed," Bessie said with a sigh. "I can't believe how much has happened in just this one day. It seems like at least a week has passed since Mack's death, and yet it was only twenty-four hours ago that I found him." She shuddered involuntarily as she recalled that unpleasant moment.

Rockwell put his arm around her and led her slowly towards the building's exit. "And tonight you found Bambi," he remarked. "These have been some very traumatic days for you, haven't they?"

"They've not been as bad for me as they have been for Mack and Bambi," Bessie said firmly. "I can't allow my emotions to get the better of me. We have to figure out what's going on."

Rockwell grinned at her. "Don't say that too loudly, or Inspector Corkill might hear you. You know how he feels about anyone getting in the way of his investigation."

"I think he's starting to like me," Bessie replied. "He remembered to call me 'Miss Cubbon' when I was leaving and he's also given me permission to keep track of how Bambi is doing."

"No one can resist your charms forever," Rockwell grinned. "Not even grumpy old police inspectors."

"He isn't that old," Bessie argued.

Rockwell laughed. "I notice you didn't say anything about how grumpy he is," he teased. "But no, I'd guess he's about my age, just a bit north of forty and fighting it as much as possible."

Now Bessie laughed. "Don't fight it," she counselled. "You can't win, so you might as well enjoy the wisdom and experience that come with your age."

"Sound advice as always," he replied.

"Is Inspector Corkill single?" Bessie asked curiously.

"No offense, Bessie, but he might be a little bit too young for you," Rockwell grinned

"But he seems the perfect age for Helen Baxter, and she's in there right now, probably flirting up a storm with him."

Rockwell laughed. "Poor Pete. He is single, although that's fairly recent. His wife got tired of the hours and the unpredictability and walked out, maybe six months ago. From what I've heard, he isn't in any hurry to replace her."

They had reached the hospital entrance now and the inspector dropped Bessie's arm to hold the door for her. His police car was parked immediately outside the door, in front of the "No Parking - Emergency Vehicles Only" sign.

"Are you sure collecting me counts as an emergency?" Bessie couldn't help but ask.

"It's been a long day," Rockwell replied as he helped Bessie into the car. "I didn't have the energy to try to find a legal parking space around here."

Even though Bessie didn't drive, she knew that parking around the hospital was always difficult to find. She slid back in the seat, suddenly exhausted and grateful that the inspector had parked so near to the door.

"I'm afraid I'm going to fall asleep on the journey home," she told Rockwell after he'd slid into the driver's seat.

"Go ahead and nod off," he suggested. "We have a lot to discuss, but it's probably best to wait until we get to your cottage to talk. You have a quick nap and I'll concentrate on my driving and then we'll figure out who killed Mack once we get you home."

"That sounds like a good idea," Bessie smiled. She leaned back in her seat and let her eyes close. Even if she didn't sleep, the rest would feel wonderful.

CHAPTER NINE

"Bessie? Bessie, we're home."

Inspector Rockwell's voice slowly began to penetrate the fog in Bessie's brain.

"Aunt Bessie? Are you awake?"

Bessie sat up in her seat and slowly opened her eyes. The inspector had parked his car in the small space next to her cottage. She blinked when she noticed that another car was already there.

"I can't possibly have company at this hour," she muttered.

"That will be Hugh and Doona," the inspector told her. "They wanted to get involved, so I told them they could meet me here. Hugh brought Doona over, and I said I'd run her home when we're done."

As Bessie emerged from the car, she was grateful again for a convenient parking space. She stretched slowly and then sighed. She was getting too old for such late nights.

Doona was by her side before she'd finished her stretch. "Bessie, my goodness, how are you? I can't believe you've found two more bodies. I should have gone to the blinking conference with you. I'm picking you up tomorrow for sure and I'm not letting you out of my sight at that conference."

Bessie sighed as her friend took her arm and the pair walked up to Bessie's front door.

"You know I hate it when you fuss," she reminded Doona. "And anyway, Bambi should be fine. I only found the one body."

"It's still one too many," Doona argued as Bessie opened her door and then flipped on lights. Bessie turned and looked at her friend. Doona's heavily highlighted hair was something of a tangled mess and her brilliant green eyes looked worriedly back at Bessie.

"I'm fine, Doona," Bessie insisted. "Stop fussing."

Doona shook her head and then headed over to the kitchen counter where she began to fix a pot of coffee. Inspector Rockwell had followed the women into the room and now Hugh brought up the rear.

"Bessie, love, we need to find you a nice safe hobby. Maybe skydiving or something?" Hugh laughed and then gave Bessie a huge hug.

"It's great to see you," Bessie told the young policeman. She'd known Hugh since his childhood and while he was now in his mid-twenties, he still looked no more than fifteen. Bessie sometimes had trouble taking him seriously, but she was coming to enjoy his company more and more and lately she'd been pleased to find that he was brighter than she'd realised and dedicated to his career in police work.

"I'm just as worried about you as Doona is," Hugh confided to Bessie in an undertone. "But I'm smart enough not to fuss at you about it."

Bessie laughed. "Let's all sit down," she suggested. Doona had flipped the coffee pot on and the foursome sat quietly while the smell of brewing coffee filled the small cottage's kitchen.

Once the pot was ready, Doona filled four mugs, waving Bessie back into her chair when she tried to get up and help. She put out cream and sugar as well as a plate of biscuits she had filled from Bessie's generous stock.

"Thanks," Bessie told her friend as Doona sat back down.

"I can make tea if anyone would rather," Doona belatedly offered. "I just thought we all needed coffee for now."

"Indeed," Rockwell smiled at her. "I think we all need rather a lot of coffee."

"So, Bessie, what's new with you?" Hugh asked with a cheeky grin.

"Oh, not much," Bessie grinned back. "Just the odd murder,

nothing special. Although, to be fair, Inspector Corkill seems to think it was all just a tragic accident, so maybe we don't actually have anything to talk about except the weather."

Rockwell shook his head. "Whatever Pete is saying publicly, Mack's death was no accident," he told the others. "And I know I don't have to remind you all that everything we discuss here is strictly confidential, but I will anyway."

"The police are sure it was murder?" Bessie asked.

"Absolutely," Rockwell told her. "The half-eaten brownie that was found next to Mack's body was nothing like the ones on the so-called 'dessert bar.' We're waiting for the lab results and it's the weekend, so it might take a while, but we suspect that it contains a large portion of finely ground peanuts."

"But wouldn't Mack have tasted the nuts?" Bessie questioned.

"The coroner is speculating that there was enough chocolate flavour in it to mask any other flavours. Short of taking a bite of it, I'm not sure how we can check that. What it does mean is that someone brought that brownie with them to the conference."

"Maybe they brought it for themselves, in case they got hungry, and Mack got it by accident?" Doona suggested.

"That's always possible," Rockwell conceded. "But it doesn't explain why Mack didn't have his adrenaline injectors with him. Both his current girlfriend, Bambi, and his former girlfriend, Marjorie, have stated that he always carried three injectors with him at all times. There were none on the body or in the room with the body and only one was found in Mack's hotel room. Bambi identified it as Mack's quote 'emergency spare' end of quote."

"So it's murder," Hugh announced. "Time to look at means, motive and opportunity."

Bessie grinned. Hugh was very fond of talking through those three points.

"For means, the main question is who knew about his allergy?" Rockwell told the others. "Anyone could have bought or baked the brownie and brought it along, but who knew it would kill Mack?"

Bessie shook her head. "Just about everyone who knew Mack knew about his allergy," she told them all. "Certainly anyone who'd ever organised a conference where he spoke, or ate a meal with him, or did any site excavations with him would have known. I suspect that includes just about every person that was there last night. Oh, they'll be a handful that didn't know the man, but not many."

"And that's part of the problem," Rockwell sighed. "There were over a hundred people there last night, and aside from a very few, they've all admitted to knowing Mack. Of course, the ones who claim they didn't know him could be lying and have to be considered as well. For now, I suggest we focus on the people that Bessie knows well. The others will have to be investigated by Pete and his men."

"So we could be wasting our time here," Hugh sighed. "The killer could be someone Bessie's never even met."

"Indeed," Bessie agreed. "But I think it's still worth considering the people I do know. It seems more likely to me that the murderer is someone associated with the conference in some way, not just a random member of the audience."

Rockwell nodded. "I'd tend to agree with that," he said. "Especially in light of the missing slides and the attack on Bambi. If the killer were just a random audience member, why take the slides? And why come back today?"

"Okay, so we know that everyone who is involved in the conference knew about Mack's allergy, right?" Doona checked.

"Yes, so we aren't going to be able to eliminate anyone on means," Bessie sighed.

"Before we get into motive, what about opportunity?" Rockwell asked Bessie. "Mack had shut himself up in the cuillee while everyone else went to the dessert bar. Who could have snuck back into the Moore Lecture Theatre while everyone else was eating?"

Bessie sighed. "Again, as far as I know, it's pretty wide open. I certainly wasn't watching everyone and people were all over the place, going to the loos and possibly in and out of the building, even. Henry and Doug, the two employees from Manx National Heritage, were in the Moore Theatre straightening out the chairs when I found Mack, but they said they'd only just started because they were serving the cakes and biscuits for the first twenty minutes or more after Mack's talk."

"Let's try it from another angle, then," Rockwell suggested. "Who would Mack have opened the door for?"

Bessie shrugged. "That rather depended on what sort of mood Mack was in," she replied. "He might not have been willing to open the door to anyone so that he could get ready for the questions that were sure to come, or he might have welcomed just about anyone so that he could bask in the glory of his shocking news."

"Just how shocking was his news?" Doona interjected.

"Very shocking," Bessie answered. "Archeologists have been searching the island for evidence of Roman occupation or settlement since they started exploring the island. Poor old Harold Smythe has pretty much devoted his entire career to the hunt. And Mack claimed he'd found it."

"And now his slides are missing," Rockwell added.

"Indeed," Bessie replied. "Which makes it even more difficult for anyone to prove or disprove his claim."

"That sounds like you think Mack made it all up," Doona said.

Bessie sighed. "I don't know what to think," she confessed. "It's almost impossible for me to believe that an archeologist of Mack's standing would fabricate such a hugely important find, but Harold hasn't been able to find any evidence to support Mack's claims, and I thought he had the contacts with the farmers if anyone did."

"For what it's worth, the police haven't been able to find anything to back up Mack's claim either," Rockwell told her. "They've been in touch with as many land owners as they can around the island and they haven't yet found anyone who admits to working with Mack in the last year or more."

"How did the murderer get Mack's injectors away from him, though?" Doona asked. "I wouldn't have thought he would have just handed them to someone without a fight."

"Unless someone managed to get close enough to simply take them out of his pocket. He might have dropped some or all of them as well," Bessie said. "He always kept them very close to hand. I think he kept them all together in a little bag; I suppose the bag could have fallen out of his pocket, maybe if he took his jacket off or something."

"Let's leave that for a moment," Rockwell suggested. "If we believe that just about everyone at the conference had the same means and opportunity, we need to discuss motive. Bessie, what are your thoughts there?"

"The way I see it, there are two possible motives, personal and professional," she said.

"Oh, let's talk about the personal one first," Doona grinned.

Bessie smiled back at her. "Mack was, well, something of a womaniser, I guess is the best way to describe it. Marjorie told me that he always had a beautiful blonde girlfriend on his arm, but he also always had a second girlfriend in the background."

"Sort of like a chain-smoker," Hugh suggested. "Lighting his next cigarette with the previous one."

Bessie blinked. "I hadn't thought of it like that," she said, "but I guess I can see the analogy. Anyway, Marjorie reckons that his secret girlfriend might be at the conference. Maybe she was tired of his games and decided to get rid of him."

"That's possible," Rockwell said. "Any idea who the mystery woman is, though? No one has admitted to the police that they were involved with the dead man other than Bambi."

"You need to look at all of the blonde women at the conference," Bessie told him. "Mack definitely had a type. Any blonde under the age of fifty could have been involved with him."

"Of course, hair colour can be changed," Doona interjected, smoothing down her own lightened locks.

"So I guess you need to question every woman under fifty," Bessie laughed. "That's got to be a quarter of the conference, maybe."

"Inspector Corkill is organising background checks into as many people as he can," Rockwell told them. "He's looking for places where Mack's path crossed with anyone else at the conference. Besides that, we already know that Marjorie was a former girlfriend. What are the chances that we'll find a few more of those when we dig deeper?"

Bessie flushed. "I know you'll find at least one," she said. "I'm only telling you because I trust you not to harass her, but Liz Martin from my Manx language class dated him very briefly when she was at university."

"Liz did?" Doona asked. "I'm shocked. She doesn't seem like the type to date a man like that. I thought she and her husband had been together forever, anyway."

"They have been," Bessie told her. "She only went out with Mack a couple of times, but it was after she'd already met her future husband. That's why she didn't tell Inspector Corkill about it. She really doesn't want to upset Bill."

Bessie poured herself another cup of coffee. She'd never get to sleep later, with all this caffeine in her system, but sleep was less important than figuring out what happened to Mack. She added a couple more biscuits to the plate in front of her. She was sure she'd put three on there earlier, but they seemed to have disappeared.

"Maybe we can figure things out before Inspector Corkill finds out about Liz and Mack," Doona said. "She and Bill are such a happy couple; I'd hate to see them having problems over this."

Rockwell remained silent, simply taking notes as the conversation about Liz washed over him.

"Anyway, beyond that, I know that Mack propositioned my friend Helen last night as well," Bessie told the group. "She probably didn't want to mention that to the police. I think she was embarrassed."

Doona shook her head. "I am so very sorry that I didn't come along to this conference with you. I really wish I could have met this guy. I suppose I would have been disappointed, though, if he didn't try to chat me up."

The inspector made a sound that turned into a cough and drew everyone's attention. "I think that covers the personal side of the motive issue," he said. "I want to add that it seems to me that someone with a personal connection with Mack would be more likely to be able to get the injectors away from him. But what about the professional side of things?"

"Well, Harold was furious with Mack. First Mack went behind

everyone's back and got George to let him give the first talk at the conference and then Mack announced that he'd found exactly what Harold has been looking for pretty much his entire adult life. I can certainly see Harold wishing that Mack would suddenly drop dead, even if I can't see him killing him."

"Do you know of anyone else who might have a motive to do with Mack's talk or his professional life?" Hugh asked, earning a nod from the inspector.

"Not really," Bessie replied. "But then I don't keep track of the games academics play. It seems like someone is always mad at someone about something, but I don't pay any attention unless it impacts one of my friends."

"So there could be more there, if we look for it?" Rockwell asked.

"Absolutely," Bessie agreed.

"No one knew what Mack was going to talk about, right?" Hugh checked.

"That's right. Most of us who were planning to attend the conference didn't even know he was going to be here. He wasn't on the schedule. I'm not even sure when he talked to George and made the arrangements to come."

Rockwell was scribbling furiously. "That's interesting," he told Bessie. "And it might just narrow down our list of suspects. The person who brought the brownie must have done so knowing that Mack was going to be there. We just have to figure out who knew."

"From what I heard, Mack called some people and invited them himself," Bessie said. "He wanted a big audience for his big announcement. Maybe you should focus on people who decided to attend at the last minute."

The inspector nodded. "The next thing we have to talk about is the missing slides," he said after he'd drained his coffee mug and then refilled it. "Who could have taken them?"

Bessie shook her head. "Anyone and everyone," she replied. "They were sitting on a projector in the back of the Moore Theatre. Did they take the whole carousel or just the slides?"

"Just the slides," Rockwell told her after he'd checked his

notes.

"Anyone could have taken off the carousel, dumped the slides into a small bag or even a pocket and then snapped the carousel back in place. It would have taken less than a minute and if they were challenged they could just say they were getting them for Mack. There were only about ten slides anyway. Didn't Mack have copies?"

"Bambi seemed to think so, but we haven't found any," Rockwell answered.

"Which brings us to what happened to Bambi today," Doona said. "John, you said when we talked earlier that it looked like an overdose. Is that still what the police are thinking?"

"It was definitely an overdose of something," Rockwell answered. "We're hoping that when Bambi wakes up she'll be able to tell us how it happened."

"She wasn't suicidal," Bessie said insistently. "I talked to her after Mack's death and she was fine, sad but not depressed."

"So that leaves accidental overdose or attempted murder," Hugh said. "Did she do drugs?"

Bessie frowned. "I thought she was on something when we talked last night," she admitted. "She was spacey and unfocussed, but she was also bored and out of her element. I think attempted murder is more likely."

"We'll know more once we've spoken to her, but in the meantime, let's work from the assumption that it was attempted murder," Rockwell said. "Means, motive and opportunity?"

"I can guess that the motive was just to shut her up," Bessie said. "While the police seemed to think Mack's death was an accident, she was running around telling everyone, including Inspector Corkill, that Mack had been murdered. If I had killed Mack, I would have wanted to shut Bambi up."

Rockwell nodded. "I think that's the clearest possible motive we'll find," he said. "As far as we know, she didn't know anyone here before the conference, aside from Mack. Of course, people could be lying to us, but Bambi herself said she didn't know anyone when Corkill interviewed her yesterday afternoon."

"Do you know what she overdosed on?" Doona asked.

"Not yet. It's far too soon to have any lab results. Until we're sure, we almost have to assume that anyone and everyone had access to whatever it was."

"Well, that complicates things," Hugh sighed.

"How did the drugs get into her system?" Bessie asked.

"Again, it's too soon to be sure. If she didn't take them voluntarily, then they were probably hidden in something she ate or drank."

"I didn't see her at dinner," Bessie said. "And the only thing I saw her with after dinner was a bottle of water."

Rockwell checked his notes. "One of the men sitting with her in the foyer before the last talks of the day told Inspector Corkill that she had a bottle of water in her hand when she sat down. He wasn't sure where it came from, but it was the same type as all the others that were all over the foyer. That was all he remembered seeing her eat or drink."

"And then Claire and Joe collected all the empty bottles for recycling," Bessie said. "Inspector Corkill wasn't happy about having to send hundreds of bottles away for testing."

"I can't imagine," Rockwell shuddered. "It will blow his lab budget for the next six months or more."

"Maybe when Bambi is up to answering questions she'll be able to help," Doona suggested. "Maybe she'll confess to having taken something before she got there or something."

Rockwell shrugged. "As she's still alive and reasonably well, Corkill may well decide it isn't worth worrying about testing all the bottles. We'll have to see what happens in the next twenty-four hours or so."

Bessie topped up her coffee cup again and frowned at her plate. It was empty, which had to mean that she'd eaten the biscuits, but she had no recollection of having done so. She sighed and took a few more from the plate in the centre of the table. Caffeine and sugar were all that were keeping her going at the moment.

"One last question for all of you, and then I'd better let you get some sleep," the inspector said. "If you had to pick out the murderer tonight, who would you choose?"

Hugh grinned. "One of the women," he announced. "Maybe that Liz who doesn't want her husband to know she cheated on him."

"Liz couldn't possibly have killed anyone," Bessie protested. "She's incredibly sweet and she has two small children to look after."

"Maybe she thought Mack was a threat to her marriage and, therefore, her children's happiness," Hugh argued. "Mothers will kill for the sake of their children."

"I still don't see it and neither does Doona, right, Doona?" Bessie asked.

Doona shook her head. "I can't see Liz killing anyone," she agreed. "But then, I can't imagine her dating Mack, either, so I guess I don't know her as well as I thought."

"If she used to date him, he probably would have trusted her enough to take the brownie from her," Hugh argued.

"And presumably she could have figured out a way to get close enough to him to grab his injectors," Rockwell added.

"But why would she steal the slides?" Hugh asked.

"And how did she even know he was going to be here?" Bessie added.

"Maybe Mack called her and told her he was coming and suggested they get togther," Doona said. "Although, from everything I know of Liz, I think that's extremely unlikely. I still can't see her being involved."

"So who would you pick, Doona?" Hugh asked.

Doona frowned. "I wish I'd gone along to this conference. It would be easier if I'd actually met these people."

"I'm just interested in your impressions," Rockwell told her. "There's no prize for getting it right or penalty for getting it wrong."

Doona grinned. "In that case, I'll go for Harold Smythe. Not only did he have a strong motive, I don't like his surname. Smythe is just a fancy version of Smith and it annoys me."

Everyone laughed.

"But Harold said he didn't even know Mack was coming until right before the conference started," Bessie argued. "And he certainly didn't know what Mack was going to say."

"So maybe he brought the brownie for himself and once Mack finished speaking he saw that he had the perfect chance to get rid of him," Doona suggested.

"It's possible," Rockwell said. "The theft of the slides makes it seem more likely that Mack's murder had something to do with his talk."

"But how did he get Mack's injectors from him?" Bessie played devil's advocate.

"Maybe he just asked if he could have a look at them," Doona suggested. "Mack must have trusted Harold if he took the brownie from him in the first place." Her eyes lit up. "Maybe Mack felt the attack coming on and he gave Harold the injector and asked him to help. Then all Harold had to do was stand there and wait until Mack died."

"Why didn't he call for help after he was sure Mack was dead?" Hugh asked. "He could have said he tried to help but he was too late."

"And why take the injectors away with him?" Rockwell added.

Doona frowned. "Well, if you're all going to pick holes in my theories, I'll keep them to myself."

Rockwell grinned. "The whole point of the exercise is to think about every possible suspect and then poke holes in every theory," he told Doona, giving her hand a pat.

Doona smiled back. "So who would you pick, John?" she asked him.

He shook his head. "This isn't even my case," he said with a sigh. "Inspector Corkill would probably file a formal complaint about me with the Chief Constable if he knew I was even discussing it. I'm just lucky I have friends in the Douglas Constabulary who've shared the information I've managed to get so far with me."

"You must have a personal favourite suspect," Doona pushed him. "You know everything you say here is confidential."

Rockwell passed a hand over his eyes and then grinned tiredly. "I suppose it's only fair that I add my opinion to the conversation," he admitted. "I guess I'm leaning towards an unknown person, though, which isn't much help."

"What do you mean by 'an unknown person?' Unknown in what way?" Doona demanded.

"I mean someone who has a connection to Mack that we haven't uncovered yet," he explained. "I haven't met any of the suspects myself. I'm just working from Pete Corkill's notes. It seems to me that some of the people he's talked to must be hiding things."

Bessie smiled. "I'm inclined to agree with Inspector Rockwell," she told them. "But I'll go one further. I think we're looking for a woman, either Mack's current secret girlfriend or someone that he used to date in the past."

"Why?" was Hugh's blunt question.

"I can't see Mack accepting a snack from Harold or any of the other men at the conference. Especially not after the bombshell he'd just dropped. While I'm sure Mack never expected to be murdered, he would have been wary of someone ostensibly bringing him a treat after he'd announced his controversial findings," Bessie answered.

"Here's a thought," Hugh interjected. "What if his secret lover gave him the brownie to bring with him or something? Maybe she isn't even here."

"If that's the case, who took Mack's injectors, who stole the slides and who drugged Bambi?" Rockwell asked.

Hugh frowned. "Okay, maybe not," he muttered.

"All of those things don't have to be connected," Rockwell conceded. "But I'm wary of coincidences, especially where murder is involved."

"So if you're sure it was a woman who killed Mack, do you think she took the slides to confuse things?" Doona asked Bessie. "Or do you think she has a professional interest in what Mack was doing and that's why she took the slides?"

"The slides confuse things," Bessie admitted.

Rockwell yawned. "I think we need to leave it there for tonight," he said, clearly reluctantly.

"We all need some sleep. Bessie's giving her paper tomorrow afternoon and we've all promised to be there," Doona reminded the others.

"I'm looking forward to it," Hugh said with a noticeable lack of enthusiasm.

Bessie laughed. "You really don't have to come," she told the young man.

"I want to come," he insisted. "If nothing else, I want a good look at all of the suspects."

Everyone laughed and then the party broke up. Hugh headed out, closely followed by the others.

"Make sure you lock up tight," Doona reminded Bessie.

"Yes, I know." Bessie rolled her eyes at Inspector Rockwell.

"I'll pick you up at half seven," Doona continued. "That should get us to the conference in plenty of time for breakfast."

Bessie glanced at the kitchen clock and winced as she counted just how few hours sleep she was going to get.

"I'll see you in the morning," she told Doona. "And I guess I'll see you at my talk," she said to Rockwell.

"You will indeed," the inspector smiled at her.

Bessie locked her door, making faces at the absent Doona as she double-checked that it was locked tightly.

Upstairs, she raced through her getting-to-bed routine, promising herself she'd make more of an effort with her teeth the next day. She climbed into bed, convinced that all of the caffeine in her system would keep her awake. What felt like ten minutes later she was shocked awake by the alarm she had nearly not bothered to set.

CHAPTER TEN

Bessie had fully expected her internal clock to wake her at her normal time and had set the alarm as a backup only. Now she'd overslept and she needed to hurry to make sure she was ready when Doona arrived.

She showered, dressed and quickly ran a brush through her grey hair, grateful that she wore it quite short. Downstairs, she eyed the coffee pot longingly. There was no point in brewing an entire pot, though, not when she was going to be out all day. She sighed and made herself a cup of tea instead. It did little to help combat her tiredness, but she promised herself several cups of coffee at the conference breakfast.

She was only a little bit surprised to see Inspector Rockwell's car pull into the parking area next to her cottage at half seven. Doona waved to Bessie from the backseat as Bessie locked up her cottage. The inspector climbed out the driver's side to help Bessie into the car.

"I figured I might as well come along for the whole day of the conference, rather than just come for your talk," he explained to Bessie as they made their way out of Laxey.

"Your wife doesn't mind?" Bessie asked curiously.

"She's across with the kids," Rockwell told her. "She takes them back to see her mother most weekends at the moment. Her mother hasn't been well and this gives my wife a chance to pick up groceries and tidy up the house for her for the week ahead."

"I see," Bessie answered.

"Anyway, I've leased a little terraced house just a few streets over from Doona so that I can stay in Laxey when I have to work late. I decided to stay there last night to save driving back to Ramsey after our late meeting, so it just made sense for me to pick up you and Doona this morning."

"And it's much nicer going to these things with friends," Doona interjected from the backseat. "I was worried that I wouldn't have anyone to sit with all day."

"You can sit with me," Bessie laughed. "At least until my talk."

"I wasn't sure if you had other things you needed to do," Doona replied.

"Not really," Bessie said with a shrug. "Anyway, you know Marjorie and Liz; I expect they'll both be there."

Doona nodded. "All true, but John doesn't know any of them."

Bessie laughed again. "In that case, I suppose it's helpful that you'll be there to sit with him, then," she told Doona.

The museum car park was mostly empty when Rockwell pulled into it a few minutes before eight. Bessie smiled at the security guard at the door who was checking everyone in.

He knew Bessie on sight and smiled as she introduced her friends. "John Rockwell and Doona Moore have come in with me today," she explained. "They both registered for the day."

"They're both on my list," he assured Bessie. "Breakfast should be set up in the upstairs foyer."

"Thank you," Bessie started to move past him, but he caught her arm.

"I don't suppose you've heard from Dr. Smythe or Ms. Stevens this morning?" he asked, his tone anxious.

"I haven't, no," Bessie said. "I would have thought they would both be here by now."

"They were supposed to be here at seven," the man told her. "But so far I haven't seen either of them. Henry has been following the schedule and instructions that he worked out with Dr. Smythe in advance, but no one seems to be sure what's going on."

Bessie glanced at Rockwell, who shook his head. "I don't know," she told the man. "We all had a very late night. Maybe they both simply overslept."

"I hope so," he replied gloomily.

Inside the museum foyer, Rockwell pulled out his phone and stepped away from Bessie and Doona to make a quick call.

"Dr. Smythe and Ms. Stevens are both at the Douglas station answering a few questions," he told the women when he returned a minute later.

"They've been arrested?" Doona gasped.

"Not at all," Rockwell assured her. "Pete Corkill had a few questions to ask them both and it was easier for him to have them brought to him there than to run down here again, that's all."

"So they'll both be here soon?" Bessie asked.

"I would hope so," Rockwell replied.

The trio made their way to the lifts and up to the top floor. Bessie made a beeline for the coffee pots, filling cups for herself as well as for her friends.

"Ah, I needed that," the inspector told her after his first sip. "I haven't bothered to get appliances for my little house, but I'm thinking a toaster and coffee pot are going to be essential."

Doona grinned as she filled a plate. "I didn't realise the food here was going to be so lovely," she said as she scooped fresh fruit onto her plate. She added a plain croissant and some sort of fruit Danish to the pile.

"There's seating in the Kinvig Room," Bessie told her, pointing towards the open door.

Bessie filled her own plate, consciously ignoring the section of the room that was marked off with police tape. Rockwell walked over to the small group of chairs and took a look before he rejoined Bessie and made his own breakfast selections.

"Did you learn anything from the crime scene?" Bessie asked as they worked their way down the food table.

"Not a thing," Rockwell grinned. "But I didn't expect to. I just couldn't resist having a peek."

"I suppose if Bambi had died, Inspector Corkill would have blocked off the entire foyer today," she remarked.

"Undoubtedly," Rockwell agreed.

Inside the Kinvig Room, Doona had joined the small crowd that was already eating at one of the tables provided. Rockwell and Bessie headed towards her, but Bessie was intercepted.

"Bessie, how's Bambi this morning?" Claire Jamison looked like she'd had even less sleep than Bessie. Her dark hair was pulled back into an untidy ponytail and behind her thick glasses Bessie could see dark circles under her eyes.

Bessie glanced at Rockwell and then back at the girl. "You'd have to call Noble's for an update," she told her. "And I'm not sure if they're giving out any information at the moment."

That wasn't strictly true. Bessie knew that they absolutely were not giving out any information. They'd told her that both last night and early this morning when she'd called. Once she'd given her name, however, thanks to Inspector Corkill's kindness, they'd shared limited updates.

This morning Bessie had been told that Bambi was going to be fine, but she wasn't yet well enough to speak to the police. Bessie was tempted to tell the very worried-looking Claire Jamison the good news, but she'd promised to keep it confidential.

"But you must know something," Claire insisted now. "You went with her in the ambulance last night."

"I did, and as soon as we arrived, I was sent to the lobby to fill out a huge stack of paperwork while the medical team did their job. By the time I'd waded through the few questions I could answer, Inspector Corkill had arrived. He's the one who won't be letting any information be released, I suspect. I haven't spoken to him since last night."

"I'm so worried about her," Claire said with a frown. "We only talked a few times, but she was taking Mack's death so hard. I was afraid she might try something, but I thought she'd wait until after she got back to the UK."

"You think her overdose was a suicide attempt?" Rockwell asked.

"What else could it have been?" Claire asked in a confused tone.

"An accident," Bessie suggested. "Did you get the feeling that

Bambi was taking drugs? Because I wondered."

Claire shook her head. "I don't know much about drugs," she said. "Bambi just seemed like a sweet kid. She was a little, um, distracted at times, but she was also bored and more than a little fed up with that boyfriend of hers."

"So she and Mack were fighting?" Rockwell asked.

"I guess so," Claire answered, her eyes darting around the room. "Oh, look, there's Joe. I need to talk to him about...." She trailed off as she walked away from Bessie and the inspector.

"That was strange," Bessie remarked as they joined Doona.

"I've no doubt that everyone's nerves are at the breaking point," Rockwell replied. "The last two days have been, well, intense, I suppose. I'm guessing dead bodies and drug overdoses aren't usual at these sorts of conferences."

"No," Bessie agreed. "Usually the most exciting thing that happens is that someone's slide gets stuck in the projector and everyone worries that it might melt before they can get it out."

"I imagine everyone will be asking you about Bambi," Rockwell added. "It's only natural for people to be concerned and probably nosy as well."

Bessie sighed. "I wish I could tell them that she's going to be okay," she whispered to her friends.

"But you can't," the inspector said sternly.

"So I shall be trying to avoid the question," Bessie answered.

"Anyway, I'm assuming that was Claire Jamison, from everything you've told me," Rockwell said.

"Oh, sorry, I should have introduced you," Bessie said. "I was just so flustered."

"It's not a problem," he assured her. "I just figured, since she started the conversation, I should try to get a few questions in. I'm officially off-duty this weekend, and, of course, out of my jurisdiction."

"Which one is Helen Baxter?" Doona asked. "I want to meet the woman who's brave enough to flirt with Peter Corkill."

Bessie laughed. "I didn't know you knew him," she said curiously.

"Oh, the Isle of Man Constabulary is just one big happy

family," Doona replied. "We all get together for dinner and drinks all the time."

"Really?" Bessie asked in surprise.

"No, not really," Doona laughed. "But Inspector Corkill filled in for Inspector Kelly for a few weeks when I first started in the office, long before John got here."

"What did you think of him?" Bessie asked.

"He was totally professional at all times," Doona told her. "I don't think I saw him smile even once while he was there and I'm sure the younger officers were terrified of him."

"He's a very good policeman," Rockwell said firmly. "And those guys usually need a firm hand to keep them in line."

"I can't argue with that," Doona grinned at him. "But you manage to keep them in line and seem human at the same time."

Rockwell laughed. "I'll take that as high praise," he replied.

The room had been filling up slowly and now Bessie nudged her friend. "That's Helen," she whispered, gesturing as the pretty blonde standing uncertainly in the doorway with a drink in her hand. Bessie smiled at her and then waved. A relieved look flashed over Helen's face and then she headed towards them.

"Ah, Bessie, I must say I could have used another five or six hours of sleep before I saw you again," Helen said, as she dropped into a chair across the table from the trio.

"Good morning, Helen." Bessie smiled at her. "I don't think I ever thanked you for your help last night," she said quickly. "I'm not sure what I would have done with all that paperwork if I'd had to handle it on my own."

Helen laughed. "You would have managed," she replied. "And if you hadn't, we still would have taken good care of Bambi."

Bessie performed quick introductions, forcing herself not to laugh as Helen focussed her big blue eyes on the attractive police inspector.

"John Rockwell, it is ever so nice to meet you," she cooed. "How is it that you know Bessie?"

Rockwell grinned at her. "I'm a CID inspector with the Laxey station," he replied. "I met Bessie when I was investigating a murder and we've somehow managed to become friends from there."

"Bessie makes friends with everyone," Helen laughed. She turned to Doona and winked. "And aren't police inspectors unbelievably attractive these days?"

Doona flushed. "As I work in the constabulary as well, I think I'd better keep my own counsel on that," she told Helen.

Helen laughed again. "Are you a police officer as well?" she asked Doona.

"Oh no, I just man the front desk. I'm strictly a civilian employee."

"And friends with Bessie as well?"

"We met in a Manx language class a couple of years ago," Doona explained. "She helped me get through a very tough divorce."

"And are you married?" Helen asked Rockwell.

"I am, yes," he answered quickly.

"What a shame," Helen said with a cheeky grin. "But then I've still got Pete Corkill to work on, so I shouldn't complain."

"Pete's a good guy," Rockwell told her. "But he's only just recently single and he's had a bad time of it. Please take it easy on him."

Helen smiled. "I'll be good," she promised. "He actually seems like a decent guy and I sure could use one of those."

The inspector looked as if he wanted to say more, but after a moment he took a sip of coffee instead.

Helen sighed. "That coffee really hit the spot," she told them. "Now I need to get something to eat, I suppose. I'll see you later."

"She's very, um, bubbly," Doona hissed after Helen was out the door.

"Actually, she's a really nice person and a dedicated nurse," Bessie told her friend. "She's just something of a flirt as well."

"I noticed," Rockwell said dryly.

Now Bessie pointed out Liz Martin to the inspector. Liz was standing in one corner, holding hands with her husband, Bill.

"I didn't know she was bringing Bill today," Bessie remarked.

As if aware that she was being discussed, Liz waved at Bessie and then headed towards her, dragging Bill along behind.

"Good morning, Bessie," she said when they arrived, giving Bessie a huge and fake looking smile. "Hi, Doona."

"Hello," Bessie answered. "And it's nice to see you here as well," she told Bill, whom she had met at the informal class gathering that Marjorie had organised a few weeks earlier.

Bill nodded, but didn't speak, and Bessie got the feeling that he was unhappy about something.

"This is my friend, John Rockwell," Bessie said.

"Oh, isn't he, I mean, didn't you say, that is," Liz flushed. "Sorry, I'm all at sixes and sevens today. Aren't you a police inspector?" she asked Rockwell directly.

"I am, although I'm off-duty today. I just came to hear Bessie's talk."

"Oh, that's too bad," Liz said, clearly disappointed.

"Liz, what's going on?" Bessie demanded of her young friend.

Liz sighed and glanced at Bill. He shook his head and then turned and looked away. She moved closer to him and rested her head on his chest for a moment before straightening up and blowing out a long breath.

"I need to make a statement to the police," she said finally. "I've told Bill all about how I dated Mack a few times many years ago and now I need to tell the police as well. I can't see how it could possibly have anything to do with Mack's death, but Bessie was saying that the more the police know the faster they can find the murderer, so I need to tell someone."

"Let me get Inspector Corkill on the phone and see what his plans are for today," Rockwell offered. "I'm sure he'll be happy to come and take your statement or send someone to talk to you in his place."

"I hope, that is, I'd like it if Bill can stay with me," Liz said hesitantly. "We don't have any secrets and I sort of need his support."

"I'm afraid that's out of my hands," Rockwell said apologetically.

Liz nodded and Bessie could see her blinking back tears. Bill sighed and then his arm went around his wife. Liz leaned back into him and sighed as well.

"If only I hadn't been so stupid all those years ago," she said quietly.

"We all do stupid things when we're young," Bessie replied. "What's important is that we learn from our mistakes and don't make the same ones again."

"Oh, I definitely learned my lesson," Liz answered.

"And so did I," Bill said. "I learned that I need to make sure that I'm taking such good care of you that you never even notice any other men."

Liz laughed as tears streamed down her face. "Oh, honey, you already do that."

Bill wrapped both arms around her now, and gave her a gentle kiss on the end of her nose. "I'm sorry I've been giving you such a hard time about this," he told his wife. "I love you."

"Not as much as I love you," Liz replied, squeezing him tightly.

Bessie glanced over at Doona and rolled her eyes. Doona had to turn her burst of laughter into a cough so as not to offend the couple.

Rockwell made a phone call and then assured Liz and Bill that someone would be there soon to take her statement. The pair wandered off towards the foyer to wait and Rockwell turned back to Bessie and Doona.

"This is turning into a very interesting morning," he remarked.

Bessie grinned. "I can't wait to see who comes over to say hello next," she told him.

She didn't have long to wait, either. She'd just finished the last of her breakfast when Joe Steele dropped into the seat across from her.

"Good morning, Aunt Bessie," he said with a small smile.

"Hello, Joe, how are you?" she asked.

"I've been better," he admitted.

Bessie introduced her friends before she picked the conversation back up where it had been. "But what's wrong?" she asked him.

Joe shook his head. "I don't understand women," he said.

Rockwell laughed. "Welcome to the club," he told the younger man. "It never gets any easier."

Joe sighed. "I thought Claire and I were really hitting it off," he began hesitantly. "But now that the conference is nearly over she seems to be trying to get rid of me."

"Joe, you just met the woman two days ago," Bessie reminded him gently. "And they've been very strange days at that. I suggest you follow her lead. If she isn't ready to make plans to see you again, let it go. You can always flood her with phone calls and emails after the conference."

"I guess," Joe replied glumly. "She'd invited me to visit her in Anglesey," he told Bessie. "And then, this morning when I mentioned trying to arrange flights, she said maybe I should wait."

"So maybe she's just trying to slow things down a little bit," Doona suggested.

Just then the woman in question walked back into the room with her drink in hand. She smiled and waved at Joe and then headed towards them.

"I just got off the phone with Harold," she told Joe excitedly. "He's going to let me give my talk again this morning to make up for the interruption last night."

"That's great," Joe said enthusiastically.

"I know. I was so unhappy about it being cut short last night. I didn't get to talk about the most important things I'd found. Anyway, I've got to dash back to the hotel and get my notes and slides. Did you feel like a walk?"

Joe's eyes lit up. "I'd love to walk with you," he told Claire. He grinned back at Bessie and the others. "See you guys later," he said as he took Claire's arm and the pair headed towards the door.

"Ah, young love," Rockwell said in a cynical tone.

"I think they're very cute together," Bessie said.

"He's too immature for her," Doona argued. "She'll get tired of him soon enough."

Bessie sighed. "I suppose you're right," she conceded. "He is rather young for her."

Just then Harold Smythe strode into the room. His expression was dark and thunderous and Bessie could feel everyone in the room shrink away from him. She took a deep breath and then smiled and waved at the man. For a moment he looked at her blankly and then he crossed to her in a couple of steps.

"Bessie, this whole conference is just one disaster after another," he said as he sat down next to her. "If I could have changed my flight, I'd have abandoned this sinking ship last night."

"I'm glad you're still here," Bessie told him, patting his arm gently. "There are still some excellent talks to come and I'm especially looking forward to what you and Marjorie have to say in your concluding remarks."

Harold laughed humourlessly. "What can we say? Watch out for peanuts if you have an allergy? If you think someone was murdered, keep it to yourself?" He shook his head. "If someone had set out to derail my career, he couldn't have done better than what's gone on this weekend."

"I rather think someone set out to derail poor Mack," Bessie said sharply. "I understand you're disappointed in how the conference has fallen apart, but I do think you're feeling a bit too sorry for yourself."

Harold blushed. "You're right, of course," he said sheepishly. "It's just all so difficult."

"I'd like you to meet my friends," Bessie told him, introducing Harold to Rockwell and Doona.

"It's nice to meet you both," Harold replied, clearly not really interested.

"They both work for the Isle of Man Constabulary," Bessie told Harold, hoping to surprise him.

She was unprepared for the deep flush that spread across his face. "Oh, my, well, then, um, have you been friends with Bessie for long?" Harold stammered out.

Bessie nodded, but her reply was interrupted by the sound of bells.

"What on earth?" Doona exclaimed.

"It's my phone," Harold said as he jumped up. "I need to answer this."

The trio watched the man as he raced out of the room.

"Harold's actually a very nice man and he's usually quite

interesting to talk with," Bessie told her friends with a wry smile.

"I guess today is unusual," Doona grinned.

Bessie smiled. "This conference was his baby and it couldn't really have gone much worse, could it? I feel sorry for him and for Marjorie as well. She had a big part in planning and organising the conference as well."

"Speak of the devil," Doona grinned and waved to their friend as she walked into the room. She was clutching a coffee mug tightly and it seemed to take some time for her eyes to focus on Doona. Bessie watched her walk towards them.

"You look like you haven't slept in a week," she told Marjorie after she'd introduced Rockwell to the woman.

"It feels like that as well," Marjorie admitted. "But really, I wasn't sleeping well for at least a week before the conference because I was so worried about it. It turns out all the things I was worried about haven't happened, and yet the conference has been disastrous. Anyway, I haven't slept at all since Mack died."

Bessie patted her arm. "Harold said something similar," she replied. "But there have been some good moments, and today should be interesting."

"We should have cancelled the rest of the conference after Mack died," Marjorie said. "But the police didn't want anyone to leave anyway, so it seemed like a better idea to keep going."

"Are they going to let people leave today?" Bessie asked.

Marjorie shrugged. "You'll have to ask Inspector Corkill about that," she said. "I'm not going anywhere, even though I'd love to be anywhere but here."

"I'd hate for you to miss my talk," Bessie said quietly.

Marjorie flushed. "Of course I'm looking forward to your talk," she told Bessie. "I just wish, oh, I don't know, I guess I wish that George Quayle had just said no to Mack. Then I could go back to worrying about whether or not we have enough teacups and what to do if a speaker gets sick, instead of worrying about getting arrested."

"You're not going to get arrested," Doona told Marjorie. "We all know you didn't have anything to do with Mack's death."

"I'm not sure Inspector Corkill would agree," Marjorie sighed.

"And I did hate Mack enough to kill him, you know. I'm just too much of a coward to actually follow through with it."

"You still hated Mack, even after all these years?" Bessie asked.

Marjorie frowned. "Yeah, I did. And I hate to admit that, even to myself. I should have been over him and getting on with my life, but I still felt so angry at him. When he suggested that we could, um, sleep together again, I probably would have stabbed him right there if I'd had a knife to hand."

"So he didn't know that you were still angry?" Bessie questioned.

Marjorie looked thoughtful for a moment. "I think it was more that he didn't really believe that I could still be angry. I'm not sure that he understood why I was angry in the first place. He didn't feel like he'd done anything wrong. He just didn't do monogamy, and that didn't mean he didn't care about me." She shook her head. "Mack was just Mack. He thought everyone loved him and life was just one big game."

"You are so much better off without him," Dona told her friend. "You were way too good for him in the first place."

Marjorie managed a weak smile. "Thanks, Doona," she said. "I'm so glad I moved here when it all went wrong. I've never felt so welcome and at home anywhere in the world."

"There is something special about this place," Rockwell told her. "I felt it when I moved here as well."

Bessie smiled. "I hope that means that neither of you is ever planning on leaving," she told them. "I'm ever so glad you're both here."

"I'm not going anywhere," Marjorie told her emphatically. "I've built a life I love here and I've even learned the language."

Bessie and Doona both laughed at that. "How is it that you've only been here a few years and you can speak Manx like a native?" Doona demanded. "I grew up here and once I get past moghrey mie I'm lost."

Marjorie smiled. "I've always been good at languages," she told Doona. "I'd already studied Welsh, Irish, and Scottish Gaelic anyway, so adding Manx wasn't difficult."

Doona and Bessie both laughed again. "Not difficult?" Bessie said. "I've taken your class three times and I can't get past the very basics."

"You just need to practice more," Marjorie told her. "We should be having this conversation in Manx, for instance."

Bessie groaned. "I have enough to worry about with my talk this afternoon. Please don't make me speak Manx in the meantime," she said a bit desperately.

Now Marjorie managed a small chuckle. "See, you have the wrong attitude," she told her friend. "Speaking in Manx should be fun, not a chore. Liz and I chat all the time in Manx."

"But Liz is good at it," Doona interjected.

"Because she practices," Marjorie argued with a smile.

"When is your next class starting?" Rockwell interrupted the argument. "I've been thinking I might like to give it a try."

Marjorie smiled at him. "I try to do four sets of classes every year, rotating around the island," she told him. "The class that Bessie and Doona are taking has two more classes to go. We were supposed to finish tomorrow, but we had to add a class on to the end because of an unexpected cancellation."

Bessie and Doona exchanged glances. Neither wanted to remember the events that had led to that cancellation.

"Next week I'll start the advanced class in Laxey for those who want to go on or those who took the beginning class in the past and want to learn more," Marjorie continued.

"I don't think I've learned enough to move on yet," Bessie said. "Maybe I'll try another beginner's class, though."

Marjorie smiled at her. "You could try the advanced class if you want," she told her encouragingly. "But it does move faster and we cover a lot. You really need to know your basics."

Doona shook her head. "That lets me out as well," she said with a sigh. "I'm going to need to retake the first one again as well."

"Maybe we should all try it together?" Rockwell suggested. "And drag Hugh along as well."

Bessie laughed. "That could be fun," she said. "Then when we all get together we could all speak Manx."

"The next set of classes starts in July in Port Erin," Marjorie told them. "Then in October I'm teaching them in Peel. If everything goes to plan, I'll be in Douglas in January and back in Laxey or maybe Ramsey next April."

"I may just have to wait for next April, then," Rockwell told Marjorie. "Work is just too uncertain to commit to classes elsewhere on the island."

Marjorie nodded. "That's why I move them around," she told him. "If you're really interested, though, I'd be happy to send you some of the materials that we use in the classes and you can get started on your own. I'm sure Bessie and Doona with help you with pronunciation and practice with you."

"I'll give it some thought," he promised Marjorie. "And I'll let you know."

"Marjorie!"

Every head in the room turned towards the door.

"Marjorie, come here," Harold was yelling into the room.

Marjorie blushed and shook her head. "What's wrong with him?" she asked no one in particular as she stood up.

"Hurry up," Harold shouted, his arms waving as if to hurry her along.

"I'd better go see what's wrong," Marjorie told Bessie and the others. "I'm sorry I'm just rushing off."

Bessie's polite reply was lost on Marjorie as she rushed from the room behind Harold.

"What was that all about?" Doona demanded.

"I think we'd all like to know the answer to that," Bessie replied. "I suppose we'll find out eventually."

A few minutes later, Harold was back in the doorway.

"Ahem, um, good morning." He spoke loudly and then paused and waited for the room to grow quiet.

"Ah, yes, well, thank you for your patience this morning. I realise that we're a little bit behind schedule, but with everything that's gone on, well, I suppose we're lucky to be carrying on at all."

"He's not going to cancel today, is he?" Doona whispered to Bessie.

"I certainly hope not," Bessie replied.

"Anyway, there have been some changes to today's schedule. I just wanted to let everyone know what's going on. Because of the interruption last night, we wanted to give Paul Roberts and Claire Jamison another chance to present their work. Paul will begin in a few minutes in the Ellan Vannin Theatre downstairs and Claire will be speaking here, in the Kinvig Room."

"Good for them," Bessie said quietly. "I just hope they get decent audiences."

"The series of short talks and the talk by William Corlett that were originally scheduled for this morning will still take place. They have been moved to two o'clock, with the short talks being scheduled for the Ellan Vannin Theatre downstairs. Dr. Corlett will speak in here."

"But that's when you're speaking," Doona said to Bessie.

"Maybe they'll put me in the Blundell Room, then," Bessie said.

Doona frowned but didn't reply.

Harold continued. "Dr. Cross will speak at two o'clock as scheduled, however, she will speak in the Blundell Room. Miss Cubbon's talk will now take place in the Ellan Vannin Theatre at four o'clock and the final concluding remarks by myself and Ms. Stevens will take place in the same location immediately after Miss Cubbon has finished. If anyone has any questions about the schedule, it's posted on the board just outside of the lifts. I now need to ask everyone to vacate this room so the museum staff can get it ready for the presentations."

Bessie grinned at Doona. "There, you see, they've moved me as well. It's going to be another long day, though."

The trio got up slowly and followed the crowd out into the foyer.

CHAPTER ELEVEN

"Moghrey mie, Bessie," Henry whispered to her as she passed him. He was waiting for the room to clear. He had a large wheeled cart that was empty and ready to fill with the plates and cups from breakfast.

"Kys t'ou, Henry?" she asked.

"I've been better, I'll tell you," he said. "But I can't tell you right now. I've got to get everything sorted out in there and quick."

"And there you are, Bessie," the loud voice boomed across the spacious foyer. Bessie forced a smile onto her face as George Quayle crossed the room towards her.

"Hello, George, how are you today?" she asked.

"I'm doing well," he answered heartily. "You, on the other hand, look well knackered."

Bessie laughed. "I had a very late night last night," she told him.

"Oh, aye, we all did, didn't we?" he replied. "After you took off in the ambulance, the rest of us had to wait around to talk to Inspector Corkill. He did his best, mind, and he didn't ask much, but it was still late by the time I got out of here. And then, once I got home, well, I just couldn't get to sleep. I kept thinking about that poor young girl and how upsetting it was, what had happened to her. I called Noble's first thing this morning, but they won't tell me how she's doing."

"They aren't telling anyone anything," Bessie told him.

George shrugged. "I hope she's okay. I'll tell you something, though, the next time Marjorie and Harold ask me to sponsor a conference, I'll think twice."

Bessie frowned. "Oh, but none of this is their fault," she said.

George laughed. "I know, and I'm sure I won't be able to say no when they ask; I never have before. I guess I should be happy that I'm off the hook for Mack's excavation. That wouldn't have been cheap."

"I'm sure it wouldn't have been," Bessie agreed.

"Inspector Rockwell, how very nice, if rather unexpected, it is to see you," George said, as if he'd just noticed Bessie's companions.

"Bessie's a friend," the inspector replied. "Since I was planning to come for her talk anyway, I decided I might as well come for the whole day."

"Is that so?" George grinned and turned to Doona. "And who is this lovely young lady?" he asked Bessie.

"This is my friend, Doona Moore," Bessie replied. "We take Marjorie's Manx language class together."

George took Doona's offered hand and gave it a squeeze. "Moghrey mie," he said to her with a wink.

"Oh, moghrey mie," she replied, pulling her hand away.

"Why haven't I seen you here all weekend?" George asked Doona.

"History isn't really my thing," Doona replied. "I'm just here today to support Bessie."

"She's lucky to have such loyal friends," George said. "But if history isn't your thing, what is?" he asked Doona in a suggestive tone.

Doona blushed and glanced over at Bessie. Bessie frowned. George was flirting outrageously and it was making her and Doona both uncomfortable.

"How's Mary today?" she asked him pointedly.

George laughed. "You mustn't mind me," he told Doona with a grin. "When my wife isn't with me and I meet a beautiful young woman I can't seem to help but flirt. The problem is, I'm terrible at it and I know it. Luckily, no one ever takes me seriously, so I never end up in trouble with Mary."

"It's fine," Doona said uncertainly.

"Anyway," George turned back to Bessie, "in answer to your

question, Mary is just fine. She told me you're coming over for tea next week and I'm ever so pleased. It would do her a world of good to make some friends."

"She's a lovely person and I'm looking forward to getting to know her better," Bessie told him.

"So, what's your theory on our little murder mystery, then?" George asked Inspector Rockwell.

"Douglas is out of my jurisdiction," he replied. "Inspector Corkill is the one coming up with the theories here."

"Oh, come on," George chuckled. "Even out of your jurisdiction, you're still a cop. You must have your own ideas about what happened. Shall I tell you what I think?"

"If you like," Rockwell said in a deliberately casual tone.

"I think Bambi killed Mack and then tried to kill herself when the guilt got to be too much for her," he announced loudly.

Bessie winced as she realised just how many people must have heard his remarks.

"It's certainly one theory worth exploring," Rockwell said diplomatically. "I'm sure Pete Corkill is considering every possibility."

"You know, someone suggested that I had a hand in it," George said in an indignant voice. "As if I had any motive for murdering anyone. I didn't even know the poor man had a nut allergy, so that lets me out anyway."

"Whenever something like this happens, all sorts of wild and crazy theories get suggested," Doona told him soothingly. "It's Inspector Corkill's job to sort out the crazy ones from the rest and then investigate from there."

George appeared to be only half-listening. His eyes were focussed past Doona's head towards the lifts. A moment later, Harold reappeared.

"Okay, ladies and gentlemen, the speakers are all ready," he said in a loud voice. He only had to repeat himself twice before the crowd finally noticed him and went quiet.

"Sorry about the delay," Harold told everyone. "The first sessions are now ready to begin."

"So where are we going?" Doona asked Bessie as the foyer

began to empty.

Bessie frowned. "Last night I was planning to go to Claire's talk and I missed it, so I suppose I'd like to go there. But Paul is a very good speaker and I think you and the inspector might enjoy hearing him more."

"We could flip a coin," Doona suggested.

"I'll throw in my vote," Rockwell offered. "Having had the chance to meet her, I'd like to hear what Claire has to say."

Accordingly, the trio made their way into the Kinvig Room and took seats near the back. Claire was in the front of the room, flipping anxiously through her notes and talking with Joe Steele, who looked ready to try to pull down the moon if Claire asked him to.

"The poor man is head over heels, isn't he?" Doona whispered to Bessie.

"She could do a lot worse," Bessie whispered back. "He's a nice enough person and he's well educated. He's just awfully young and he's trying way too hard."

A moment later, Joe slid into a front-row seat and Claire stepped behind the podium.

"Ah, good morning," she said brightly. "I suppose I should start by apologising to those of you who heard the first half of this talk last night, because I'm going to start back at the beginning. I hope you don't find hearing it all again too boring."

A polite chuckle went through the crowd and then Claire began. Bessie was relieved to find that she was a talented speaker. The last thing Bessie wanted was for her friends to be bored. Bessie herself found the talk fascinating and when it ended she was almost ready to visit Anglesey herself.

"We should have a holiday to Anglesey," Doona said as she turned to face Bessie once the talk had finished.

Bessie laughed. "I was just thinking that very thing," she told her friend.

"Have you ever been there?" Doona asked her.

"No, and before today I wasn't even tempted to go," Bessie replied.

"I was there for a policing conference a few years ago,"

Rockwell told them. "It's a lovely little island, although obviously not as cut off from things as we are here. I actually enquired about a job there after I left because I was so taken with the place, but they didn't have any appropriate openings."

"Their loss is definitely our gain," Bessie said with a smile.

Claire fielded a few questions from the audience and then thanked them all for coming. Bessie and her friends remained seated as the room slowly cleared. The session was due to run for two hours and Claire had taken less than one. There was nothing on the schedule now until lunch, so they were in no rush to get anywhere.

"So, how was that?" Claire asked Bessie as she walked towards the door with Joe hot on her heels.

Bessie grinned at Claire's flushed face. "It was wonderful," she replied honestly. "You're a gifted speaker and you'd clearly done your research and knew your topic well."

Claire turned an even brighter pink. "Oh, thank you," she said. "I always get so nervous and then I tend to talk too fast." She shook her head. "Maybe by the time I retire I'll be used to it."

Bessie laughed. "You certainly didn't talk too fast today, and you didn't look nervous, either."

Claire grinned. "So my acting skills are improving, even if my nerves aren't."

Joe put an affectionate hand on her shoulder. "I told you that you'd be amazing," he said. "And I'm never wrong."

Claire smiled at him. "I can't tell you how much your support means to me," she told the young man.

"It's easy to support someone who's brilliant and beautiful," he said with a bashful grin.

Bessie stood up. "I'm counting on you both supporting me this afternoon," she said laughingly. "In spite of the fact that I'm neither."

"Actually, Harold told me that you're one of the most talented researchers he's ever come across," Joe said in reply.

"Really?" Bessie was deeply touched. She had a great deal of respect for Dr. Harold Smythe.

"He said your talk is going to be one of the highlights of the conference," Claire chimed in. "He told me that you make dusty old documents relevant and interesting and that he was looking forward to your keen insights."

Bessie blushed. "My goodness, I had no idea," she stammered, feeling somewhat overwhelmed by the kind words.

"He also told me that you're something of an amateur detective," Joe continued. "Does that mean you're going to solve Mack's murder as well?"

Bessie shook her head. "I'm nothing like an amateur detective," she said firmly. "I've had the great misfortune to get caught up in a couple of murder investigations recently, but I've only ever discovered the culprit by accident or circumstance. I'm more than happy to leave the police to sort out what happened to Mack and Bambi."

"And the missing slides," Joe said.

"And the missing slides," Bessie agreed.

"There's still an hour until lunch," Claire said. "Joe, I'm going to take my notes and things back to the hotel. Would you like to walk back with me or are you staying here to talk with people and get another drink?"

"Oh, I guess I'll walk back with you," he replied. "I could use some fresh air."

Bessie and Doona exchanged glances. Surely everyone could see through that excuse?

The couple disappeared out of the room and Bessie and her friends followed slowly. The foyer was mostly deserted.

"I bet some people have snuck downstairs for the last part of Paul's talk," Bessie speculated.

"Do you want to do that?" Doona asked.

Bessie thought about it and then shook her head. "Maybe it's because I'm so tired," she said. "But I'm feeling rather overloaded on history right now. I'd really just like to grab a cup of tea and sit somewhere quiet."

"Maybe I'll explore the museum for a short while," Rockwell said. "I've never actually been here before."

"You haven't?" Bessie said in her most scandalised tone. "How long have you lived on the island? You should be ashamed of yourself for not making the effort earlier. And you should have dragged your children around as well. They should get a good grounding in the history of their adopted country."

"Sorry," Rockwell said, looking down at the floor.

Bessie took his arm. "Come on, then, let's make up for lost time," she said, heading towards the lift.

"I thought you wanted a tea break," the inspector protested.

"Your education is more important than a tea break," Bessie said sternly. "Doona, are you coming?"

Doona laughed. "You've already dragged me around this place at least twice," she reminded her friend. "But I wouldn't miss this tour for the world."

"Of course," Bessie began as they emerged from the lifts and walked past the museum's front entrance, "if you did this properly you would start with the movie. With Paul giving his talk in the Ellan Vannin Theatre, though, we'll have to skip it for today. It's well worth a trip back to see it, however, when you have a chance."

"Yes, ma'am," the inspector replied with a grin.

"Don't get cheeky with me, young man," Bessie said mock-sternly. "If you don't behave I'll give you a test when we get to the end."

"Was she like this when she took you around?" the man appealed to Doona.

Doona laughed. "Exactly like this," she told him. "She should have been a history teacher."

"Quiet," Bessie told them both, trying not to laugh.

The pair grinned at each other and then both looked soberly at Bessie. "We'll be good," Doona told her friend.

"Okay, then," Bessie winked at them. "The first thing we're going to see is the art gallery."

She led them into the darkened space and waved an arm. "Go ahead and take a look around," she suggested. "There are some marvelous pieces in here and some important ones as well."

Doona and the inspector dutifully wandered around for a short time, looking at the artworks and reading the information provided about each piece. Bessie waited patiently for them in front of the portrait of James Stanley, Seventh Earl of Derby.

"Ah, there you are," Rockwell said as he came around the corner and spotted Bessie. Doona was only a step behind him.

"I remember him," Doona said with a laugh as she looked at the portrait. "John, may I present James Stanley? He was the 'Lord of Mann and the Isles' during the English Civil War. He actually came and lived on the island for a while and then went back to fight for the king, along with an army of Manxmen that he more or less dragged with him. He was captured and executed and then Cromwell's forces sailed across and took over the island." She smiled at Bessie. "Did I get that all right?" she asked.

"More or less," Bessie grinned. "I'm so pleased that you paid attention when I took you around."

Doona grinned. "I hope you're paying attention," she said to Rockwell with a smug smile.

He laughed. "I'm doing my best," he told her.

"Shall we go on?" Bessie asked. The trio worked their way through various rooms, stopping again in front of a case full of ancient pottery.

"That's a very ugly pot," Rockwell said.

Bessie laughed. "It's 'Ronaldsway' pottery and it is fairly basic. The Ronaldsway culture is fascinating in that it developed in different ways from what was happening elsewhere in the British Isles at the time."

"What sort of time are we talking about?" the inspector asked.

"Late Neolithic," Doona said excitedly. "I remembered that as well."

"Well done," Bessie grinned.

"Show-off," Rockwell said, sticking his tongue out at Doona. She responded in kind.

"Children," Bessie said severely.

"So not everyone was doing such ugly pottery in the late Neolithic?" Rockwell asked.

"No, they weren't," Bessie told him. "They also weren't doing the same things with flint tools. There are other things that were unique to the culture as well, but I don't want to stand here all day talking about just one thing."

"Why Ronaldsway? Isn't that the name of the airport?"

"The artifacts were found when they were excavating for an expansion of the airport in the late 1930s," Bessie explained.

The trio made their way through the Bronze Age, then the Iron Age and into the Viking period. The skull of a young woman who had apparently been sacrificed, the top of her head sliced open, fascinated Rockwell. Doona was more interested in the beautiful collection of beads that had once been a necklace adorning a pagan woman.

They continued to make their way forward through time. "I wish we had enough time for me to tell you all about everything we're seeing," Bessie told Rockwell as they walked.

"It's all really interesting," Doona told him. "You'll have to come back sometime with Bessie and get the full tour."

"I actually think I'd like that," Rockwell grinned.

"This is William Christian's hat," she told him, pointing to a display case. "Or, more accurately, it was William Christian's hat."

"And William Christian was?"

Bessie shook her head. "Hugely important in Manx history. We saw his portrait in the art gallery," she reminded him. "He was either a great Manx patriot or a traitor, depending on your view of his story."

"He's the one who surrendered the island to Parliamentarian forces during the Civil War, right?" Doona asked.

"Exactly. Charolotte de La Tremoille, the Countess of Derby, James Stanely's wife, refused to surrender, even after she was informed that her husband had been executed," Bessie replied.

"And this William Christian surrendered anyway?" Rockwell asked.

"In exchange for promises that the new government in England would recognise ancient Manx rights," Bessie said.

"Interesting," Rockwell replied, looking more closely at the hat.

"He's probably better known as 'Illiam Dhone,'" Bessie added. "That's his name in Manx."

"That might be easier to remember than any of the other

Manx I've heard," Rockwell joked.

They moved from the seventeenth century, into the eighteenth and beyond. There were sections on old toys, farm equipment, and the difficult lives of fishermen, farmers and miners.

Bessie walked slowly through the exhibit on the Second World War.

"It's strange thinking of things that happened in my own lifetime as being history," she remarked.

"I didn't realise that the island housed German prisoners during the wars," Rockwell told Bessie.

"It was a very different island in those days," Bessie told him. "We were a bit isolated from it all up in Laxey. The closest camp was in Ramsey, but that didn't mean that the whole island wasn't changed. Again, that's a story for another day. Or maybe many, many stories."

Everyone's mood lifted as they headed into the section that showed the island as a tourist destination. Rockwell sat inside the model horse tram and watched video footage of the huge crowds of people that used to flock to the island in the summer months.

"The island must have felt very different in those days as well," he said to Bessie.

"I remember it well," Doona laughed. "When I was a teenager we would spend the whole summer complaining about all the tourists and then, when they'd gone, we'd complain about how boring all the locals were."

Bessie grinned. "Again, Laxey missed out on a lot of the worst of it, but as you say, the island had a somewhat different feel, at least in the summer months. Much like it feels different now during the TT."

"Ah, I haven't been here for a TT yet," Rockwell said. "I'm not sure if I'm looking forward to it or dreading it."

"You probably won't be sure after it's over, either," Doona laughed. "It brings a lot of people to the island and keeps many of the hotels and restaurants in business, but it also closes down a lot of the island's roads off and on for a fortnight and that can be frustrating."

"And it keeps the police extra busy," the inspector told them. "I was told when I took the job here that no one is allowed to take any time off during the fortnight and that I should expect to work extra hours."

"Ninety-nine per cent of the people that come and enjoy the TT are wonderful," Bessie said. "Unfortunately, there are so many of them that even one per cent of them can cause an awful lot of trouble."

"I guess I'll find out next month," Rockwell shrugged.

The tour ended at the museum library, but it was closed on Sundays. They wandered back past the gift shop, where the inspector spent several minutes looking over the extensive collection of books on Manx history.

"I give up," he said finally. "Which one is the best for a basic history?" he asked Bessie.

Bessie laughed and then made a few suggestions. Rockwell bought everything she recommended and then added a few extras that had caught his eye. The clerk at the desk was happy to hold all of them in the shop until the conference finished so that he didn't have to carry them around for the rest of the day.

"You're really starting to feel at home on the island, aren't you?" Bessie asked as they made their way back towards the front of the museum.

"I am indeed," Rockwell told her. "And the more at home I feel, the more I want to know about the place."

With a few minutes left to fill before lunch, the trio made their way back up to the education level foyer. Paul's talk had, seemingly, just finished and the foyer was full of people grabbing drinks before lunch. As Bessie and her friends crossed towards the table with the tea and coffee, the lifts "pinged" open behind them and even more people began to join the crowd.

"This is crazy," Doona gasped as the noise level in the space began to rise.

"Let's head downstairs," Bessie suggested. "We can be the first in the lunch queue."

"That sounds like a plan," Rockwell grinned. He turned back towards the lifts and led the other two out of the room.

CHAPTER TWELVE

As it happened, they weren't first in the queue for lunch. Bessie laughed as they rounded the corner to the café and spotted Hugh standing in front of the closed door. His nose was pressed to the small glass window in the door but he quickly straightened up and swung around as they approached.

"Oh, hi, um, I was just looking to see if you guys were in there," Hugh stammered out.

"You were trying to get a good look at what's on offer," Doona teased. "Wipe the drool off your chin."

Hugh blushed and then laughed. "I was just taking a peek," he replied. "There were like a hundred people wandering around the upstairs foyer when I got here," he continued. "Since I wasn't sure where you all were, I figured I'd catch up with you here."

"And here we are," Bessie grinned at him. "And lunch is a classic British carvery. I'm really looking forward to it."

Hugh's eyes lit up. "I was feeling sorry for myself, because I'm missing me mum's Sunday lunch, but this makes up for it for sure."

Doona shook her head. "If I worried about food as much as you do, I'd weigh five hundred pounds."

"I'm a growing boy," Hugh said, patting his flat stomach.

"I'm a growing girl," Doona laughed. "I'm just growing in the wrong direction."

"Women worry too much about their weight," Rockwell said. "All these models and actresses who weigh next to nothing give women unrealistic ideas of how they should look."

"That's easy for you to say," Doona told him. "You're in terrific shape and I know you work out every day."

Rockwell grinned. "Only during the week. I take weekends off," he said. "And I enjoy working out; I don't just do it to keep my weight down."

"Maybe I've tried the wrong sorts of exercise, then," Doona replied. "I've certainly never found any that I enjoyed."

"We should start promoting exercise at the station," Rockwell said. "We could convert the storeroom at the back into a small gym. I could bring my weights and equipment from home and everyone could use them. I'm sure we could get one of the local fitness clubs to do classes for us once or twice a week, as well."

Doona shook her head. "It all sounds like hard work," she said.

"Once you get started, you'd be hooked," Rockwell said enthusiastically. "I'm going to talk to the Chief Constable about the idea next week. There are already shower rooms back there."

"Yeah," Doona said with a frown. "For the folks we've arrested."

"But no one ever uses them," Hugh chimed in. "We hardly ever have anyone in the short-term lockup anyway and I can't remember the last time we kept anyone overnight."

The discussion was cut short when the door to the café opened. Henry stuck his head out.

"Is it just you folks waiting for lunch?" he asked, sounding surprised.

"We're a little early," Bessie said apologetically.

"I thought we'd have a crowd by now," Henry told her. "I guess everyone is too busy talking upstairs."

"It was really crowded," Bessie replied. "Maybe no one has noticed the time."

"I'll run up and make an announcement," Henry said. "But in the meantime, you guys can get started on the buffet." He glanced around, then spoke again in a whisper. "They let me eat a little bit ago and it was delicious," he told them with a huge smile.

Everything smelled wonderful and Bessie quickly filled a plate almost to overflowing with thickly sliced roast beef, Yorkshire pudding, roast potatoes, carrots, broccoli, sprouts and peas. At the end of the table, she stopped and poured a generous helping of gravy over everything.

Inspector Rockwell was a few steps ahead of her, and he'd already settled into a chair at a table in the back corner of the room. Bessie joined him now and the pair waited for Doona and Hugh to finish fixing their plates before they dug in.

"You never talk about your family," Bessie said to the inspector. "I don't even know your wife's name."

Rockwell looked startled and then shrugged. "She's called Sue," he said. "We have two kids, Thomas is fourteen and Amy is twelve."

"And how are they finding the island?" Bessie asked.

"They're having real trouble adapting," Rockwell replied. "They miss their friends and our family back in Manchester and they don't like the school in Ramsey, either."

"Oh, dear," Bessie frowned. "I'm sorry, I didn't mean to pry," she said.

"It's fine," Rockwell assured her. "Sue and I are considering a number of different options."

Bessie bit her tongue before she blurted out questions about what options they might be considering. "We'd all really miss you if you moved back to Manchester," she said after an awkward pause.

"I'm hoping it doesn't come to that," the inspector said.

Within minutes, the small room began to fill with hungry conference attendees and the noise level rose accordingly.

"So how's Grace?" Bessie asked Hugh, figuring that she'd started prying into people's personal lives, so she might as well continue.

"She's fine," Hugh said with a shrug. "We don't see all that much of each other at the minute. She's busy with school and marking papers most nights, but we try to spend weekends together when we can."

"I want to meet her one day," Bessie told the young policeman.

"Yes, ma'am," Hugh flushed and focussed on his dinner.

"I'm glad you got this corner table," Bessie told Rockwell. "It feels out of the way of the crowd."

"You'll have to point out all of the suspects to me," Hugh said. "I don't know anyone."

"Let's not call them suspects," Rockwell suggested. "People don't tend to like being thought of that way."

"None of the people we discussed last night is here yet," Bessie told Hugh as she scanned the crowd.

"Ah, Helen Baxter has just walked in," Doona hissed.

Hugh nodded. "Actually, I have met her," he told the others. "She works out at Ramsey Cottage Hospital once in a while and me gran is in and out of there every other week for something or other. How did she know Mack again?"

"Apparently she didn't," Bessie told him. "But she tried to talk to him early in the evening and he was quite rude to her, apparently. She told me that later on that evening he actually propositioned her, though."

"Why was he propositioning strangers if he was here with Bambi?" Doona asked angrily. "I know you said he always had a woman on the side, but surely he could survive with just Bambi for the few days they were going to be here?"

Bessie shrugged. "I don't know, maybe he was just flirting or maybe Helen misunderstood him. If he was seriously trying to get her into bed, though, that suggests that his secret girlfriend wasn't at the conference."

Rockwell frowned. "But the mystery girlfriend is my favourite suspect," he said.

"Surely, if she were here, Mack wouldn't have been trying to pull another woman as well?" Bessie asked.

Rockwell shrugged. "Some men flirt with every attractive woman they meet," he told her. "Even when they have no intention or even interest in following through."

Doona shook her head. "I've met my fair share of them," she sighed. "Although I guess I'm getting older, because it's been a while."

"George Quayle was flirting with you just this morning,"

Bessie reminded her friend.

"Who's that?" Hugh interrupted, nodding towards the door.

"Speak of the devil," Bessie grinned.

George Quayle stood in the entrance, surveying the room. He waved and shouted greeting to various people, including Bessie.

"He looks familiar," Hugh said, frowning.

"He's only been back on the island for a short time, but he's making a real name for himself," Rockwell told Hugh. "He's friends with the Chief Constable; you may have seem them together at some event or somewhere."

"That must be it," Hugh nodded. "How did he know Mack?"

"According to him, he didn't," Bessie replied. "Or at least not very well."

"You sound suspicious of that," Doona challenged her friend.

Bessie shrugged. "I find it odd that George insisted that Harold and Marjorie change the conference programme to accommodate Mack," she said thoughtfully. "I've never known George to do anything like that before. He's usually very hands-off when he funds something. It makes me wonder if there wasn't something behind it."

"Like Mack blackmailed him into it?" Doona asked.

"Or George agreeing so he could get Mack here so he could kill him?" Hugh chimed in.

Bessie shook her head. "I think both of those ideas are a bit dramatic," she said. "It was just somewhat out of character, at least as far as what I've seen of the man in the last year or so that he's been here."

"It is strange," Rockwell agreed. "I think I need to try to have a chat with Mr. Quayle."

"Don't let Inspector Corkill hear you say that," Bessie cautioned him.

Rockwell grinned. "Good point; maybe I'll call Pete and tell him to have a chat with the man."

"Oh, the lovebirds are here," Doona announced.

Bessie waved back at Claire and Joe as they took their places in the buffet queue.

"The pretty brunette is Claire Jamison and the man with her is Joe Steele," Bessie told Hugh.

"Didn't you say that neither of them knew Mack before the conference?" Hugh asked.

"Joe told me that he met him Friday night and Mack was rude to him about his background in paleontology," Bessie replied.

"That isn't much of a motive," Hugh replied.

"I'm surprised their paths had never crossed before, though," Bessie added. "Joe said he's been studying in London for almost six months and Mack was based there. The archeology world isn't that big, even in London. I would have expected that they'd have at least met once or twice before this weekend."

"Something else to ask Pete about," Rockwell sighed.

"What about Claire?" Hugh asked.

"She's another one who said she'd never met him, but Mack did do some excavating on Anglesey. Maybe she was doing research somewhere else during the time he was there, though. Harold didn't think Mack was on Angelsey for long."

"Speaking of Harold," Doona smiled, "he's the, um, plumpish man in the doorway."

Hugh grinned. "He looks like a history professor," he remarked.

"He does, rather," Bessie agreed.

"He also looks very pleased about something," Doona added.

"I wonder what's going on," Bessie said. "He wasn't looking that happy this morning."

"Well, he doesn't look like a murderer," Hugh said.

"Most murderers don't look like murderers," Rockwell said with a sigh. "If you could tell who'd done it just by looks, our job would be a lot easier, wouldn't it?"

"Surely no one here looks like a murderer?" Doona asked, looking around the room.

"That guy looks shady," Hugh said, after he'd done his own scan of the occupants.

Bessie followed Hugh's line of sight and then laughed. "Poor Paul. He's always complained that people don't give him much respect because he looks like an aging hippy. Now you think he looks like a murderer."

"Who is he?" Hugh asked.

"An archeologist and a very nice man," Bessie answered. "And there's no way he killed Mack. He didn't arrive on the island until after Mack died."

"Your friend Marjorie looks upset," Hugh remarked, as she walked into the café.

Bessie sighed. "This whole conference has been horrible for her. I'm almost surprised she's here today."

"I didn't know you knew Marjorie," Doona said to Hugh.

"I interviewed her when we were investigating Moirrey Teare's death," Hugh said. "That's how I know Liz Martin as well. I talked to them both very briefly, just to verify what happened in the class you all took together. And here's Liz now." Hugh nodded towards the door where Liz had just entered, still holding her husband's hand.

"That's her husband, Bill," Bessie told Hugh.

"And both Marjorie and Liz knew Mack before this weekend, right?" Hugh checked.

"They both dated Mack at different times," Bessie told him. "At least I hope it was at different times."

"Oh, I hope so, too," Doona exclaimed. "Liz and Marjorie seem to have become good friends. I'd hate to see them fight over Mack."

"What about Bill?" Hugh queried. "He must have known Mack before if he went to school with Liz. Maybe he knew they'd dated and he was jealous?"

"As far as I know, he was home watching the children the night Mack was killed. I certainly didn't see him at the conference before today," Bessie replied.

"Well, I'm going to keep an eye on him," Hugh said, narrowing his eyes and studying the man still standing near the door.

Bessie looked around, just as Harold finished filling his plate with food and then came across to Marjorie, who was still queuing. The pair had a quick conversation. When he'd finished speaking, Harold headed for a table near the back with his lunch while Marjorie continued to wait for her turn at the carvery.

"Well, whatever Harold said, it seems to have cheered Marjorie up a little bit," Doona remarked.

"Indeed," Bessie replied. "I think that's the happiest I've seen her all weekend."

"Maybe Harold has figured out who the murderer is," Doona speculated.

"I think it's more likely he's found out something about Mack's research," Bessie told them. "And from the looks on both their faces, I'd be willing to bet it's something that makes Mack look bad, as well."

"So will he make a big announcement any minute now?" Doona demanded.

Bessie frowned. "Actually," she replied, "he's far more likely to wait and make his announcement during the final session of the conference. He and Marjorie are meant to be summing up the entire weekend in twenty minutes or less. He doesn't have Mack's flair for the dramatic, but I bet he won't able to resist waiting until he has the entire conference hanging on his every word."

"But I want to know what's going on now," Doona said in a whiny voice.

Bessie laughed as Rockwell shook his head. "Patience," Bessie told her friend.

"Uh oh, everybody act casual," Doona hissed.

"Why?" Hugh demanded.

"Inspector Corkill's just walked in," Doona said under her breath.

By the time Doona had finished speaking, Inspector Rockwell was on his feet, crossing to greet his Douglas counterpart.

"Pete, always nice to see you," Rockwell said, offering his hand.

Bessie blew out a relieved breath when the other inspector took it with a smile that didn't look entirely forced. "John, I didn't know you'd be here today," he said.

"Bessie's a good friend," Rockwell explained. "I wanted to hear her talk and I figured the least I could do is drive her up for the day."

"Well, lunch looks tasty anyway," Corkill replied, looking past Rockwell to meet Bessie's eyes. "And now if I could just have a minute of Miss Cubbon's time?"

Bessie stood up quickly, aware that every person in the room was watching the inspector's every move. "Of course, Inspector Corkill," she said politely.

The inspector turned on his heel and Bessie followed him wordlessly out of the café. Bessie glanced back when they reached the door and gave Doona what she hoped was a reassuring smile. Bessie couldn't begin to imagine what the inspector wanted with her.

Inspector Corkill led Bessie to a small private room nearby that Bessie hadn't even known existed.

"I couldn't say anything in front of everyone," the inspector began, "because we're still restricting all information about Ms. Marks' condition."

Bessie heart sank. "She's still okay, isn't she?" she asked anxiously.

"Oh, she's fine," Corkill quickly assured her. "In fact, she's more than fine. Her doctor is prepared to let her go home, and I'm struggling to find any reason to keep her here. I was hoping you could talk to her."

"Me?" Bessie asked. "Why me?"

Corkill smiled. "You seem to have made quite an impression on the young lady," he told Bessie. "She's actually asking to see you. I was hoping, while you were visiting, you might be able to get more information from her than we have so far. I'd also prefer if she stays on the island for a few more days, just until we wrap up this thing with Mack and figure out exactly what happened to her."

"I'm happy to go and talk to her," Bessie told him. "I don't know that what I say will make much difference, but I'd really like to see her."

"Good," Corkill looked relieved. "Let's go."

Bessie shook her head. "There are some short talks I wanted to go to at two, and I'm supposed to give my talk at four," she told the man. "There simply isn't time now. I'll have to go and see

Bambi after the conference is finished."

Corkill frowned. "I really have to stress to you how important it is that you speak to Ms. Marks quickly," he told her. "Her father is putting a great deal of pressure on the Chief Constable to get her off the island. He won't let me see her at all. I haven't even been able to question her."

Bessie sighed. "But I've been looking forward to this conference for months," she said sadly.

"I'll drive you over and back," Corkill told Bessie. "We may well be able to get there and back in an hour, if you talk fast."

Bessie couldn't help but chuckle at that. "Give me a minute and I'll just let Harold know I'm leaving," she told him.

Bessie walked back to the café. Marjorie and Harold were sitting together, talking intently. She crossed to them, ignoring the curious stares she knew she was getting from the rest of the room.

"I hate to do this," Bessie said as a greeting, "but I need to run a quick errand. I can't see any reason why I won't be back by four, but I wanted you to know, just in case." She braced herself for the angry remarks she knew she deserved.

"Ah, Bessie, I'm sorry I didn't warn you about changing the start time of your talk, but it sounds like the later start time will work better for you anyway. Anyway, with everything else that's gone wrong, I'm not too worried if your talk starts a few minutes late, besides," Harold said tiredly.

Bessie grinned and then headed back towards the door. She waved at Doona and the others and then rejoined Inspector Corkill in the hallway outside the café.

"Okay, I'll probably have to miss the short talks, but as long as I'm back by four o'clock it should be okay," she told him. "That should be plenty of time to talk to Bambi and get back."

"I certainly hope so," the inspector said. "And before I forget, thank you."

Bessie didn't have time to stare at him in surprise, but she would have liked to do so.

CHAPTER THIRTEEN

Bessie followed Inspector Corkill through the museum and out the front of the building. His police car was parked in the emergency vehicle space right outside the door. Corkill held the passenger door open for Bessie and then climbed in himself.

"As I said, Nigel Marks, Bambi's father isn't letting her speak to us," Corkill told Bessie as they made their way out of the car park. "She's issued a statement through the solicitor that her father brought with him, at least."

"Her father brought along a solicitor?" Bessie asked, amazed.

Corkill let out a sharp bark of laughter. "Yeah, he rushed to his daughter's hospital bed, stopping just long enough to gather up his solicitor on the way."

Bessie shook her head. "Poor Bambi," she remarked.

"Oh, you'll want to call her Margaret now, at least in front of Mr. Marks," Corkill told her. "Mr. Marks doesn't approve of Bambi as a nickname."

Bessie laughed. "I can kind of see his point on that one," she told the inspector.

He shrugged. "Anyway, according to her statement, Ms. Marks has no idea what happened to her. She says she was just sitting and talking to some people, drinking some bottled water, and then she suddenly got so sleepy she couldn't stay awake. The next thing she knew, she was in hospital."

"That's unfortunate," Bessie said with a sigh.

"Aye, I was hoping for quite a bit more," Corkill admitted. "At any rate, what we need to find out is where she got the water from."

"She didn't say in her statement?"

"Nope."

Inspector Corkill pulled his car up to the front doors of Noble's Hospital and then turned and smiled at Bessie. "I'm going to let you out here," he told her. "I'll park and then I think it's better if I wait for you in the lobby. I'd rather Mr. Marks didn't know we were, um, communicating with one another."

"Fair enough," Bessie replied. "I just hope I can find out something useful."

"Me too," Corkill muttered.

Bessie made her way into the building, stopping at the information desk to find out in which ward Bambi was staying.

"Ah, Ms. Marks is in our private patient wing," the woman behind the desk told her. "I'll just have Sue escort you over there."

Bessie considered arguing, but she'd never actually been to the private wing. Maybe a guide would come in handy.

Sue turned out to be a volunteer that Bessie guessed had to be close to her own age, possibly even older. She walked slowly down the hospital corridors, using a Zimmer frame to assist her.

"I know what you're thinking," she said to Bessie as they made their slow way towards the private wing. "You're wondering why they have an eighty-seven year old woman with a Zimmer frame showing people around the place."

Bessie grinned. "I was rather wondering that," she admitted.

The other woman cackled with laughter. "Well, at least you're prepared to admit it," Sue said. "Most people won't, you know, but the thing is, I need my exercise and besides, the private wing is lovely and posh. I love visiting over there. Sometimes the nurses will slip me a fancy biscuit. They've got the nicest ones in the whole hospital, even nicer than what's in the doctors' lounge, and those are some nice biscuits them doctors have got, I can tell you."

Bessie laughed. A moment later they reached a set of double doors.

"You need to know the code," Sue told Bessie seriously. She

pulled a slip of paper from her pocket and then typed the four-digit number that was written on it into a panel by the door. A bell chimed softly and then the wide doors slowly swung open.

"Come on, then," Sue urged Bessie. "They don't stay open long, these doors, or else they'd have all sorts in here sniffing around the posh bickies."

It only took Bessie a moment to move through the doors and into the thickly carpeted corridor. Recessed lighting gave the hallway a soft glow that was warm and inviting. Bessie waited patiently as Sue clomped along behind her, obviously moving as quickly as she could as the doors slowly swung shut.

"The information desk is just down the hall," Sue told Bessie, taking a very slow lead again. Bessie fought down the urge to rush past the woman. She felt fortunate that her own age hadn't yet slowed her down.

At the desk, Sue greeted the woman behind it. "Good afternoon, Debbie, I've brought a visitor for Ms. Marks," she told her.

Debbie frowned. "I'm afraid you'll have to speak to Mr. Marks, the patient's father, first," she told Bessie.

"That's fine," Bessie smiled. "Where can I find him?"

"It's fine?" Debbie seemed surprised. "Well, um, he's just in with his daughter. If you wait here a moment, I'll let him know you've arrived."

She got up from behind the desk and took a few steps before turning back to Bessie. "I'm sorry, I didn't get your name. Mr. Marks will want to know."

"I'm Elizabeth Cubbon," Bessie replied.

"Oh, Laxey's famous 'Aunt Bessie,' right? My cousin, Barb, used to hang out at your place all the time about twenty years ago," Debbie grinned. "I'll go tell Mr. Marks he should feel honoured that you're here."

Bessie chuckled. "I don't think he'll see it that way," she said.

"Probably not," Debbie agreed cheerfully.

Only a moment later, Debbie was back. "Well, he's willing to talk to you at least," she told Bessie. "He's asked you to wait in the television room for a few moments and then he'll be in."

"I'll show her the way," Sue announced.

Debbie grinned at Bessie. "How about if I show her and you go down to the kitchen and see if they can spare you a biscuit?" she asked Sue. "I think I just heard the kettle boil as well, so maybe you'll be in time for a cuppa."

"Oooo, how lovely," Sue said. "I'm off then."

Debbie and Bessie watched Sue's painfully slow progress for a minute, before Debbie turned back to Bessie.

"Let me show you where to wait," she said, heading off in the opposite direction from where Sue was still visible.

"Please don't complain about Sue," Debbie said in a quiet voice as they made their way down the corridor. "Her son is one of the surgeons and everyone on the staff loves her, but I know many of our visitors find it frustrating when she takes so long to show them where they're meant to be going."

"I would never think about complaining about her," Bessie assured her. "She's very sweet and I always like to see older people finding something useful to do with their time."

Debbie grinned as she opened the door with the "Television Lounge" sign on it. "I'm not sure how useful she actually is," she laughed. "But we'd all miss her if she wasn't here."

Debbie flipped the light switch and Bessie looked around the comfortably furnished room. Several large couches were angled so that everyone would have at least a decent view of the large television on the back wall. There was a small refrigerator and a few cupboards along one side wall.

"We keep drinks and snacks in there for the patients," Debbie told Bessie. "Feel free to grab a cold drink or a biscuit while you wait. Mr. Marks will be here in his own time."

Bessie thanked the woman and then Debbie went back to her post, leaving Bessie to explore the room. Bessie checked the refrigerator, not because she was thirsty, but because she wondered what the private patients had on offer. She was disappointed to see a fairly standard selection of fizzy drinks and bottled water, rather than the champagne and imported bottled drinks she expected. The cupboards were equally disappointing, containing nothing more elaborate than custard creams and digestives. She was disappointed yet again when she pulled back the curtains at the window to reveal a somewhat depressing view of the car park

"I guess I shouldn't mind having to have my care on the NHS," she muttered to herself as she sank down on one of the couches.

A moment later the door swung open and Bessie got back to her feet. The man who strode in was probably close to fifty, with dark hair and dark eyes. He was immaculately dressed in a black suit and Bessie reckoned that she'd be able to see her reflection in his shoes if she got close enough.

"Mr. Marks?" she asked politely.

"No, I'm Clive Henderson," the man said sharply. "I'm an old family friend as well as the family's solicitor."

"How very nice for you," Bessie said. "And what are you hoping to get me to agree to or sign before you'll let me visit with Bambi?"

The man shook his head. "You misunderstand me," he said smoothly. "I'm merely here as an old family friend. Mr. Marks and I are very aware that Margaret needs some help in getting her life back together, that's all."

"Look," Bessie said, trying to hide her annoyance, "I'm here because I was told that Bambi wanted to talk to me. If she doesn't actually want to see me, just say so. Believe it or not, I have better things to do with my time than stand here talking to you. If she does want to see me, then stop making this so difficult and let me see her."

The man shook his head. "I don't want to argue with you, Mrs. Cubbon, but we're being very careful about what influences we let come into contact with Margaret at the moment and...."

Bessie held up a hand. "You know what? I've had enough. If you think I'm likely to be a bad influence on Bambi, then there's no point in our continuing to talk. Please tell her that I was here and I'm sorry that I couldn't see her."

She headed towards the door, but was stopped when another man walked into the room. Of a similar age to the overly polished solicitor, he looked as if his sharp edges had recently been worn away. His hair was shot full of grey and his eyes looked tired and swollen. He was wearing jeans and an old button-down shirt that looked as if it needed laundering.

He smiled at Bessie, but it looked forced. "Miss Cubbon? I'm Nigel Marks." He held out a hand and Bessie took it, somewhat reluctantly.

"Nigel, I'd have to advise you...." Clive Henderson began.

The other man raised a hand to stop him mid-sentence. "Clive, why don't you go down to the café and have some lunch? I'll have a chat with Miss Cubbon and then join you in a few minutes."

The solicitor drew in a deep breath and Bessie could almost hear the wheels turning in his head as he studied his friend. "I'll see you downstairs, then," he said finally, spinning on his heel and marching stiffly from the room.

"It was nice meeting you," Bessie called after him.

Nigel Marks's bark of laughter drowned out any reply that Clive Henderson might have made. "I feel like I should apologise for Clive," he told Bessie. "He is genuinely trying to look out for Margaret's best interests, even if he doesn't always go about doing so in the best way."

"I'll take your word for that," Bessie said dryly.

Marks laughed again. "You are not at all what I was expecting," he told Bessie. "Margaret only told me a little bit about you. Clearly nowhere near enough."

"Really?" Bessie asked. "You're exactly what I was expecting from Bambi's description."

Marks flushed and then shook his head. "I feel as if I've been insulted," he told Bessie. "And I'm sure it's deserved."

Bessie really wanted to see Bambi, and being argumentative and difficult with the man was hardly going to help her cause. "She's a lovely girl," she said now. "Very bright, with a good head on her shoulders."

The man beamed at Bessie. "She is at that," he agreed. "In spite of everything my ex-wife and I put her through."

Bessie considered half a dozen replies before she went carefully neutral. "I'm sure you did your best."

Marks shook his head. "I did no such thing," he told Bessie. "I was self-absorbed and immature and both my ex-wife and I used Margaret as a weapon in our fights." He sighed. "I wish I could say that I'm going to change and things are going to be different now, but I can't promise anything. I certainly intend to try, but Margaret is in her twenties now. It's definitely too late to give her a happy childhood."

"It's never too late to be the best father you can be," Bessie told him. "You could start by calling her Bambi, if that's what she prefers."

"It seems such a small thing," he told Bessie. "But she only ever wanted to be called that to annoy me. I hate to give in to that childishness."

Bessie shook her head. "Maybe if you start treating her as an adult, she'll outgrow some of what you think of as childishness," she suggested.

"And calling her Bambi, after some movie deer, is treating her as an adult?" he demanded.

"Respecting her choice as to what she would prefer to be called is treating her as an adult," Bessie said.

"I can see why Margaret likes you," he sighed. "She told me to make sure to call you 'Miss Cubbon,' as that's what you prefer."

Bessie grinned. "You're welcome to call me 'Bessie,'" she said. "Nearly everyone does."

The man grinned back at her. "And you must call me Nigel, of course."

"I really would like a chance to see Bambi," Bessie told him.

"Certainly," he agreed quickly. "I'll show you to her room and then I'll join Clive for a drink downstairs. You and Mar, er, Bambi can have a little bit of privacy."

"I'd appreciate that."

Bambi's room was only a few doors away, and Nigel didn't even go in with Bessie. He stopped in the corridor. "Tell my daughter that I'll be back shortly. If you leave before I get back, thank you for everything."

Bessie wasn't sure what she was being thanked for, but she shook the man's hand anyway. Once he was a few paces down the hall, she slowly pushed open the door to Bambi's room.

"Ah, Bessie, thank goodness you're here." Bambi was sitting in a chair in a small seating area just inside the door. "I'm just about to die from sheer bloody boredom," she continued, pressing the button to turn off the television she had been staring at as Bessie entered.

Bessie grinned at Bambi as she sat on the couch next to her. "I brought you a book," she said, pulling a paperback from her bag. She wasn't, strictly speaking, telling the truth. She always had a book in her bag for unexpected times when she needed some entertainment, and this one just happened to be the latest, but it was one she'd read many times before and she didn't mind giving it to Bambi.

"Agatha Christie?" Bambi's wrinkled her nose. "Is she any good?"

Bessie smiled. "She's absolutely brilliant," she assured the girl. "And reading is always better than television."

Bambi laughed. "I rarely watch television," she told Bessie. "I'm usually too busy with my life. But now, I'm stuck in here with Mr. Stick-Up-His-Butt guarding the door."

"Ah, that would be the charming Mr. Clive Henderson?" Bessie asked.

Bambi shook her head. "'Charming' and 'Clive Henderson' do not belong in the same sentence," she replied. "Uncle Clive is many things, but charming is definitely not one of them."

"I can't stay long," Bessie told the girl. "I'm supposed to be giving my talk soon, but I was pleased that you wanted to see me. I've been worrying about you."

"I'm fine," Bambi answered airily. "I've done much worse things to myself in the past. This was just a small overdose of sleeping pills or something."

"But how did you come to overdose on them?" Bessie asked.

Bambi shrugged. "I have no idea," she replied. "I felt fine after lunch and then the only thing I had to eat or drink after that was a bottle of water. I guess there must have been something in the water."

"Where did you get the water?"

"It was just on the table, you know. There were a whole bunch of bottles of water, and tea and coffee pots and whatever. When I walked into the room, I just grabbed a bottle off the table and then went and sat down. A few minutes later a couple of people joined me and we were all chatting when I started to feel really sleepy."

"Do you remember talking to Claire Jamison?" Bessie asked.

"Sure, she was collecting empty bottles, but I'd barely even started drinking mine by that point. I promised that I'd give it to her when I was done."

Bessie frowned. "Inspector Corkill was hoping you might be able to tell us more," she told the girl. "He's convinced that Mack's murderer is the one who drugged you."

"I don't know," Bambi yawned. "I'm wondering now if I overreacted to Mack's death. Maybe it was just an unfortunate accident. I'm trying hard to be less dramatic about life, you know?"

Bessie shook her head. "Sometimes drama is called for," she replied. "Mack was definitely murdered, and if we can figure out what happened to you, we might be closer to finding out who killed him."

Bambi yawned again. "I'm sorry, Aunt Bessie, but I'm awfully tired. I wish I could help, I truly do, but I don't know anything."

"Never mind," Bessie told her. "I'll let you get some rest. When you wake up, have another think about everything that's happened since you've been on the island. You might remember something after all. I'll try to stop back this afternoon for another visit."

"That would be great," Bambi said, getting slowly to her feet. "I'm just going to have a short nap now. Maybe something will come back to me while I'm resting and I can tell you all about it later."

"I hope so," Bessie told her. "But whatever happens, your first priority has to be getting yourself fit and healthy."

"I'm okay," the girl insisted. "The doctor reckons the drugs will have worked their way through my system by tomorrow, and my father is planning to take me home as soon as we get permission from him."

"I'll definitely have to stop by later today then, won't I?"

"I'll look forward to it," Bambi replied, trying to stifle yet another yawn.

Bambi crawled into her bed and gave Bessie a wave. "See you later," she said softly, her eyes closing almost as soon as her head hit the pillow.

"Definitely," Bessie replied, making her way to the door. She glanced back at the woman and smiled. Bambi already appeared to be fast asleep.

Back in the corridor, Bessie headed towards the main section of the hospital. The hard tiled floors and bright florescent lighting felt harsh to Bessie after the plusher fittings in the private wing.

She found Inspector Corkill in the lobby as promised. He nodded at Bessie as she walked through. They both headed for the main doors, meeting just before passing through them.

"Hop in," he told Bessie as he held open the passenger door of his car.

CHAPTER FOURTEEN

Bessie sank back in the car's seat and sighed deeply. "I'm sorry," she told Inspector Corkill. "I wasn't able to find out anything useful."

Corkill sighed. "I didn't really expect you to," he told Bessie. "Ms. Marks is hiding behind her father and his solicitor. Whether that's because there's something she doesn't want to tell me or for some other reason, I wasn't expecting her to say anything useful to you. I do appreciate your trying, though, and I'm hopeful that maybe Ms. Marks will think things over and get in touch with one of us before she leaves."

"I told her I'd try to stop back later this afternoon," Bessie said. "She's planning on leaving tomorrow if her doctor gives the okay."

The inspector nodded. "I'd love to make her stay, but I'm not ready to tackle Mr. Marks and his high-powered London solicitor."

Bessie sighed. "I honestly don't think she knows anything," she told him.

"I'd still like a chance to ask her a few questions," he replied.

The rest of the drive passed quickly. Bessie repeated her fruitless conversation with Bambi to the man while they went. Bessie was back at the museum almost thirty minutes before she was due to speak.

"At least you're back with a few minutes to spare," Corkill grinned at Bessie. "Um, good luck with your speech."

"Thank you," Bessie said, hoping she didn't sound as surprised as she felt.

"I might just come up and listen," Corkill continued. "I was planning to come to the last talk of the day already. I'm hoping to talk to a few people after that's over. If I come to yours, maybe I'll learn something interesting about, well, whatever it is you're talking about."

"I'm talking about the sometimes unexpected things that wills can tell researchers. And of course you're more than welcome," Bessie said, figuring his presence couldn't possibly make her any more nervous than she already was.

"I'll just park up somewhere," he replied. "You go on ahead and I'll see you later."

Bessie climbed out of the car and headed into the museum. It had long been one of her favourite places on the island, but she was looking forward to this particular weekend being over. It felt as if it was going to be a long while before she was going to be able to enjoy the museum again.

The education level foyer was full of people as Bessie stepped off the lift. She sighed as she realised that, unless some of them left, they were all going to be at her talk. The last-minute schedule change meant that her presentation was the only thing scheduled in the added time slot.

Glancing around the room, she felt a flood of relief when she spotted her friends. She slipped through the crowd, saying polite hellos to people she knew as she walked.

"Did you have any luck with Bambi?" Rockwell asked as soon as Bessie has greeted them all.

"Unfortunately, no," Bessie said with a frown.

"Any idea what Pete's next move is going to be?" he asked Bessie.

"He said he's going to come to my talk and the one Harold and Marjorie are finishing the conference with," Bessie replied. "And then try to catch a few people before everything breaks up."

"Time to let Bessie focus on her speech," Doona told Rockwell sternly. "We can worry about murder later."

"I'm not sure I want to think about my speech," Bessie laughed nervously. "There are an awful lot of people here."

"Harold asked me to let you know that they've moved everything to the Kinvig Room," Doona told her. "Apparently there is some other event this afternoon and the museum needs to use the Ellan Vannin Theatre for that."

"I think I'll be happier in the smaller space," Bessie confided. "The Ellan Vannin Theatre is really big and I hate being up on a stage like that."

"Do you want to go somewhere quiet to gather your thoughts before you start?" Doona asked her friend.

"I'd love to," Bessie said, grasping the idea like a lifeline.

"Marjorie told me to tell you to use the Blundell Room," Doona told her. "I hope you know where that is?"

Bessie smiled. "I do indeed."

She headed off down the hall and was pleased to find that the door to the room was unlocked. After she'd switched on the light, she locked the door behind herself and sank into the closest chair. Pulling her notes out of her handbag, Bessie checked that they were in order and then began to read through them. A knock on the door startled her.

She opened the door to Harold Smythe's smiling face. "Just giving you a five-minute warning," he told her. He was gone before Bessie could challenge him as to the cause of his dramatic mood change.

Bessie clicked the door lock again and sat back down, but her mind refused to focus on her notes. Instead, she kept seeing Mack, just two days earlier, locked in the cuillee.

Who would he have opened the door for? she asked herself. Who would he have trusted enough to eat whatever they gave him? Who was locked in with the dead or dying man when Bambi tried the door?

Bessie shook her head, trying to get her focus back on the paper she was about to present.

Who could have taken Mack's injectors from him? And who had the missing slides? There were two missing sets, Bessie thought. Why would the murderer take them both? Or were there two different culprits at work? She frowned. This paper was going to be a disaster.

She stood up and paced around the room. As she walked, she accidentally knocked over a water bottle that someone had left sitting next to one of the seats. As she stood it back up, her mind was racing.

She was ready for Harold's knock a minute later.

"Ready to go?" he asked her.

"I am," Bessie replied grimly. She couldn't remember anything in her long life that she'd dreaded as much as she was dreading what she was about to do. "I just need a quick word with Inspector Rockwell," she told Harold. "And I guess Inspector Corkill as well," she added.

Harold frowned, but didn't ask any questions. Bessie stood near the door to the Kinvig Room and waited while Harold found the two inspectors and sent them out to her. She spoke quickly and they were both looking as grim as she felt when she'd finished speaking.

"You know her better then I do," Corkill said to Rockwell. "Is there any way to stop her?"

"It's probably not worth the effort trying," Rockwell shrugged. "We'll be better off going along with her than arguing at this point. Anyway, if it all goes spectacularly wrong, Bessie will end up with all of the blame."

Corkill looked like he might argue, but instead he pressed his lips together and marched back into the conference room.

"Good luck, Bessie," Inspector Rockwell told Bessie with a grin.

"Thanks," Bessie replied grimly.

Rockwell went back into the room and found a good seat. Bessie nodded to Harold who was standing near the podium. He stepped up and began his introductions.

Bessie was too nervous to listen to him, however. Instead, she paced back and forth, shuffling her notes nervously. The sound of polite applause told her when it was time to go in.

She tried hard to smile at the crowd as she made her way to the podium, which seemed far away. Doona's bright smile made her feel a bit better and Hugh's goofy grin almost drew a smile. Bessie spotted Marjorie, clapping loudly from her seat in the front row. Claire Jamison and Joe Steele were together in the row behind Marjorie, holding hands. George Quayle gave Bessie a wave and Bessie finally did smile when she spotted his wife, Mary, sitting beside him.

Bessie found Liz, Helen and Paul Roberts scattered throughout the crowd as she took her place at the podium. She put her notes down, took a deep breath and then looked out at the audience.

"The wills that people leave behind are often very informative in ways that their creators may not have intended. How people chose to distribute their belongings, who they select as trustees for their estates and who they nominate as guardians for their minor children all give researchers important information about family relationships within any given family."

She paused and took another deep breath. "We all have people we trust, people whom we believe have our best interests at heart. I'm sure Mack Dickson had people that he trusted. Unfortunately, one if those people took advantage of that trust to commit his murder."

Bessie took a sip of water as people gasped and began to murmur among themselves. When she put her glass down, the room fell silent again.

"Mack was a talented archeologist and a very gifted speaker. I've no doubt that there are people in this audience who found him difficult to work with. He had his own way of approaching things and he often seemed to care little about other people's feelings or whose toes he stepped on as he rushed to achieve his own success. But Mack wasn't stupid. He knew that he'd upset quite a few people here the night he died."

She drew another breath. "I speculated that night, as I went to find Mack to try to get the question-and-answer session started, that there were very few people who Harold could have asked to go and see if Mack was ready yet. And that's what has been on my mind this afternoon. If so many of the people at the conference were upset with Mack after his speech, for whom would Mack have opened the door to the cuillee?"

Bessie took another drink, but this time the room remained completely silent, all eyes fixed on Bessie.

"I don't have any evidence," she said almost conversationally, "but I have some thoughts that I'd like to share with you all. Maybe someone will have something to say when I'm finished."

Bessie watched the colour drain from the one face she'd been focussed on. For her that was more than enough evidence that she was correct. She caught Inspector Rockwell's eye and he nodded once, his expression serious. Presumably, he'd seen the same thing.

"Anyone who knew Mack well knew certain things about him. He loved big dramatic presentations and he loved beautiful blondes."

A few people chuckled at that. Bessie tried to give Marjorie a reassuring smile, but her friend was already crying silently.

"I know someone who dated him, many years ago, and she told me a couple of interesting things about Mack. One was that he was always involved with at least two women at any given time and the other was that he didn't really understand why the women found that unacceptable."

Again, there were a few nervous chuckles.

"This woman I'm talking about, Mack's former girlfriend, was actually propositioned by Mack on Friday night, in spite of the fact that their relationship had ended disastrously many years ago. That fact suggested a couple of things to me. It suggested that Mack was looking for some, um, extra attention, shall we say, in spite of being here with his girlfriend, and it also suggested that he was willing or perhaps even eager to reconnect with old girlfriends. Of course, there is no shortage of beautiful blondes at this conference to consider as possible ex-girlfriends of the man."

Bessie watched as Liz blushed. She hoped her friends would forgive her for making them uncomfortable and unhappy, but she couldn't stop now.

"The more I thought about it, the more convinced I became that the only people Mack would have opened the cuillee door to would have been current or former girlfriends. He had to trust this person enough to not only open the door, but also to accept a brownie from them. The murderer also had to get close enough to grab Mack's life-saving adrenaline injectors. I'm going to guess that the murderer also accidentally grabbed Mack's second set of slides when she took the injectors. That would account for one missing set, at least."

"Drugging Bambi wouldn't have been difficult," Bessie continued. "Her water bottle was on the floor next to her chair. Anyone could have easily walked past, pretended to trip over the bottle and then switched it for one full of sleeping tablets. The foyer was noisy and chaotic and no one was paying attention to such things."

Bessie shrugged. "I'm convinced, therefore, that the murderer is a woman. One who once had a significant place in Mack's life. I know a few women here that fit that description, and I'm sure the police have been looking at them very closely. I suspect, however, that the murderer has yet to acknowledge that she knew Mack prior to this conference. I'm sure that once the police start investigating her thoroughly, however, they will find plenty of evidence to support my theory. It would probably be easier for everyone involved if she just confessed. Perhaps she'd like to have a word with Inspector Corkill after I finish my talk."

Bessie looked back down at her notes, not wanting to see the agony on one woman's face any longer. She drew a deep breath and then began her speech again.

"As I was saying, wills provide researchers with a great deal of information. They often include surprisingly detailed inventories of people's belongings."

Claire Jamison stood up. "When did you figure out it was me?" she asked Bessie as tears streamed down her face.

"Just this afternoon, when I accidentally kicked over a water bottle. I remembered watching you talk with Bambi about the bottles and I realised how easily you could have switched hers for a drugged one."

"I didn't want to kill her," Claire said. "I just wanted her to shut up. The police were happy to call Mack's death an accident. If she'd kept quiet no one would have suspected anything."

"I'm afraid you rather underestimated the local police," Bessie told the woman. "Inspector Corkill knew it was murder. He just wasn't making noise about it."

Claire shook her head. "He called me, you know? Mack

called me on Thursday, just before I was due to fly over here. He was laughing and talking about how he was going to give everyone the shock of their lives. He said he'd seen my name on the programme, you know? He suggested we meet up for a drink after his talk. I knew he thought that I'd be thrilled to jump back into bed with him again. He had no idea how much I hated him."

Inspector Corkill got to his feet. "Ms. Jamison, I have to caution you against saying anything at all without your advocate or solicitor present."

Claire gave the man a shaky smile. "It's okay," she said. "I knew I was going to get caught. Oh, I tried my best, but I'm strictly an amateur when it comes to murder."

Joe Steele got up and took her hand. "Claire, it was all just an unfortunately accident, right? I mean, maybe you took him the brownie, but you didn't know it would kill him, did you?"

Claire laughed lightly. "I'm sorry, Joe, really I am. You are such a sweet, dear man. But I knew exactly what I was doing with that brownie. I baked it myself Thursday night, after I told Mack how excited I was that I was going to get to see him again. That much was true, you know. I'd been waiting and hoping for a chance to see him again. I started planning how I'd kill him as soon as he left me."

"Ms. Jamison, please. I think we should have this conversation in my office," Inspector Corkill said, taking a few steps towards the woman.

"Bessie wants to hear my story, don't you, Bessie?" Claire asked. "And I bet everyone else here wants to hear it as well. How I hung up the phone and started baking. I'd made brownies so many times for Mack when we were together. He loved my brownies, and he loved this batch just as much. I put in extra chocolate, you see, lots and lots of extra chocolate. He never even tasted the ground peanuts."

She shook her head. "But I've started at the end of the story and I haven't told you about when Mack and I met. How he swept me off my feet and promised me the world. He was researching Roman finds on Anglesey and then he was accused of, well, stealing someone else's research. He denied it, of course, but after an initial investigation the university's chancellor asked him to just leave quietly."

Claire sighed. "So off he went, without even saying goodbye. My heart was broken beyond repair and then, a week later, when I'd finally stopped crying and managed to drag myself into my office, I discovered that when he left, some of my research notes had gone with him."

Joe put his arm around her and gave her an awkward hug. "You should have called the police," he murmured.

"The police aren't interested in personal quarrels," Claire told him. "I called Mack and demanded that he return my notes. He did send them back eventually, and I warned him that he'd better not ever use so much as a single word from them in anything he did or he'd be sorry. Surely I should get credit for warning him?" she asked Inspector Corkill.

"I take it he used your research in a paper, then?" Bessie asked from the podium.

Claire smiled grimly. "He was subtle and clever with it," she told Bessie. "Just little bits, here and there, often things that he might have stumbled over himself, if he'd actually done any research on Anglesey. But I was with him when he was on Anglesey and I know exactly how he spent him time. It wasn't doing research."

"Look, I think this has gone on long enough," Corkill said. "Let's go down to the station and you can put everything into a formal statement," he told Claire.

"There isn't much else to tell," Claire shrugged. "I baked the brownies and then I dyed my hair brown. Everyone knew Mack loved blondes. I figured no one would connect me with Mack if I were a brunette. After Mack's speech I went and got a drink and then told everyone I needed the loo. When I went back out, the foyer was empty and it was easy to sneak back into the lecture theatre. Mack let me into the cuillee and he was ever so pleased that I'd brought him a treat. We made plans to get together for a drink as soon as he was done speaking. When he gave me a big hug, I was able to grab the bag he kept his injectors in out of his pocket. I didn't realise until later that he'd also put a second set of slides from his talk in the same bag. I've mailed them to a friend," she said to the inspector. "I'll give you his name and address and someone can collect them from him."

Corkill nodded. "Let's get going, then," he suggested.

Claire shrugged. "I wanted to just leave him," she continued, seemingly unable to stop herself. "I was at the door just as he took his first bite of brownie, and then someone started knocking." Claire looked down at the ground and shuddered. "It was so horrible. I actually reached into my bag for Mack's injectors. I was going to try to save him, but I couldn't. I knew if he survived I would be charged with attempted murder."

Joe was looking at Claire with a stunned look on his face. After a moment, he let his arm fall from her shoulders and sank back down into his seat.

"It only took a few seconds for him to die," she said. "It felt like hours, but it was only a few seconds. Then I straightened him up a little bit because he'd struggled so much while he was trying to find his injectors. I crept back out and everyone was still eating and drinking and having fun. No one seemed to even notice that I'd been gone."

"What happened to the other set of slides?" Paul Roberts demanded. "I want a look at them."

Claire shook her head. "I don't know anything about them," she told him. "I only found one set in the bag Mack had in his pocket."

"What about Bambi?" Bessie asked.

"You were right about that," Claire told her. "I made a big fuss about collecting water bottles and then swapped hers almost right in front of her face. She was too busy flirting with everyone around her to notice."

"Okay, I think you've confessed to just about everything," Corkill said. "Time to get to the station and call your advocate."

Claire gave him a thoughtful look. "I guess you're right," she said finally, with a strange smile. "We should go."

The Kinvig Room was silent as Claire picked up her handbag and then let Inspector Corkill take her arm. Everyone watched the pair exit the room and then all eyes focussed on Bessie once more.

"I don't suppose anyone one really wants to hear about nineteenth-century wills at this point, do they?" Bessie asked the group.

In the end, Bessie did give her talk. If the audience didn't give her remarks their full attention, that was understandable. She cut a few paragraphs out here and there, trying to make up the time that solving Mack's murder had taken up. The question-and-answer session was fairly short. Many people wanted to ask Bessie questions about Mack and the murder, but they didn't feel that they should do so during her presentation. Very few could think of anything to ask her about wills.

Harold got up at the end to thank her.

"Let's have a nice round of applause for Elizabeth Cubbon," he requested. Bessie smiled as she stepped back from the podium. She couldn't help but wonder if people were clapping for her speech or for her role in finding Mack's killer. Perhaps it was a bit of both.

"Anything that Marjorie and I have to say will, perhaps, feel anticlimactic after what we've just heard," Harold told the crowd. "However, we do have a lot to talk about in our summary of the weekend's events. We're going to take a short break, maybe ten minutes, for everyone to grab a drink and stretch their legs and then we'll resume in here with our conclusions, including a discussion of what Mack claimed to have discovered."

Harold's last sentence was about the only thing that could have distracted the crowd from Claire's unexpected arrest. As everyone made their way into the foyer for tea and coffee, excited voices eagerly discussed Mack's death, Claire and what Harold might be going to talk about in equal measure.

Bessie made her way from behind the podium towards her friends.

"Congratulations," Rockwell told her. "That was very cleverly done."

Bessie shook her head. "I don't feel like I want congratulating," she said sadly. "I don't know that I've ever felt sorry for a murderer before, but I feel desperately sorry for Claire.

I almost wish I hadn't said anything."

Hugh frowned at her. "But she killed Mack. It was clearly premeditated from what she said, as well."

"Mack broke her heart and stole her research," Bessie replied. "And he wasn't a very nice person, either."

"That doesn't give her the right to end his life," Rockwell said soothingly. "Moirrey Teare was thoroughly unlikeable, but she didn't deserve to die, did she?"

"No," Bessie said softly. "But the person who murdered her wasn't any more likeable than Moirrey. Claire's different, somehow."

"I understand what you're saying," Doona told Bessie, giving her a hug. "Claire was treated very badly by Mack, until she behaved in a way that was totally out of character for her. But no matter what Mack did, she shouldn't have killed him."

"I know," Bessie sighed. "I just feel, I don't know, miserable."

The foursome made their way towards the door.

"Maybe some sweet milky tea will help," Doona suggested. "And half a dozen chocolate biscuits."

Joe Steele was the only person still in the room. He was sitting in the same seat that he'd dropped into during Claire's confession and his face still wore a dazed look.

"Joe?" Bessie stopped next to him and touched his shoulder. "I'm sorry, Joe, truly I am."

Joe shook his head and then looked up at Bessie. "She stood there, in the same room with him, and watched him die," he said in disbelief. "I could just about understand plotting to kill the man. I'm sure she isn't the first woman to come up with crazy ideas to get rid of a man who hurt her. I could even understand her baking the brownies and colouring her hair. Taking his injectors, well, that's a little bit harder to get my head around, but even then...." He trailed off and looked at the ground.

"You won't ever be able to understand," Doona told him, sitting down next to him and starting to rub his back gently. "Take it from someone else who once dated a murderer, you won't ever understand how they could seem so wonderful while hiding a secret that big. You'll always feel like you should have been able to tell somehow, that you should have noticed something or felt something was wrong. And you'll always feel like you were being used somehow." Doona sighed.

"I think we all need a cup of tea," Bessie announced in the brightest tone she could manage. "Come on, let's go."

Doona stood up and pulled a reluctant Joe to his feet.

"Tea and biscuits," Bessie told the man, "are the classic British panacea."

Joe looked like he might argue, but he followed them from the room. The foyer was crowded and noisy.

"You lot wait here," Rockwell told the others. "I'll fight my way over to the tables and bring back tea for everyone."

"You don't have enough hands to manage that," Hugh said. "I'll come as well."

The pair was quickly swallowed up by the crowd. "Hugh just wants to make sure some biscuits come back with the tea," Doona told Joe.

He managed a weak smile. "Maybe some sugar will help," he replied.

"It can't hurt," Bessie told him, patting his arm. "I'm sorry that I didn't realise that it was Claire sooner, before you two had become so involved."

Joe shrugged. "We weren't that involved," he told her. "She kept sort of pushing me away. I couldn't tell if she was really interested or just being nice. I was sort of falling for her, so I'm a little bit sad, but mostly I just feel like an idiot. It never even crossed my mind that she might have killed Mack."

Rockwell and Hugh were back a moment later with mugs of hot tea. Doona and Bessie laughed when Hugh passed around the plate full of biscuits he'd brought with him.

"What's so funny?" Hugh demanded, looking from Bessie to Doona and back again.

"Try a chocolate one," Doona urged Joe, ignoring Hugh. "Chocolate can fix almost anything."

A moment later, Harold was trying to talk over the crowd. "Okay, everyone, um, everyone? Hello?"

Bessie grinned at Doona. "Maybe the museum should try to

get George to pay for a microphone and speakers for the foyer."

"Um, right then," Harold continued once everyone had fallen mostly silent. "Marjorie and I are ready to begin, if you'd all like to find seats in the Kinvig Room."

Bessie and her friends were still standing near the door, so they were among the first back into the room. Rockwell steered the group towards the front. "This should be interesting," he said to Bessie. "I get the feeling that Dr. Smythe has a lot to talk about."

They settled into their seats in the front row and waited while the room slowly filled to capacity. Bessie had a feeling that they were about to discover what had happened to the other set of missing slides.

CHAPTER FIFTEEN

Marjorie walked to the podium as soon as the audience was settled.

"I had a number of things I intended to say this afternoon," she told the crowd. "But in light of everything that's taken place in the last couple of hours, and knowing what Harold has to discuss, I'm going to keep my remarks short."

She paused for a breath and gave Bessie a grin. Bessie smiled back, happy to see her friend recovering from the ordeal that the conference had turned out to be.

"Harold and I spent many months organising this conference, and I'm pleased that in spite of, um, difficult circumstances, shall we say, a great deal of very interesting research was presented and discussed. I'd just like to thank, very sincerely, each and every person who took the time to be here, either as a speaker or as an audience member. Every person contributed something to the parts of this conference that were successful."

"I guess she'd consider Mack's death as a less successful part?" Doona whispered to Bessie.

"Those of you who were able to hear Dr. William Corlett's talk are aware that there is an effort being made to establish a centre here on the island to provide a focus for any and all research about the Isle of Man. This would, of course, include archeology and history, but also language and literature, music, popular culture," she shrugged. "Basically anything with any Manx component could be a part of the centre and I think everyone who works for Manx National Heritage is excited by the idea. We will be asking all of our conference participants to consider submitting a copy of their paper to us. We would like to publish all of the papers from this weekend in a single volume. All proceeds from the sale would go towards helping with the initial funding of the new centre."

A whisper went through the crowd and Bessie grinned. She'd be happy to have her paper included in such a publication.

"A great deal more information will be forthcoming over time," Marjorie told the group. "For today, I think, perhaps, it is more important to tie up a few loose ends. I'm delighted to turn things over to Dr. Harold Smythe, who will be sharing some of his most recent findings with you all."

Harold bounced up the podium and smiled brightly at the audience. "Thank you, Marjorie. I'm delighted to be here this afternoon to share with you some important information. I assume that the vast majority of you were also here on Friday evening when Dr. Mack Dickson shocked us all by showing slides of various Roman settlement finds that he claimed to have unearthed right here on the Isle of Man."

Harold cleared his throat and then looked nervously at Inspector Rockwell. "I suppose I must start my comments with a small confession," he said, almost sheepishly. "After Mack finished speaking, in the excited chaos that followed, I, er, well, that is, you see, I...." Harold took a deep breath.

"I pulled off the slide carousel with Mack's slides in it and dumped the slides into my briefcase. No one saw me do it, but I could have bluffed my way through it if I'd been spotted. I simply wanted a few minutes to study them more closely, but before I could do that I was grabbed by first one person and then another. Everyone wanted to talk to me about Mack's speech and I never got a moment alone to look at them."

Harold gulped his water, watching Rockwell nervously. When the inspector did nothing, he continued.

"I was so flustered after Mack's death that I almost forgot about the slides. With the police questioning everyone, and everything else that was happening, I didn't feel like I could say anything. Of course, I should have told Inspector Corkill that I had them and given them to him immediately. In fact, I decided to give them to the inspector the very next day, but I took a quick look at them before I did so. What I saw made me more reluctant to hand them over to the police. Lights, please?"

The lights dimmed and Harold clicked a remote that brought a slide up on the screen behind him.

"Those of you who were here Friday night will recognise this as one of Mack's slides, one that he claimed came from a photo that he'd taken in the last few weeks. This one, however," Harold clicked again and a second slide appeared, "is from a talk that was given at a poorly attended conference on Italian political history about five years ago in Italy."

The audience buzzed with excitement. The two slides were identical.

The lights came back up and Harold grinned at the crowd. "When I studied Mack's slides closely, I thought some of them looked vaguely familiar. So far, this is the only one of Mack's slides that I can definitely prove was copied from elsewhere. This particular collection of coins was actually unearthed near Rome itself about ten years ago and is considered relatively insignificant there. After all, Roman finds ought to be found near Rome."

Everyone chuckled at that. "I've sent copies of Mack's slides to a number of experts in Roman remains and I intend to spend some time with Paul Roberts, one of the world's leading experts on the subject, as soon as the conference wraps up. I'm confident that the experts will be able to identify every one of the slides that Mack claimed were his own."

"But why would Mack do something like that?" a voice from the crowd shouted out.

Harold shook his head. "I can only guess that when he came back out for the question-and-answer session he was going to announce that his talk was all an elaborate hoax. I know he did something similar at a conference about seven years ago, getting everyone in the crowd excited and then using his follow-up talk to discuss how easily he'd managed to create a believable fake presentation."

Bessie shook her head. "Mack was up to something more complicated than that," she whispered to Doona. "I wish I knew what it was."

Harold continued. "I must add, as well, that I was lucky to get that slide identified so quickly. I suspect the others will be harder to trace. Mack was very clever when he made his selections. If they are all as obscure and believable as the one I've managed to track down, it could take years to sort them all out. I mustn't speak ill of the dead, but it is just possible that Mack was hoping to advance his career with his 'finds.'"

"Does that sound more likely?" Doona asked Bessie.

"I'm afraid it does," Bessie shrugged. "Mack could have refused to show the slides to anyone after his talk. George Quayle had already offered to fund an excavation. Mack could have done quite well out of his charade."

"But surely his career was on the line if he was caught?" Doona demanded.

"Maybe," Bessie replied. "But Mack was always doing things like this." She shook her head. "Maybe not quite like this," she clarified. "But he was often getting himself into some sort of trouble or another and then talking his way out of it. You heard what Claire said. He got into trouble in Anglesey and managed to get away with his reputation intact. Mack could be very convincing when he needed to be and I'm sure he had a backup plan in case he was caught right away."

Doona shook her head. "I'm not sure if I wish I'd met the man or not."

"I'm going to wrap things up for today," Harold told everyone. "Anyone who is interested in what we discover as we dig deeper into Mack's so-called 'findings,' should send me an email. I'll send out periodic updates as we go along."

"So that's that, then," Rockwell said as the crowd began to disperse. "The murderer is in custody. The missing slides are all accounted for. And Mack's big announcement turns out to have been a clever hoax. I think that's quite enough excitement for one day, don't you?"

Bessie grinned. "I'm still supposed to go back for another chat with Bambi," she reminded the inspector. "I can't imagine that she'll have anything to add to today's revelations, but at least

I can fill her in on what she missed."

Rockwell grinned. "I'll drive you over. Doona and I can wait in the lobby while you talk to her and then we can go out for a celebratory dinner, on me."

"Um, I'll pay my own way, like," Hugh interjected. "But I'd love to come as well."

The inspector laughed. "You're more than welcome," he told him. "And dinner is on me, but you can pay for the bottle of champagne."

"That sounds like a fair deal," Hugh grinned.

Bessie needed several minutes to extract herself from the crowded foyer. Nearly everyone seemed to want a quick word with her about Mack, Claire and the Roman hoax. When Marjorie saw her, Bessie found herself engulfed in a huge hug.

"I can't thank you enough for figuring out what happened to Mack," Marjorie told Bessie. "I feel like I can finally sleep again tonight."

"I do feel sorry for Claire," Bessie admitted to Marjorie. "Mack treated her quite badly."

"He treated a lot of us quite badly," Marjorie replied. "Maybe we should have all banded together like in Agatha Christie and took turns to stab him."

"You don't mean that," Bessie told her friend.

"I suppose not," Marjorie said with a sigh. "But I must admit I feel, I don't know, free somehow now that Mack's dead. I feel like I can finally get on with my life in a way I didn't before. And I feel like a horrible person for feeling that way."

Bessie hugged her friend tightly. "Well, at least something good has come out of Mack's death, then," she said. "I just hope that doesn't mean you're going to be tempted to leave the island."

"Oh, good heavens, no," Marjorie exclaimed. "This is home now and I'm not going anywhere."

"There was something you didn't tell the police," Bessie said. "Can you tell me now?"

Marjorie flushed and looked down at the floor. "I really don't think...." she began. She sighed and then looked at Bessie. "I was with Mack in the cuillee for a short time before his talk," she said.

"You were?"

"When he went in to get ready, I followed him into the cuillee." Marjorie's eyes filled with tears again. "I'm so embarrassed to admit it, but he, well, he just about persuaded me to forgive him. We actually made arrangements to meet for a drink after the question-and-answer session." Marjorie blushed even brighter. "We were going to meet at my house. I wrote my address on the back of my business card and Mack tucked it into the bag with his injectors. I was worried that the police would find it, but I guess Claire found it instead. I can't believe he made drink plans with her as well. I'm such an idiot when it comes to men."

"Marjorie, I'm so sorry," Bessie said, wishing she could do something to help her friend. "Why don't you bring an overnight bag tomorrow night and after class you can come over to my cottage. We'll drink a bottle of wine together and talk about anything and everything. My spare room is reasonably comfortable, especially if you've had a bottle of wine."

Marjorie laughed through her tears. "I'd love that, Bessie, thank you."

Bessie hugged her one more time and then moved on. She had a quick word with Harold, congratulating him on his discovery. Luckily for Bessie, nearly everyone in the room wanted to talk to him as well, so he could do little more than shake her hand before someone else pulled him away.

Joe was standing next to the tea table, mindlessly eating chocolate biscuits as Bessie made her way around the room.

"Are you going to be okay?" she asked him with real concern.

"Yeah, I am," he replied. "I'm having dinner with Helen Baxter and a couple of her friends. I'll be flying back to London tomorrow to continue my research and my studies, but I hope to get back here one day soon, maybe after the new research centre opens."

"When you come back, give me a call," Bessie told him, handing him a slip of paper with her contact details on it. "I'd love to see you again."

"I'll do that," Joe promised, tucking the paper into a pocket. "Thanks for everything."

Bessie and her friends arrived at the lift at the same time as Liz, who pulled Bessie into a huge hug.

"Thank you for figuring it all out," she told Bessie, as tears filled her eyes. "I know Bill will be pleased that it's all over and done with and no one will be asking me any more questions."

"I think we're all glad it's all over and done with," Bessie told her.

At the front door to the museum, Hugh headed off to find his car and head for the restaurant they had agreed upon. It wouldn't be busy on a Sunday night, and no one would mind if he took up a table for four on his own while he waited. Bessie suspected that he'd order himself a snack anyway, something to keep him going until the others arrived.

Rockwell drove Bessie and Doona to Noble's. Inside, Bessie bypassed the information desk and headed straight for the private wing. She tapped in the code that she'd seen Sue use and smiled to herself as the doors swung open. When she arrived at the information desk, she was pleased to be told that she was expected and cleared to visit Bambi.

"Ms. Marks is going back to London tomorrow," the nurse on duty told her. "We've just had a call from the police giving the final okay."

"She must be happy about that," Bessie replied.

The nurse shrugged. "You go on down and ask her yourself," she suggested.

Bessie walked down the hallway and knocked lightly on Bambi's door.

"Come in," a voice called.

Bambi was sitting in the same chair she'd been in earlier. Her father and Clive Henderson were side by side on the couch. Bessie could feel tension in the atmosphere as she stepped into the room.

"I hope I'm not interrupting anything," she said tentatively.

"Not at all," Clive said smoothly, getting to his feet. "We're just finalising our travel plans for tomorrow. The sooner we can get this young lady back to London, the better."

Bambi snorted and muttered something under her breath.

Her father shook his head and then stood up and smiled at Bessie.

"Miss Cubbon, thank you for coming back to see Mar, er, my daughter again. I'm sure she appreciates your efforts," he said.

"It was no problem," Bessie assured him. "As it happened, it's been quite an exciting afternoon and I wanted to share some of what Bambi missed at the conference with her, if she's interested."

"Yes, Inspector Corkill was here a short time ago. He filled us in on your, um, unmasking of Dr. Dickson's murderer. I'm sure the police are very grateful and I know my daughter will sleep better knowing that that woman is behind bars."

"Oh, for Pete's sake," Bambi erupted. "I'm sitting right here. I can speak for myself."

Bessie grinned at her, addressing her directly. "I'm sure you've heard that Claire also admitted to switching your water bottle for a drugged one," she said.

"Yeah, which was disappointing, because after you left I started thinking about it and I was pretty sure I'd figured out that she'd done it," Bambi replied. "I couldn't wait to see you again to tell you, but now everyone knows she did it."

"I'm sure Inspector Corkill appreciates that you were able to confirm Claire's version of events," Bessie told her.

"Yeah, well, he would appreciate it a lot, if certain people would let me talk to him," Bambi said with a scowl.

"Margaret, we've been all through this," Nigel said sternly. "I think you need to get your things packed up and then get some rest. Thank you for coming, Miss Cubbon."

Nigel took a step towards Bessie, as if to usher her out the door. Bambi stepped forward and held up a hand.

"I think I'd like to take a short stroll with Aunt Bessie," she announced. "Just down the corridor for a cup of tea. We'll be right back."

Before her father or his solicitor could reply, Bambi almost dragged Bessie out into the corridor. "Hurry," she whispered in Bessie's ear. They were halfway down the hall before Bessie could reply.

"Are you planning on running away?" she asked the girl.

Bambi laughed. "Oh, it is so tempting," she told Bessie. "But no, I really just want ten minutes alone with you and a cup of tea."

"I'm surprised they aren't following us," Bessie said, glancing behind them as Bambi pushed open the door to the television room.

"They won't want to cause a scene," Bambi assured her. "One of them will wander in casually in about five minutes, just to check that I'm okay."

"So what did you want to talk to me about?" Bessie asked curiously as the girl filled the kettle with water and switched it on.

"Mack was planning to move to America," she said.

"Mack was planning what?"

Bambi laughed. "He was planning to move to America. Apparently some little university in some obscure town in the middle of nowhere offered him a ridiculously inflated salary to come and start an archeology programme for them. I think they thought that having a British archeologist would give them some class or something."

"I thought he was planning a big excavation here?" Bessie asked.

"He was hoping to get a big lump of money from George Quayle for a dig here, but then use it to pay for his relocation to the US," Bambi told her.

"But that's fraud," Bessie exclaimed.

"And that's why my father doesn't want me to tell anyone about it. He says that I could be prosecuted because I knew about the plan."

"But the plan didn't work," Bessie said.

"I know, but my father is all about covering his butt. Or in this case, my butt. I wasn't going to tell you, but after everything you've done, finding Mack's killer and all, I figured you deserve to know."

"But why wasn't the university in the US covering his moving costs?" Bessie asked.

Bambi shrugged. "I don't know the whole story," she replied. "Maybe Mack was trying to get as much as he could out of George before he moved on. I know that there's something in George's past that Mack knew and was holding over him. It's just possible that the whole exercise was just a fancy way for Mack to get George to hand over a bunch of blackmail money."

"Mack was blackmailing George?" Bessie shook her head. "Poor Mary."

"Yeah, apparently a lot of the money is Mary's and George can't just do whatever he wants with it. The whole Roman remains thing might have been dreamed up between George and Mack, for all I know."

Bessie sighed. "The police should know all of this," she told the girl.

"And they will," Bambi told her. "Just not right away. My dad is being super about everything right now and I need to play nice with him. I promise I'll give a formal statement to someone in London in a few days, once we get settled. For now, though, I'm keeping quiet and I hope you will as well."

"Everything you've told me is just hearsay," Bessie replied. "The police wouldn't be interested in hearing it from me." Bessie knew that wasn't strictly true. Inspector Rockwell would be very interested, and she planned to tell him everything she'd been told as soon as she had a moment alone with him. There was no evidence that George Quayle was involved in anything illegal at this point, but Bessie would feel better knowing that Rockwell was keeping an eye on him.

The kettle came to a boil and clicked off just as the door to the room swung open. Nigel Marks stuck his head in. "Everything okay in here?" he asked brightly.

"Everything's fine," Bambi replied in a monotone. "Bessie and I were just having a little girl talk, but she needs to get going."

"I do, actually," Bessie said. "I'm having dinner with some dear friends."

"I'll walk you out," Nigel suggested, offering Bessie his arm.

"Take good care of yourself," Bessie said to Bambi. "If you ever come back to the island, please give me a call."

"Thank you for everything," Bambi told her, giving her a quick hug. "You should look me up the next time you're in London."

"I might just," Bessie grinned, knowing full well that she rarely travelled to London and, even if she did, she would never contact Bambi there.

Bessie took the offered arm and followed Nigel from the room. He waited until they were nearly to the wing's exit before speaking.

"I hope she didn't say anything, um, off the wall," he said. "She's still suffering badly from the drugs she was given by that woman."

"We just chatted about Mack and their relationship," Bessie told him. "I think she's still a bit overwhelmed by everything that happened this weekend."

"I can certainly understand that," Nigel replied. "I certainly never wanted my baby girl caught up in a murder investigation."

"No, of course not," Bessie said. "At least now she can go home and start sorting out her life."

"Yes, we've been talking about a lot of different options," he told Bessie. "I think she's probably going to go back to school, maybe in fashion design."

"Good for her," Bessie grinned. "I hope I see her work in glossy magazines some day."

"Me too," Nigel replied.

The pair crossed the lobby slowly, with Bessie shooting a warning look at Inspector Rockwell as they went. She'd rather Nigel didn't know that the inspector was one of her friends.

"Bessie, there you are," Doona crossed the room. "All set?"

Bessie thought about performing introductions, but Nigel didn't give her time. "I'll just leave you with your friend, then," he said, giving her a small bow. He'd disappeared back down the hall before Bessie had a chance to reply.

"Should I feel insulted that he didn't want to meet me?" Doona laughed.

"Count your blessings," Bessie answered wryly.

Inspector Rockwell joined them and they were quickly off to join Hugh at the restaurant on the Douglas promenade. Half an hour later, the foursome was seated around a large table in the nearly empty restaurant. Everyone had ordered and the champagne that Inspector Rockwell insisted on had been delivered.

"To Bessie, a brilliant historian, incredible detective and wonderful person," Doona said, raising her glass.

"To Bessie," Hugh and Rockwell repeated.

Bessie blushed a bright red. "Now don't you fuss like that," Bessie chided her friends. "I'm none of those things, really."

Doona laughed. "You're all of those things and more. I forget to mention what a great friend you are. Your friendship means the world to me, it truly does."

Bessie blushed even more. She thought about arguing further, but worried it might just bring on more compliments she didn't feel were entirely deserved. Instead, she took a sip of champagne and then smiled at her friends.

"To friendship," she said, raising her glass.

"To friendship," the others repeated.

Glossary of Terms

Manx to English

cuillee	back room or small room off a kitchen
Ellan Vannin	Isle of Man
fastyr mie	good afternoon
kys t'ou	how are you?
moghry mie	good morning
skeet	gossip
ta mee braew	I'm fine
Treoghe Bwaaue	Widow's Cottage (Bessie's home)

English to American Terms

advocate	Manx title for a lawyer (solicitor)
aye	yes
bickies	cookies (informally)
biscuits	cookies
car park	parking lot
cuppa	cup of tea (informally)
fairy cakes	cupcakes
holiday	vacation
knackered	tired
lift	elevator
pavement	sidewalk
pudding	dessert
queenies	scallops
sponge	cake
telly	television
Zimmer frame	walker

Other Notes

CID is the Criminal Investigation Department of the Isle of Man Constabulary (Police Force).

The phrase "knickers in a twist" means that someone is very upset about something, usually something that the other person considers relatively unimportant.

"Noble's" is Noble's Hospital, the main hospital on the Isle of Man. It is located in Douglas, the island's capital city.

When talking about time, the English say, for example, "half seven" to mean "seven-thirty."

When island residents talk about someone being from "across," they mean that the person is from somewhere in the United Kingdom. (across the water)

There is an English expression, "mutton dressed as lamb," which refers to a woman who is dressing too young for her age. Often shortened to "mutton."

A "carvery" is a buffet meal where roasted meat is sliced to order.

Sunday lunch is typically a large family meal in the UK. It generally consists of a meat roast and many trimmings.

The NHS is the National Health Service, which provides medical treatment for every person who lives in the UK, mostly without charge, although some types of care might have a co-payment. Wealthier patients have the option of accessing private treatment if they prefer, which may offer faster treatment options or access to amenities like private rooms.

When someone in the UK is "on the pull" they are looking to

attract a member of the opposite sex (or the same sex if that is how they are inclined). Similarly, "chatting up" is flirting.

The TT (or Tourist Trophy) is a motorcycle road-racing event held on the island every May/June. It is held in a time trial format over approximately thirty-seven miles of closed public roads. The course takes in the mountains as well as travelling through several small towns and villages.

A few notes on the Manx Museum (with apologies for my creative license):

There really is an upper level in the museum that is used to host conference and other special events. If the various rooms on that level have names, however, I do not know what they are. In order to make sense of all the events that move around throughout this book, I have chosen to name the rooms. I have named them all after well-known historians who have studied the island (more details below).

I don't believe the main theatre on the ground floor has a name, either, although I've called it the "Ellan Vannin Theatre" in this book. (Ellan Vannin is the Manx name for the island.)

The historians whose names I've borrowed:

A.W. Moore wrote his two-volume *History of the Isle of Man* in 1900 and the volumes have subsequently been reprinted by the Manx Museum and National Trust.

R.H. Kinvig published his *The Isle of Man: A social, cultural and political history* in 1975.

William Blundell's *A History of the Isle of Man* was written between 1648 and 1656 and subsequently published in two volumes by the Manx Society in 1876 and 1877 from the original manuscript.

Acknowledgements

Special thanks to my wonderful editor, Denise, who tries hard to make my work the best it can be, before I go back in and mess things up again! Any and all mistakes that remain are mine.

Thanks to my first, best beta reader, Barb who is also my biggest supporter (and my mom).

I can't say enough wonderful things about Kevin, who supplies me with such stunning photos for my covers. Thank you, Kevin!

And an extra special thanks to my amazing beta reading team (in alphabetical order), Charlene, Janice, Margaret and Ruth. Your input is invaluable to me.

Coming January 16, 2015:

Aunt Bessie Decides
An Isle of Man Cozy Mystery
by Diana Xarissa

Aunt Bessie decides that she and her closest friends should have an enjoyable night out.

Elizabeth Cubbon (known to almost everyone as Aunt Bessie) has made many friends over the lifetime that she's lived in the village of Laxey, but few have been as close as the ones she's made recently. Bessie relied on Doona Moore, Hugh Watterson and John Rockwell to help her through several recent murder investigations she's found herself caught up in. Now she wants to treat them all to an open-air performance of a Shakespearean play on the grounds of historic Peel Castle.

Aunt Bessie decides that it doesn't much matter what show the troupe is performing as long as she and her friends can relax and have fun.

Two members have recently left the theatre company. Now the troupe has thrown aside its usual repertoire in favour of a play written by one of their own. When those two former members appear in the audience, though, someone decides to get rid of one of them for good.

Aunt Bessie decides to give the show another chance, but a second performance almost ends in a second tragedy.

With all of the suspects blaming one another, and several of them turning up on the doorstep of Bessie's cottage, it's time for Bessie to decide to solve this murder herself.

Aunt Bessie Assumes
An Isle of Man Cozy Mystery
by Diana Xarissa

Aunt Bessie assumes that she'll have the beach all to herself on a cold, wet, and windy March morning just after sunrise, then she stumbles (almost literally) over a dead body.

Elizabeth (Bessie) Cubbon, aged somewhere between free bus pass (60) and telegram from the Queen (100), has lived her entire adult life in a small cottage on Laxey beach. For most of those years, she's been in the habit of taking a brisk morning walk along the beach. Dead men have never been part of the scenery before.

Aunt Bessie assumes that the dead man died of natural causes, then the police find the knife in his chest.

Try as she might, Bessie just can't find anything to like about the young widow that she provides tea and sympathy to in the immediate aftermath of finding the body. There isn't much to like about the rest of the victim's family either.

Aunt Bessie assumes that the police will have the case wrapped up in no time at all, then she finds a second body.

Can Bessie and her friends find the killer before she ends up as the next victim?

Aunt Bessie Believes
An Isle of Man Cozy Mystery
by Diana Xarissa

Aunt Bessie believes that Moirrey Teare is just about the most disagreeable woman she's ever had the misfortune to meet.

Elizabeth Cubbon, (Aunt Bessie to nearly everyone), is somewhere past sixty, and old enough to ignore the rude woman that does her best to ruin the first session of the beginning Manx language class they are both taking. Moirrey's sudden death is harder to ignore.

Aunt Bessie believes that Moirrey's death was the result of the heart condition that Moirrey always complained about.
The police investigation, however, suggests that someone switched some of the dead woman's essential medications for something far more deadly.

Aunt Bessie believes that she and her friends can find the killer.

But with Doona suspended from work and spending all of her time with the dead woman's long-lost brother, with Hugh caught up in a brand new romance and with Inspector Rockwell chasing after a man that might not even exist, Bessie finds herself believing that someone might just get away with murder.

Island Inheritance

An Isle of Man Romance

By Diana Xarissa

Carly thinks her life is just about perfect. She recently bought an adorable little house in her hometown in Pennsylvania. She has a job she loves, teaching first grade at the same elementary school she once attended. And she has the same boyfriend that she fell in love with in that very school, when they were both in third grade. He'll get around to proposing one day, she's just sure of it. Carly doesn't want to change anything in her life.

Doncan thinks his life is just about perfect. He's followed in his father's and his grandfather's footsteps and is an advocate (lawyer) on the Isle of Man dealing mostly with estates and trusts. This earns him a generous income that allows him to drive a luxury car and live in a fabulous penthouse apartment. He's never short of female company and he doesn't want to change anything in his life.

When Carly's grandmother inherits a cottage on the Isle of Man, Carly makes the journey to the island to settle the estate. Doncan wants the paperwork signed and the cottage safely sold to his cousin who is ready to tear it down and build luxury apartments in its place. Carly falls in love with the old cottage and the beautiful island, while Doncan tries hard to keep her happy so she will sign on the dotted line. Suddenly both of their lives are changing in ways neither of them ever imagined.

Island Escape
An Isle of Man Romance
By Diana Xarissa

Katie's life changes dramatically only a few months before her planned wedding. With the wedding cancelled, an unexpected opportunity to do some research on the picturesque Isle of Man seems the perfect escape. She can get away from all the sympathetic looks and gossipy remarks and focus on her career while nursing her broken heart.

Finlo Quayle is the gorgeous owner of the island's only charter airline. William Corlett is the intelligent and sexy man who runs the Institute that is funding Katie's research. Katie finds herself being fought over by two very different men, both of whom attract her in very different ways.

Now the only thing Katie is sure of is that she isn't going to let a ghost make any decisions about her love life for her.

ABOUT THE AUTHOR

Diana lived on the glorious Isle of Man for more than ten years before returning to the United States with her family. Now living near Buffalo, New York, she enjoys having the opportunity to write about the island that she loves so much. It truly is an amazing and magical place.

Diana also writes mystery/thrillers set in the not-too-distant future under the pen name "Diana X. Dunn" and fantasy/adventure books for middle grade readers under the pen name "D.X. Dunn."

She would be delighted to know what you think of her work and can be contacted through Facebook, Goodreads or on her website at www.dianaxarissa.com.

17237330R00133

Printed in Poland
by Amazon Fulfillment
Poland Sp. z o.o., Wrocław